EMBERS IN THE Sea

JENNIFER M. EATON

Month9Books

D1528154

ePub ISBN: 978-1-945107-95-5 Mobi ISBN: 978-1-945107-96-2
Paperback ISBN: 978-1-945107-82-5

Published by Month9Books, Raleigh, NC 27609
Cover design by Najla Qamber Designs

Month9Books

For Mom and Dad.
Wish you were here to enjoy this journey with me.
Sorry about the curse word, Mom.
Stop laughing about it, Dad.
Miss you.

YA Classification Guide

Age of protagonist: ___18___

Gore?   yes   (no)

age 10+   (14+)   17+

EMBERS IN THE SEA

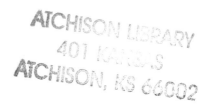
1

Homework sucks.

I tucked back the dark bang that flew in my face, shifted my seating, and balanced *Philosophers of the Pre-Modern World* on my crossed legs.

Squinting in the morning sunshine, I forced myself to read the passage from Colton's *Lacon* one more time:

> *"Time is the most undefinable yet paradoxical of things; the past is gone, the future is not come, and the present becomes the past, even while we attempt to define it."*

I closed the textbook and tossed it on the grass. "Why should I even care about what some old cleric guy said two hundred years ago?"

"Because he's a famous old cleric guy." Matt plucked the book from the lawn and dusted a few stray grass clippings from the cover.

"I came to college to study photography, not to be confused beyond reason by dead philosophers."

Matt handed me the book as we stood. "Philosophy is supposed to broaden your mind."

"Yeah, well, I'm broad enough." Knowing I'd gained a few pounds since the last time we'd seen each other, I sensed a witty retort forming on his lips. "Don't say it."

He held up his hands. "I wouldn't think of it."

A group of people pointed at us from across the courtyard, and my fingers twined around my mother's necklace, pressing the charm into my palm.

When I first came to Columbia University, this secluded lawn nestled between Lewisohn and Earl Halls was one of my favorite places to relax. Digging my fingers into the cool grass felt like a hug from home, despite the New York skyline looming just over the trees. But each semester I had to dodge more and more Jess-watchers. Why they were still interested in me after all this time, I didn't know.

It had been nearly two years since David left Earth to help his people populate Mars, and there'd been no impromptu spaceship sightings yet. But alien chasers still flocked to Columbia University thinking today might be the lucky day.

"How about we go this way." Matt tugged me away from the wide-eyed group. Several of them raised camera phones, then looked at the sky.

It was always the same, as if just because Jessica Martinez walked outside, a spaceship would magically pop out of nowhere and whisk her away.

"You know, it wouldn't hurt you to smile once in a while." Matt waved at a guy holding a late model Nikon camera with a cheap lens attached to the front. "You always look ticked on the tabloid covers."

I left the walkway and stomped across the grass. "These aren't paparazzi. They're just gawkers, and they're driving me crazy. I wish they'd just let it go."

Matt laughed. "Let it go? You're Jess Martinez: the girl who saved the world from Armageddon. Twice. I think you need to cut people some slack."

I stopped under a tree at the corner of the visitor center and watched a bird hop back and forth from the grass to the cement walkway. "I just want to be normal again. I want people to stop staring at me all the time."

"Then you better stop wearing those tight jeans because, damn, girl, I'd snap a few pictures too if I thought I could get away with it."

I smacked his shoulder, like I always did when he complimented me in his own, Matt-like way. It felt like we were back in New Jersey, back when I was "just Jess" and friendships weren't so much a luxury.

"So, when is your cancer symposium over?" I asked.

"I'll be here for a few more days."

A few more days. It wasn't enough. "Thanks for coming to see me. I missed you."

Red stained his cheeks. "Yeah, I missed you too." His gaze drifted to the tree. "Bobby says hi, by the way."

I cringed and tried to hide my sneer. "I can't believe you guys ended up friends after what he did to you in high school. He's such a jerk."

"Yeah, but he's a connected jerk."

"You don't need him, Matt. You're brilliant."

He shrugged. "Brilliant only gets you so far. Bobby has the charm and means to get my work noticed."

"And in return, you get him good grades?"

"I can't take his exams for him, but yeah, I help with the other stuff." We walked to the Alma Mater steps, where he reclined against the cool stone. "He quit McGuire for you, you know."

"That doesn't change the fact that he's an ass."

"He's trying to get back in your good graces … change the world so you see him differently."

I eased down beside him. "Did he ask you to say that?"

Matt's eyes widened. "Am I that transparent?"

"I can't believe he's pretending to care about cancer research just to impress me. When will he learn to take 'no' for an answer?"

"So, you're serious? You're really not into him anymore?"

"Not if he were the last guy on the planet."

A smile spread across Matt's face. "Good. You can do better. He's a weasel." He cleared his throat. "Just don't tell him I said that. He's still bigger than me."

I mustered half a grin before three people jumped in front of the steps and tried to pretend they weren't taking pictures of me.

"Wow," Matt said. "They really don't let up, do they?"

"Not too much, no."

He stood and helped me to my feet. "How about we go inside somewhere? Is there anywhere around here we can catch an early lunch?"

I folded my arms. "Seriously? We're in New York City. Name your poison."

His grin made me forget about the roving photographers. "Anywhere quiet, where we can kinda be alone."

I straightened. "Alone?"

He slipped his cold fingers around mine. "I meant it when I said I missed you."

Whoa. I slid my hand away. "Weren't you just rooting for team Bobby?"

"Yeah, well, I figure if the referee has banned Bobby from the game permanently, that kinda makes room for team Matt to swoop in and maybe win one for the eggheads of the world."

A flash of seventeen-year-old Matt, bruised and bleeding on the sidewalk after Bobby beat him up for taking me to a movie flashed through my mind, before my vision refocused on the brilliant med student Matt had become. I'd saved the world from aliens, but Matt was going to save the world from cancer. He believed it. I believed it. Matt was one of those guys who could do anything.

As long as he could avoid getting beat up again.

And with me at his side, he *would* get beat up again. Going to college hadn't changed Bobby that much, even if he was riding on Matt's gravy train.

Matt just put himself way out on a limb. But did I want to go out on that skinny little branch with him?

Maybe I did. "How about something a little more casual, like ice cream."

He held up his hands. "Whoa there. I don't know. Ice cream sparks of commitment. We've only known each other for what, eight years? I think you're moving a little fast for me. I thought I was pushing it with lunch."

I punched him in the arm.

He punched me back. I loved that. No airs. No games. No attitude. Just Matt.

Maybe, just maybe, I could get my life back. Maybe I *could* be happy again.

A startled cry echoed through the courtyard.

"What is that?" a man yelled.

Matt grabbed my hand and we followed the throng away from the steps, across 116th Street, past the sundial, and onto the South Lawn. A huge hole had formed in the clouds, widening into a shimmering circle of crystal blue.

I plucked my camera out of my backpack and joined the amateurs clicking away with their cell phones. I hid my amusement behind the lens of *Old Reliable*.

These people had no idea what a picture could be, how to focus in just the right place, how to find tone in the simplest of images, and catch the perfect light to evoke the exact mood. I hit the shutter four times as the anomaly widened, expanding past several city blocks. Nature never ceased to astound me.

A few more photography students added their lenses to the crowd. There'd be no deficit of pictures for the internet newsfeeds to choose from, that was for sure.

I snapped seven more shots. The race was on. *Click.* Who would take the best shot? *Click.* Who would be the first to get their work published?

Me. That's who. *Click. Click.*

The shape shifted and elongated, swirling until it settled over the courtyard and froze as if someone pressed the pause button.

The crowd grew silent. I lowered my camera. *WTF?*

A ball formed in my gut as the air in the middle of the circle formed a nearly transparent, shimmering bubble. A rainbow formed across its surface; the stripes brilliant, clear, and defined. Dozens of breaths hitched as an iridescent flicker glimmered across the apparition. The form pinched and molded into a colorful, swirling tube that slowly dropped from the sky.

Oh. Crap.

Matt tightened his grip on my hand as the other spectators stepped away. Half their gazes staring up, the remainder staring at me. Some stumbled into the bushes lining the walkways.

"Friends of yours?" Matt asked.

I shivered. "No. That's not Erescopian technology." At least I didn't think it was. Erescopian ships were liquid metal ... shiny opal or silver. "That just looks like ... "

"Water," Matt whispered.

Water hanging in the sky. Or more like a lake ... a huge lake with a giant elevator tube dropping out of it. So. Not. Good.

The cylinder fell in short, billowing waves before settling on the middle of the South Lawn. It was there, but it also wasn't— like it took a picture of the Butler Library columns behind it and played back a video on the cylinder's façade, hiding the tube like a chameleon. Incredible—if I wasn't standing so close to it.

Matt inched back, glanced at me, then returned to my side. If I hadn't been glued to my little patch of grass, I wonder if he'd have run.

Camera shutters triggered like crazy. Everyone gawked at me, like I was supposed to know what to do.

Yeah, 'cause Jess Martinez knows all there is to know about spaceships.

A whoosh of air rushed through the open area. The people on the other side of the cylinder stepped back, shielding their eyes as a bright, flickering light flooded them.

My fingers tightened on my camera strap. I'd seen that light before, on the tarmac two years ago, as hundreds of Erescopian soldiers left their liquescent spaceships and stepped onto the earth for the first time. It was supposed to be over. They weren't coming back.

I remembered to breathe, and tried to stop my hands from shaking. This thing didn't land in the center of Columbia by accident. They knew I'd be here. My legs trembled, itching to run, but I knew there was nowhere to go.

A siren blaring from behind the buildings broke my frozen stance. I raised *Old Reliable*, clicking off shots that probably would amount to nothing, until a human form materialized within the cylinder's hazy brilliance.

2

The figure whirled within the glow until the floods abated, leaving us in the soft radiance of afternoon and the eerie shimmer of the fluidic crystal cylinder. I shot off another round of photographs, catching the blurry shape within the glass, until the figure stepped out onto the lawn.

The wind kicked up, and perky blond curls wafted in the breeze. *No. Way.*

"Maggie?"

My best friend from high school spun toward me, giggled, and bounded in my direction.

I tried to control my gape. "How ... What ... ?"

She nearly jumped into my arms. "I just took a ride on a spaceship," she said. "That was so freaking cool!"

"What are you ... Huh?"

Her smile dazzled, detracting from the liquid craft behind her. "This thing landed right in front of your house. I thought Mrs. Miller was going to have a coronary."

Matt's grip on my hand stiffened. "Are you going to get to the part about why you were on that thing?"

She raised a brow at Matt, but turned toward me. "Oh, yeah, well, he said he couldn't feel you or something like that. So I told him you were at college in New York, and he said where's New York? And I said in New York, silly, and he said—"

I held up a hand. "Maggie."

Matt's grip became iron. Pins and needles tickled my fingers. I didn't need to ask why. She said *him*.

Maggie placed her hands on her hips. "Wait. Matt? What are you doing here?" Her eyes widened. "Oh my glob. Are you guys seeing each other?"

"I, umm, I … " He turned away.

Maggie snickered through her nose. "Damn, Matt. First Bobby, and now you're taking on an alien who can probably lift a car over his head. Do you have a death wish or what?"

Matt's lips tightened as his attention drew back to the ship.

Maggie leaned toward me. "E.T. is still rocking that hard body, by the way. Could crack a walnut with that ass, I swear."

"David's in there?" I don't know why it came out as a question. I found myself squeezing Matt's hand as hard as he squeezed mine. Grounding myself.

"Of course he is." Maggie shielded her eyes, scanning the crowd. "He's up there pushing buttons and waving his hands around like he's playing Xbox Sports or something."

"That still doesn't answer why you were on the ship."

She laughed. "His alien GPS wasn't working so I had to show him where New York was. As soon as we left Jersey, he said he could feel you again, and here we are!"

A deep hole formed in my chest.

Two years.

Two freaking years and not a peep out of David. For all I knew he was dead.

And now he was back. In a nearly translucent spaceship. Parked on Columbia University's front lawn.

Numbness settled over me as several police officers moved the crowd back. A security guard approached. His lips formed an "O" as his gaze fell on my face. He backed away, hands splayed, and scooted a different group to the sidewalk.

A confused oblivion took hold as the buzz of the crowd slipped into the background. I'd gotten so used to the idea of David being gone that I could barely compute the spaceship only a few paces away from me.

More police scampered onto the scene as the base of the cylinder shimmered into a full glow again. The blurry figure of a man stepped out and solidified, facing the bystanders opposite me. Matt released my hand and shoved his fingers in his pocket, hunching his shoulders.

A few people gasped, and several women's voices yelled something about the man's resemblance to the actor Jared Linden before camera-palooza started up again.

My heart sank to my toes, and a knot formed in my stomach. The pull started—the undeniable invisible tether that drew me toward him. My skin tingled. My arms ached, begging to touch, needing to hold.

He was here … right here in front of me, and part of me still couldn't believe it.

David's fists clenched and his dark hair shifted in the breeze as he scanned the crowd. Not searching for me, of course. He knew exactly where I was. David was as drawn to me as I was to him.

I blinked away the buzz and raised my camera. The lens worshipped the white cotton tee-shirt stretched taught across his shoulders as the focus panned over his waist to enjoy the walnut-cracking rear-end Maggie just *had* to point out.

Dammit. He was just as gorgeous as I remembered. But what the lens captured was only a façade. Beneath that human covering hid beauty most people couldn't imagine. Pearly lilac skin.

Violescent. And a heart I'd die for.

My hands trembled as I clicked the shutter button again. I needed to keep it together. Focus. He was just a guy. A story. An award-winning photo opportunity.

Yeah, if I kept telling myself that, maybe I'd believe it.

Matt shifted nervously at my side as David turned and looked directly into my lens. *Click.*

His eyes: so blue. So needful. So ... sad?

My stomach twisted as David walked toward me.

Keep cool, Jess. You can do this.

A tingling wave spread over my skin. All I wanted to do was rub all over him like a kitten on a catnip-coated scratching pole.

But I couldn't do that to Matt. I had to be strong. Ignore this insane longing.

Matt was a nice guy. Human. Hung around on Earth all the time. Was always there for me. He didn't leave for years at a time and *not call.* He didn't ... I gritted my teeth.

Dammit! After all this time, why did I still want to cover myself with sweet alien goodness? *Click. Click. Click. Click. Click.*

David's face filled the lens before he drew my camera down with one finger. "I don't really have much time."

I stared at him, letting my camera hang loose around my neck. The draw swirled inside me, but I managed not to step toward him as his words sunk in. "Excuse me?"

David sighed. "Listen—"

Oh, I was sooo not ready to *listen.*

I punched with both my hands, bashing him in the chest. "No, *you* listen. You're gone for how long, and all you have to say when you get back is you don't have much time?" I slammed him again, and he stepped back. "I waited for you. I waited for you like an idiot, wasting my senior year staring at the stars, but did you even call? No. I heard nothing from you. *Nada. Nunca.* Did you ever even ... ever even ... "

At some point during my tirade, he'd grabbed my wrists. His face was expressionless.

My hands remained fisted, ready to punch. His lips tightened as his grip relaxed. "Can I let go of you now?"

I closed my eyes and nodded, even though I didn't want him to let go of me. Not now. Not ever.

His hands fell to his sides, but I wasn't done.

Two years. *Two freaking years!* I punched his chest again. My fists thudded like striking a lightly padded wall. I shook the ache away.

David grimaced. "Are you done?"

I dug my nails into my palms. I didn't know what I wanted to do more: kiss him, or smack that annoyed look off his face. "No. I'm not done. I'm angry."

Matt appeared at my right. He gulped, his gaze trained on David. What was he going to do, protect my honor?

Maggie touched my left shoulder. "What's wrong with you?"

What *was* wrong with me? For years I've been waiting for him to come back. But now the only emotion coursing through me was anger. But was I angry at David, or at myself for still feeling this stupid connection?

David ran his hands through his hair. "I don't have time for this."

Time again. Getting hit with a bat would have hurt less.

Just how insignificant was I to him? I thought he loved me. But maybe it was never about me. Maybe it was only about humanity as a whole, and I was only part of that. God, what an idiot I was.

Matt moved a little closer.

Brave. Dependable.

Matt always called. He never left me hanging. Okay, maybe he never saved my life or anything, but he was a good guy. He'd save me if he had to. *I think.*

David's eyes narrowed, and his attention shifted from me to Matt.

Oh, crap! Next time hold your thoughts around the telepathic alien, Jess!

"I don't know you," David said.

"This ought to be good," Maggie whispered.

Matt gulped and offered his hand. "Hi. I'm, umm, Matt. I've heard a lot about you."

David just stared at him.

"Matt is Jess's boyfriend," Maggie said.

Oh. My. Gosh. She did *not* just do that!

Matt stepped back. "Can we please not tick off the already ticked-off-looking alien that's twice my size?"

David's gaze fell on me.

Happy thoughts. Happy thoughts. Nothing going on here. No-sir-ee, Bob.

David blinked, took Matt's hand, and shook. "It's nice to meet another friend of Jess's."

Wow. That went well.

He faced me. "I need to talk you." His voice—so short. So direct.

"We're already talking."

"Not here." He glanced over his shoulder. Seven or eight cameras fired off as his warm hands surrounded my fingers. "Please come with me."

I gazed into my reflection on the shimmering exterior of his ship.

"David, I don't think I should—"

Come.

His voice rumbled through my mind, shattering points inside me and breaking any desire I had to rebuke him.

His grip tightened, and I started walking.

"Jess, are you alright?" Matt asked, reaching for me.

I nodded. "Yeah."

But wait, was I? Did I really want to get on that ship? I'd just gotten my life back. Well, somewhat at least. College was going great. Getting on that ship meant Jessica Martinez's name plastered across every internet site in the world again. There was nothing I wanted less.

I dug my heels into the lawn. "Wait. I can't go with you." David raised an eyebrow. "I, I need—" I turned back to Matt. "I need ice cream. Matt and I were going for ice cream, and, and maybe even lunch." David's brow furrowed. I raised my chin, ignoring it. "Friends don't let each other down." I slipped my hand away from David and folded my arms. "So yeah, there it is. I can't go. We're getting ice cream."

David's head tilted in that adorable way that made me want to inch my palms up his arms and drag my fingers all over his ... No! No feelings. No feelings at all! I tapped my foot and looked away.

"Ice cream?" David asked.

"Yes. It's cold. You'd hate it."

A yellow hue flashed over the crystal hull of the ship. David's lips tightened as he faced his reflection. "I'm coming," he whispered.

Did he just talk to his ship?

The turquoise in his eyes darkened to a deeper blue, nearly human, as he turned to Matt. "I'll have her back in a few hours. Will that still give you ample time to get this—ice cream?"

The muscle in David's neck tensed as he spoke, and regret flowed across the tether that bound us. Had he just lied?

Matt formed several words before lowering his shoulders. "Yeah, I guess that would be all right."

"Wuss," Maggie whispered.

I elbowed her in the ribs. She answered with an innocent grin before her eyes danced all over David again.

Part of me wanted to throw something at Matt. But the realist in me didn't blame him for backing down. Anyway, David had never outright lied to me. Omit the truth, maybe, but if he said he'd have me back in a few hours ...

Something deep inside me sank. I usually trusted him. So why didn't I now? Maybe because he hadn't met my gaze. Did he know I'd felt his guilt?

But why lie to Matt?

I had a bad feeling I was going to need a double decker sundae with extra hot fudge by the time this afternoon was over.

3

Maggie gave me a thumbs-up as David led me into the cylinder below the spaceship. Matt kicked the dirt at his feet. Poor guy. He finally got the gumption to ask me out, and this happened.

Light flooded around us, followed by a chill that propelled David and me upward.

A sick, tingly feeling gnawed at my gut. The last time I was on a spaceship we ...

Oh! David slipped his hands around my waist. His strength seeped through me, into my very being, filling the holes that had lain empty for the past few years.

David had said we were connected. I knew this, because we can speak telepathically, but maybe it was deeper than that. Were those holes inside me because of him? Did I need him to fill me with his David-ness to feel complete? What did this connection really mean?

The amber glow dissipated, and David eased us off the glistening disk that had appeared beneath our feet. "Give me a second and I'll adjust the temperature so you're not too warm."

"Thanks."

I wiped the sweat that had beaded on my brow the second I entered the ship. Maggie must have been so excited to be aboard that she hadn't thought to complain about flying inside a giant oven. It had to be over a hundred degrees. Nice and hot, just like the Erescopians liked it.

The walls shimmered like mirrors before morphing into a translucent, milky white. The ceiling rose several feet higher than the roof of the smaller ship we'd traveled in two years ago, and the hallway leading to the front of the ship seemed much longer. I felt like I was standing in the foyer of a two-story mansion rather than a spaceship.

"Wow. Nice digs. New?"

"Yes. It's experimental technology. Do you like it?"

Experimental. Wow. The last ship was made of an alien metal able to transform into any shape the pilot wanted. How could you improve on that?

A smile crossed my lips when I realized I wasn't shying away from the walls. This soft, creamy white-ness warmed like a hug, chasing away the memories of the dreary dark corridors of the other crafts we'd flown in. I guess the old design could be improved on.

A purplish-blackish blotch formed in the wall, expanding outward like a giant knot in a tree. The bulge quivered before a dark, hairy form rose out of the liquidic surface, completely dry, as if it had sunk in reverse. Ten spindle-like legs shot out of the mass before the creature leaped toward me. I held up my arms and caught a gargantuan, chirping spider.

"Edgar!" I cuddled his eighteen-inch frame to my chest as he nuzzled his coarse mandibles into the crook of my neck. "I missed you too, buddy." The *grassen's* six-inch, triple fangs expanded and retracted as I scratched the bald space above his three glossy black eyes.

"Apparently she's happier to see you than she is to see me," David grumbled.

He walked toward the front of the ship and waved his arms over the panels below two huge windows that took up most of the forward wall. New York's skyscrapers blurred before blue sky and clouds encompassed the view screens.

Whoa.

Edgar crawled up and draped himself over my shoulder. His hind legs tickled my back as I raised *Old Reliable* and clicked off seven shots. "It didn't even feel like we moved."

David sunk his arms into the blue-tinted liquid that made up the console. "This ship is designed to excel in extreme pressure environments. The ride in space was even smoother. And it's fast. Really fast."

I placed Edgar on the floor. He waved his one gray leg before he scampered to the right and plunged into the shimmering liquid wall. The partition formed circles, like someone had thrown a stone into a lake, before smoothing once again. I'd never get tired of watching that.

But Edgar's sudden exit had left me alone with David, and the awkwardness that had grown between us. It didn't have to be this way. At least it shouldn't have been this way.

Dammit, all this time I didn't even know if he was alive or not. How did he expect me to react when he just showed up out of nowhere?

When I stepped toward the windows, a blob of clear liquid bubbled up to form a chair beside David. I slipped *Old Reliable* into my backpack, set the worn leather on the floor, and sat.

"Is that why you came back, to show me your new hot-rod?" The bite in my voice singed my lips. I regretted my tone, but only a little. Until he turned, that is.

The pain in his eyes sliced through me. God, did I want to wipe that expression from his face, cuddle him into my arms, and beg for forgiveness.

Wait. What? No. I was mad at him. Angry. Super angry.

His lower lip twitched and his brow furrowed.

You're reading my mind, aren't you?

"I don't have to. The indignation is radiating off your skin." He turned his chair and stared back at the panel, sucking in the side of his cheek.

Damn, did I want to cave. I missed him. I missed him like I missed chocolate during Lent. No, worse. But he needed to understand how freaking lost I'd been for the past two years.

The waiting. The wondering. The not knowing.

Every day I'd watch the news and see all the updates about Mars.

I'd been riveted to my screen when NASA released pictures of the red planet when it began turning blue. I'd celebrated when they'd confirmed it was water—oceans on Mars!

And I'd waited for a sign. Anything. Hadn't David wanted to share his accomplishment with me? Didn't I mean enough to him to call?

And then he shows up like nothing happened. And finds me with another guy. Why didn't that bother him? Was his ego so inflated that he didn't even consider Matt competition? Or was he just being David, the sweet, unassuming scientist I fell in love with?

"You were really nice to Matt," I said.

"Why wouldn't I be?"

"You didn't even flinch when Maggie said he was my boyfriend."

He tapped a point in the upper right of the console. "Because it wasn't true."

"How can you be so sure?"

He laughed. "If I tell you, you'll be mad."

"Madder than I already am? Not likely."

David turned to me, resting his left elbow on the edge of the console. "When I stepped off the ship your emotions flooded me like a cyclone. You felt pity for Matt. Nothing more. Your most direct thoughts, your desires, were centered on me."

My eyes widened. "You conceited son of a—"

"Your thoughts. Not mine."

I gritted my teeth and perused the laces in my sneakers. "Stop reading my mind. It's not right. You shouldn't know what I'm thinking."

He spun back to the console. "Like I said, that's very hard sometimes."

Was he right, though? Was I only mildly concerned about Matt? Didn't I feel anything else? Matt was a great guy. Cute. Smart. Funny. I loved being with him. But what did that mean?

I took a deep breath and grasped the arms of my chair. "You stared at me for a second when Maggie said Matt was my boyfriend. You were checking to see how I felt about him, weren't you? It wasn't any cyclone-effect. You read my mind on purpose."

"I really don't want you any angrier than you already are."

"Be honest. What did you see? How do I feel about Matt?"

He dropped his chin to his chest, as if all his muscles gave out at once. "You're very close, maybe closer than you are with Maggie. But it's friendship. I found nothing to be troubled about." His chair swiveled toward me. "Was I supposed to pretend to be worried? Did you expect me to hurt Matt? Is that why you were concerned for him?"

"No." *Yes. I don't know.* "It just seemed like you didn't even care."

David's face hardened. "You know better than that."

Did I?

He returned his gaze to the windows above the control panel. "We're here."

"Here? Where's here?"

"Just south of a grouping of islands about two-thousand five-hundred miles off your continent's west coast."

I still had no sensation of moving as we flew low and passed a torrent of bubbling water cascading from the side of a mountain and disappearing into a world shrouded in pre-dawn twilight.

Wait. Twilight? It was noon when we left. I squinted at the shadowy treetops barely visible below us. The light emanating from the ship caught the outlines of large multi-segmented leaves. Palm trees? I turned back toward the waterfall. Was it possible? "Is that Hawaii?"

We circled several times, sinking closer to the surface as the sun began to rise. Yup. Those were definitely palm trees.

"You brought me to Hawaii?" I jumped up and down—I must have looked like a complete idiot, but I didn't really care. From New York to Hawaii in under ten minutes? We could go anywhere in this thing and be back before Dad ever cried foul. How stinking cool was that?

"It's nice to see you smile again." David slid his hand into mine and tugged me back toward the shiny disk that would take us down to the beach. "This isn't the place you know as Hawaii. This is an uninhabited island about one thousand miles south of there."

Still, a tropical island! How cool is this? You are forgiven. You are forgiven. You are forgiven.

I reeled in my thoughts. How stinking shallow was I? Two years alone and I could forget it all because of a surprise trip to paradise? Did David have any idea how special somewhere like this might be to me, or did he just pluck a warm location off the map so he'd be more comfortable?

We stepped onto the disk and dropped into the elevator tube. I clung to him until the cylinder opened to the sound of the ocean and the smell of salt. A sea bird cawed overhead, not more than a shadow in the early dawn light.

David guided me from the ship. My sneakers sank into soft sand as a gentle, warm breeze shifted my hair. Soft waves lapped the beach beside the ship. Behind us, mountains rose, circling us on three sides in a private cove.

I'd never seen anything so beautiful.

"We missed it," David grumbled. "I can't believe it." He trudged around the base of the ship.

Along the horizon, the sun kissed the sea good morning, splashing fiery orange across the water.

"Missed what?"

Sand crept into my sneakers as I followed. David stopped, facing the high, dark mountain. A thin, silver, reflective blanket lay across the beach, weighted by seashells at the corners and a covered bowl of fruit at the center. The sunrise basked the scene in a reddish, warm glow.

My stomach sank to my toes. "Wait a minute. Was this supposed to be a date?"

He pointed toward the sea. "I didn't expect to have trouble finding you. And now we've missed the sunrise. And you're angry with me. And nothing is going right."

I stepped closer. "You did all this for me?"

"Well, yeah. I missed you, and I wanted to spend a few minutes with you before … " He lowered his eyes and kicked the sand at his feet.

"I'm sorry I was so upset, but you just showed up out of the blue."

He slipped his hands into mine. That sweet, lost little boy air coated his features. "So, showing up is bad, but also not coming to see you is bad." He shook his head. "I don't understand."

I plopped onto the blanket, pulling him beside me. "It's not that you showed up, it's just that you've been gone so long."

"But it was less than a full cycle."

"Well, I don't know what you mean by a full cycle, but two years is a really long time on Earth."

"I didn't … " He rubbed his palms on his jeans. "I don't know." A myriad of expressions flashed across his face before his eyes saddened. "I never wanted you mad at me. You are the only one who ever really believed in me. You are the last person I'd consciously make unhappy." He stared at me, as if memorizing the lines in my face. "I screwed up. I'm sorry."

A deep, sour prickle slithered across our bond, a regret deeper than anything I'd ever experienced. He wasn't lying. He genuinely didn't mean to hurt me.

I slipped my arm around his shoulder. "I'm sorry for the way I reacted."

"I thought about you every day. You have no idea how hard it was to keep away."

"So why did you?"

"Earth isn't exactly an easy trip unless you have one of these." He motioned to the ship. "And visiting—it's just not something my people do. We're taught to give our females space, breathing room. I didn't want you to think I was weak."

I wove my fingers around his. "Why would I think you were weak because you wanted to see me? That's crazy."

His smile warmed me in places I didn't even realize were cold. "I'll have to remember that."

"And what's all this stuff about me being the only one who believes in you? You're the guy who's building a planet. I mean, your people will probably name schools after you. You have to be totally stoked about that."

His smile faded. "Children may learn about me, but not for the reasons you think."

"What?"

"Why does it rain, Jess?"

"Huh?" That had to be the strangest turn of conversation ever. But then again, there was nothing all that normal about sitting on a beach at sunrise with an alien.

I'd been a pretty big jerk up until this point, so it wouldn't hurt me to go along with David's extraterrestrial whims. And today's scientific topic, apparently, was rain. "Well, water evaporates into the air, turns to clouds, and the clouds drop the water as rain."

"Yes, but why?"

"I don't know. It just kind of happens."

"It doesn't just happen. There has to be a reason. A catalyst."

"Well, aren't you some kind of environmental biologist? I mean, you just filled all the oceans on Mars and stuff. Don't you—"

"It didn't work, Jess." He blinked, his eyes tired and puffy.

"Huh?"

"It didn't work. The Mars project, it's over."

"Wait, what?" I straightened, kicking sand onto the blanket. "Every telescope on this planet is pointed in your direction. We watched the oceans fill. Half the planet is blue."

A beam of pride crossed his features. "Yes, they did fill, and you should see them. The ocean is so deeply blue, and the coastline— the blue swells lapping against the red sand—Oh, Jess, I wish I could take you to see it. It's really beautiful."

"So what's the problem?"

He covered his face with his hands before dropping them to his lap. "We harnessed the power of the sun, warming the planet and melting the polar caps to fill the oceans a hundred times faster than anyone believed possible. I utilized pre-existing scourge technology to inject the atmosphere with synthetic greenhouse gas and protected what we'd achieved with a series of superconducting rings." He shook his head. "That was supposed to be the hard part. I was even able to introduce a nitrogen factor to increase the density. It worked. Everyone said it was impossible, but I did it."

"I don't understand. That sounds like everything went according to plan."

"It did, but there's no catalyst for evaporation. The moisture stays in the oceans. Without movement of the water through the air, the planet won't be able to sustain life. It will die, just like it did a million years ago."

I stared at him, agape. All that time, all that work for nothing? It couldn't be possible. There had to be an answer. Maybe even an obvious one. "Can't you set up an irrigation system of some kind?"

"The planet needs to naturally sustain itself. A planet lives, just like we do. It needs moisture to travel and replenish itself just like we require blood flowing through our veins. Without a naturally circulating vapor system, there is no life, and no hope for Mars."

My stomach twisted. Two years of work, leading to another failure. No wonder he needed me. He'd become a scientific pariah again—the same problem that drove him to Earth in the first place.

"So what happens now?"

He stared at the sea, his lips pursed. The silence tore through me.

"David?"

"I told you their acceptance of my proposal to spare Earth was conditional."

I gasped. Visions of giant spaceships and billowing explosions flashed through my memory. The night the world stood still. The night humanity almost ceased to exist.

"No. No you can't let them."

He pushed up on his knees and grasped my shoulders. "There is a place in your ocean where the land beneath the sea is closest to the planet's core. A kinetic energy manifests from that point." The colors in his eyes spiraled. "This energy travels to the surface, charging the particles with enough kinetic energy to overcome the liquid phase intermolecular forces."

My mind raced. "Okay, but what does that have to do with saving Earth?"

"There's something in your ocean, Jess—something that creates kinetic energy and spreads it through the sea. It's the reason your planet is alive. It charges the water particles strongly enough that they keep their own energy until they return to the sea to be recharged." He loosened his grip. "Whatever is down there is *not* on Mars."

A chill ran across my skin. The experimental ship behind

me—a craft made to withstand a pressurized atmosphere. "You're going down there, aren't you? You're going to look for whatever is making that energy."

He nodded.

"Well, you can't take it. Whatever it is, Earth needs it!"

"I think you know me better than that." He dragged his thumb across my cheek. "I need to see it. Study it. Understand how it works. Once I do, I should be able to duplicate it on Mars."

"And that will stop your people from taking Earth?"

David sat back. "I don't know, but it's all I can come up with. I have to try."

A waft of yellow fluttered across the exterior of the ship.

"Edgar is signaling me. I have to go." David stood. "You'll be safe here."

"Wait. What?" I jumped to my feet. "You're leaving me here?"

"When my people come, they will eradicate the main continents first. Uninhabited islands will escape the initial scourge. You'll be safe here until the population phase."

My legs trembled. "They're coming? Now?"

"The Caretakers had already begun assembling the armada when I left Mars. Thankfully, the ships large enough for a full-scale scourge cannot travel as quickly as this one. We should have at least two days before they get here."

"Two days? But, but … " But everything. Earth was supposed to be safe. The Erescopians were supposed to be our friends. But now we were back where we started: on the brink of annihilation. And … *Omigosh*. "What about my father?"

David lowered his gaze. "I was hoping to find him at your home. I wanted to bring you both to safety, but I barely had time to find you."

Two more flashes of yellow rolled over the ship.

"I'm out of time." He walked toward the shimmering craft.

Was he serious? "But—"

A *thomp* echoed across the sea, and the edge of the water splashed up like someone threw the world's biggest rock into the waves.

"Hide in the trees!" David screamed, jumping through and sinking into his ship's liquid hull.

Another *thomp* reverberated from above, smashing into the beach and spraying the sand across my shoes.

Was someone shooting at us?

The cylinder below David's ship began to retract.

He was serious. He was actually leaving me here!

Yeah, you know what? Not today.

I sprinted toward the cylinder and jumped. My sneakers barely bridged the base of the retracting tube as I pulled myself inside, but the open elevator I expected closed in around me. The cold of the liquid metal stung my skin—colder, wetter, harsher than I remembered. The air iced my lungs, burning from within as I whirled upward encased in the ship's frigid grip.

My head poked out into the rear compartment, and my chest rose into the room, but nothing else. The hull started to solidify around my ribcage, trapping me inside the floor.

"David!"

The metal surrounding me constricted, pushing the breath from my lungs.

"David!" I screamed with the last of my air.

He bolted into the room and stopped short at the entrance, gaping. "Are you insane?"

I reached for him, and tried to call out again, but my voice wouldn't come. The ship rumbled as his arms slipped beneath my shoulders. My ribcage stretched as he pulled, fighting against the ship's tightening grip.

Was this where my own stupidity had finally lead me? To get crushed inside a disappearing elevator?

No. I wasn't going out like this. I refused.

Tightening my grip around David, I twisted, fighting against the ship's hold. My body shifted, slipping toward David before the floor constricted again.

David gasped. "Whatever you just did, do it again. Quickly! The ship is trying to seal itself for takeoff. It will cut you in two!"

The flooring now strangled my waist. David growled, digging his heels into the tiles on either side of me. Inside the liquid floor, my knee found something hard. I pushed with every ounce of strength I had and the metal around me gave. I slid free, falling to the ground beside David.

"You're crazy," he said, popping to his feet like a poodle on speed. "We were taking off. You could have been killed." He sprang toward the front of the ship, not even checking to see if I was okay.

I trotted after him, rubbing my bruised ribs. "Well I wasn't about to let you leave me there. Don't you know I—"

"Shut up, Jess."

I stopped short. "Excuse me?"

"I said shut up." He grabbed my wrist and flung me onto the still-forming seat beside the pilot's station. The chair came to life and seized me like I was breakfast and it hadn't eaten in weeks.

A thud pummeled the side of the ship and the window screens wavered before the island disappeared in a blur as three smaller, opalescent ships crossed paths before us. David veered us away, over the ocean.

"I thought we had two days before the other ships got here?"

He glanced at me, then back to the windows before him. "Those are sentry ships. They were already here."

A bright flash of light crossed our path. My seat tightened around me as we jolted forward.

"Why are they shooting at us?"

"I told you this was experimental technology, right?"

The ship quaked as another bolt streamed across our hull.

"Yeah."

"Well, I forgot to mention that I stole it."

"You what?"

We rolled, just missing a fourth ship as another blast of light splayed across our hull.

The side panels pulsed yellow twice.

David glanced up and then out the window. "I see it. Thanks, Edgar."

"What did he say?"

"That they're falling behind. They can't keep up with this ship. Nothing can."

We turned up toward the clouds.

"What are you doing?"

"Getting ready to dive. This is going to get interesting."

"Do I want to know why?"

"Probably not."

We stopped and hung in the air for a moment, before dipping in slow motion until we faced the ocean. The shimmering water seemed worlds away. Quiet. Soft. Peaceful.

Then we started to fall.

4

My fingers curled around the edges of the chair that had built itself up around me. I sucked in a breath, shaking, as a million prayers rolled through my mind. My heart thumped, matching the rhythm of the first time I rode the Kingda Ka roller coaster at Great Adventure. I tried not to think about how much higher this drop was.

The ocean raced toward us. The roll of the waves cast back the morning sun's brilliance, blinding me—until our black liquescent pursuers shot up directly toward us.

"Hold on!" David sunk his arms into the panel and swished twice before pushing back into his seat. The chairs came alive, filling the room with the scent of warm copper as a clear gel bubbled up around us, encasing all but our eyes, nose, and mouths.

I screamed, bracing for impact as the dark ships filled our view, then split and flew in opposite directions before we collided. But that was only two. Where was the third?

Thomp.

Our ship clattered as a panel beside David's window flashed blue.

"Just another second, Edgar!" David called out.

I clutched my chair restraints as the sea rushed towards us. A *shring* sound filled the chamber, like a knight drawing a sword out of a metal scabbard. We jolted, hitting the surface, then slid through the sea's crest like a hot knife through butter.

Bubbles covered the windows and floated away.

Thomp.

The echo beneath the water rattled my skull, but not the ship.

"Are they following us?"

"Probably, but they won't be able to dive as deep as we can." His restraints relaxed, allowing him to look at the panels over his head. "Edgar, bring us down two *sellecs*."

"Edgar can fly the ship?"

"Who do you think helped me steal it?"

The ship shuddered and the lights flickered before fading to black. My restraints loosened slightly, allowing me to move my head, but not much else.

"Are we hit?" I asked, squinting in the dark.

"No," he said. "We're fine." David shifted again in his seat. A slosh like a kid splashing in a bubble bath filled the chamber. Was he free of his chair? "Turning out the illumination at this depth is as good as hiding. They can't dive this far without losing cohesion, so they won't risk it. And if they can't see us, they can't ... "

Thomp.

The ship jarred to the right. So much for hiding.

Thomp.

We seemed to drift to the side, and I had the sensation that up wasn't quite up anymore.

Thomp. Thomp.

A weight slammed against the top of my head. I wanted to protect myself, but my hands remained immobile within the glossy grip of my chair. David grumbled a few words in his own language. My stomach sank as the gel bubbled around my face again. My ears filled, pounding with pressure. I tried to open my mouth to help pop them but my restraints locked around my jaw, securing me motionless. A scream formed in my throat, but I didn't set it free. I couldn't stay secured in that seat much longer.

The incessant *thomping* stopped. We swayed, as if floating gently on the breeze, a feather drifting in the dark. David rustled beside me again, and the liquid console splashed and trickled.

He exhaled. "They've returned to the surface."

Thank God. "Where are the lights?"

"Just a few more minutes."

Once my restraints loosened, I pinched my nose, closed my eyes, and popped my ears. I sighed at the sweet release of pressure and flopped back into my now cushy, regular, not-alive chair.

"Why were they chasing us?"

"Like I told you. I stole this ship. They don't care why."

They don't care, and they were coming. Them, and thousands more like them.

Two years ago, when the liquescent ships first came to Earth, alien-induced brilliance had shattered the darkness—wide beams of glowing orange stole the air and cracked the soil beneath our feet.

I shivered. That couldn't happen again. It just couldn't. "Are they really going to scourge my planet?" I rubbed my shoulders.

"I negotiated with the Caretakers as much as I could. They agreed to give your leaders twenty-four hours to move your population to the colder climates to the north and south."

"One day to move billions of people? That's impossible."

"I know that. That's one of the reasons I stole this ship. I knew this new technology would get me to Earth at least two days before they did. I wanted to warn your United Nations, give them more time to evacuate. But from their reaction, I'm afraid they will try to defend themselves rather than comply."

"Well what do you expect, for us to just roll over and die?"

The lights flipped on. I squinted as David leaned toward me. "No. I expected them to take the extra time given to them and get as many people to safety as possible. They can't fight our technology. It would be fruitless."

I folded my arms. "Then you don't know humans as well as you think you do." How could he sound so callous, so matter of fact? We were talking about people here, not statistics.

He grabbed my wrists and pulled me toward him. "Let's not make this our fight, Jess. Earth's only chance is to make it rain on Mars."

I nodded, looking away. I knew he wasn't my enemy, but how could he speak of moving that many people like it was nothing? "What will happen to the people who aren't moved in time?"

He turned from me. "Our focus is whatever is in the trench."

A sinking pain sliced through my core. His not answering was answer enough. All those people … He was right though. The best I could do for them was to help David. "What trench? Where are we going?"

"A crevice deep within the heart of the ocean, eleven-hundred miles west of the island I wanted to tuck you away on. Secure. Where I didn't need to worry about you."

Holy staccato rub-it-in-my-face sentences. "You're mad at me."

He shrugged. "I just wish you were safe. That's all."

Why couldn't he comprehend that the only time I really felt safe was with him? It wasn't that I was a simpering little girly-girl. I just felt stronger with him. More sure of myself. More alive. Why couldn't he understand that?

A wry smile crossed his lips.

Oh. Crap. "Stop doing that read my mind thing. I hate it."

"It's not intentional." There was that smugness again.

Stop reading my mind!

Then stop thinking at me.

Ugh! You can be so annoying.

Me? He raised an eyebrow.

Okay, so I wasn't perfect. But at least my thoughts were my own.

Or they used to be.

David turned his seat toward me and leaned forward. "I will make every attempt not to read your mind, but if you send me thoughts, I'll hear them. There's no way around that."

"Is this part of that connection thing?"

He nodded and waved his arms over the console.

So, can you hear me now, or do I have to push those thoughts at you?

He looked toward the screen and then into the murky panel. Either he couldn't hear me, or he was pretending not to.

David seemed to read my thoughts as simply as he heard my voice. It wasn't just a skill for him, but a sense, like smell, taste, and sight. How hard would it be to turn off a sense like that? Was it even possible?

"So where is this trench again?"

"About three miles ahead, and seven miles down."

"Seven miles down?" My heart fluttered. "Are you taking us to Mariana's Trench?"

"I'm not aware of this place having a name, but that is how far we need to dive."

Mariana's Trench—the deepest of the deep. The real live boldly go where no sane person should go deep. So deep the sunlight can't reach. Darkness with a capital D, hiding creatures we could hardly begin to understand.

"The pressure down there is insanely strong. Are you sure this thing can handle it?"

David sighed. "No. We are going to dive a step at a time to give the hull time to adapt. If we are careful, we should be fine."

Great. Just great. He couldn't have stolen completely proven pressure-proof technology. He had to go for an untested Maserati.

I shifted my foot under my butt and clutched my seat. Just how far would we have to dive before we'd crack, if we were going to crack? The ocean hung like a dark shroud around us, like looking out a window into a dark fog. "Are we moving now?"

"No. We're hanging at eight hundred feet, making sure the hull holds."

A black blotch appeared in the wall before Edgar rose from the surface. He scampered across the floor and jumped into my lap. With a light growl, he cuddled under my arm like a tired puppy.

David scratched behind Edgar's three hidden eyes. "You did good today, buddy."

"So I guess you two are friends again?"

"In that he hasn't tried to dismember me today? Then, yes."

Edgar rolled over and I stroked the coarse, jagged hairs on his abdomen. The three of us had been through so much. Blasting through space, getting stuck on a noxious green planet, and racing through a melting spaceship trying to save my dad. Now we were underwater, floating, hoping not to lose cohesion like we had on the way back home to Earth. I shuddered, warding off the phantom chill.

How cold would the water be if the ship were to spring a leak? I shivered and continued to stroke Edgar's belly. David wouldn't have brought us down here if he didn't think we'd make it.

A high-pitched tone echoed through the chamber. Edgar lifted his head and peeked around my chair.

"What was that?" David asked.

The tone vibrated again.

"It sounds like a submarine ping," I said.

"A what?"

Ping.

A few particles brightened by the illumination within our ship floated outside the window, but other than that, only darkness lay beyond our line of sight.

Ping.

I sat back. "Submarines are underwater ships. They send out pings to find other ships."

David scrunched his brow. "That seems very archaic, even by Earth standards."

I decided to ignore the hopefully unintentional insult. "It *is* archaic. Most subs use passive sonar now so they don't give away their location."

"So why would they ping?"

Good question. "Maybe they couldn't hear us. Does this ship make any noise?"

"A liquid ship in water? Probably not." He looked over his glistening panel. "But even in silence, this ping will find us?"

Crap. Maybe I should have paid better attention in class. "I don't know."

Edgar stretched and poked his one gray leg into the console. The lights went out, leaving us in a soft blue illumination.

"Good call," David said.

We sat in silence, staring out the window.

Ping.

My palms dampened on the arms of my chair. Who was out there, and why were they looking for us? Had the sentry ships adopted outdated Earth technology hoping to find us? And if they did find us, what kind of danger would they pose at this depth?

A soft, yellow glow shone in the distance and became larger. David's hand hovered over a pulsing crimson light within the console. A deep intensity trickled through our bond. A need to protect. His fingers twitched.

Oh, God. Was he going to shoot them out of the water? What if it actually was a sub, and not the sentries?

"No." I grabbed his wrist. "It's probably only coincidence. I bet they don't even know we're here, or they heard something and are just checking it out."

Ping.

His hand formed a fist, but flattened again as his face hardened in the sapphire light.

"David, please."

The glow in the ocean intensified, becoming a long, gray cylinder: a submarine.

Relief flooded me. "It's not the sentries."

"That doesn't mean they're not a threat." His hand still wavered over the controls.

Ping. The sound echoed through the cabin as the sub drifted closer.

Black, rigid characters that must have been letters were stamped deep into the hull just over one of the submarine's search beams.

Ping.

The sub turned, and headed straight for us.

5

Edgar chittered, waving his two front legs in the air.

"What did he say?" I asked.

"How would I know?"

"Haven't you been talking to him?"

"Yes, through the lights in the ship. I can't understand what he's saying."

Edgar jumped onto the panel, straddling the liquidic core. His hind section rose as he chirped at the screen. David leaned back, unable to reach the console with a giant spider blocking the way.

The submarine became larger. And larger.

"Is it going to hit us?"

"Get out of the way." David flailed his arm, probably hoping to shove Edgar from the controls. Instead, his arms met three bared fangs. He jerked back. "We have to move. That thing is going to hit us!"

Ping.

I covered my ears as the sound echoed off the walls. David cringed. The ship filled both our view screens. Tiny, fuzzy particles circled in the water between us.

This was it. Times up.

A deep crunch rattled our hull as we collided. Edgar slid off the console, scampered across the floor, and jumped into the wall as we drifted away from the submarine.

A harsh, scrambled static filled the chamber.

"What is that?" I asked.

"A communication."

David sunk four fingers of both hands into the console and characters flipped and changed on the screen.

"What does it say?"

"I don't know. The computers are trying to translate."

The walls around us started to glow, illuminating the compartment. The letters stopped changing and twelve ornate characters displayed across the screen.

"Damaged," David whispered.

"Damaged?"

"As in a question. They're asking if we're damaged."

Who was asking though? Those words stamped on the hull certainly weren't English.

David swirled his hands in the console again.

"What are you doing?"

"Telling them we're not damaged."

"Is that a good idea?"

"If they're friendly, it's the truth. If they're not, it tells them we are a formidable target, and it would be unwise to attack."

I soooo didn't want to be involved in an undersea dogfight. Even if I was sitting inside superior alien technology. "But you wouldn't hurt anybody, right?"

David shifted his shoulders. "Underwater weapons functionality hasn't been tested. It's the one part of the design I've always questioned." He glanced at me. "Unless we ram them, I don't have anything proven to defend ourselves with at this depth."

Great. Just great.

The buzz started again. More letters scrawled across the screen.

"Another word," David said. "Luck." He held both hands over the console. "They're ascending."

"You have to be kidding me." Did the United Nations send someone to make sure we were okay? "Does Earth know you're trying to find something to help stop the attack on the surface?"

"Yes, but I didn't have time to go into great detail."

The pinging grew less intense and faded to soundlessness.

David scanned the black sea. "Okay, Edgar, let's bring it down another *sellec*."

Already? Didn't he want to wait? Take a breath? Think over what just happened?

I guess that would be stupid. Gotta save the world and all. Sometimes I wish we could just slow things down a peg.

The light emanating from our windows shone like a beacon challenging the sea's infinite night. It could have been me, but the little fluffy things hanging out in front of the glass weren't so tiny anymore. And not really fluffy, either. More like cone shaped with lots of little legs flapping a mile a minute behind them. Kinda like little baby squid, but … not. Very cool.

I snatched my camera from my backpack and zoomed in. Each feathered creature was its own work of art. Like snowflakes wafting in the sea. *Click.* Incredible.

"We're doing okay," David said. "You wouldn't even know we were under pressure. We're going to bring it down further."

The sea didn't change. Just more … well, blackness. I guess once it's pitch black, you can't get much darker.

Something fluttered before the window.

"What was that?" I asked.

David looked up from the console. "I didn't see it."

A riffle of a huge tentacle flickered past the right of the screen, barely catching the illumination coming from my window.

"Did you see that?"

"Yes." He stood. "Whatever it is must be attracted to the light."

The blue hue illuminating the six or so inches of sea outside the ship seemed to shrink, and my little fuzzy-fluttery buddies swam off like a scattering flock of birds.

Sweat formed on my brow as the last of them skittered into the sea. What did they know that we didn't?

A blur of whitish-cream darted across the window again before disappearing in a wave of long, billowing legs. An octopus? A giant squid? I tried to snap a shot, but only a white blur appeared on my screen.

I adjusted the settings on my camera. I was not about to lose a great shot because I wasn't ready.

A *whomp* rumbled against the glass, and the creature flew up from below us, filling the screen. Its legs launched out, splaying its underside in a flattened, eight-pointed star of wiggling ivory.

I grabbed David's arm. He barely flinched.

"Should we be worried about this?" he asked.

"How would I know?"

"It's your planet."

"Yeah, well, I've never been deep-sea diving before. It looks like an octopus, but that thing's huge!"

The creature twisted its underside, and the coloring began to take on a pale blue hue. The same color as the console. The blue traveled over its surface in waves. I raised my lens. National Geographic, here I come!

"It appears it's trying to communicate," David said.

My eyes narrowed. "Really? It just looks like a bunch of flashing to me." *Click.*

Dang, I hoped those colors came through.

David waved his hand over the panel, and the blue faded out. The octopus-thingy faded too. David changed the room's coloring to a shade of purple, and the octopus altered to the same plumy pallor.

Damn. Was it mimicking, or really trying to communicate? I changed to video mode. Some aquatic scientist somewhere was going to kill over the chance to study this footage.

A beaky-like protrusion jutted out from the animal's center.

"The sensors are picking something up," David said. "Listen."

He tapped the panel and a sound seemed to seep through the glass. Kind of a mix between a quack and a squawk. A chitter echoed between us, like a kid making noises under the water.

Wait. Edgar?

The octopus spun twice and flared both purple and blue over its long appendages before closing its tentacles and disappearing into the darkness.

I clicked off a dozen more shots. *So. Darn. Cool.* I hoped whatever Edgar had said was nice.

"We found significant life signs in your oceans," David said, "but I didn't expect them to be so—*interesting.*"

"Yeah, well, Earth—you know—full of surprises."

He nodded. "Yes, I'd like to keep it that way. Let's dive."

Oh yeah. Right. Save the world. I hadn't forgotten. But the sea was more amazing than I'd ever imagined.

I slid my camera back into my pack, but left it open, just in case.

David waved over the console panels, and this time the darkness actually managed to get darker, like adding the pitch of night to blackout an already charcoaled screen. The deep, murky depths seemed to bubble closer, like a monster lurking just out of sight.

"How deep are we?"

"Eighty-four sellecs."

"Which is how far in English?"

He stared at the ceiling, like he was doing the math in his head. "About two miles."

Two miles, straight down.

I leaned closer to the window. Since I was a kid, I'd loved going to the aquarium. Didn't matter which one, or how big. When I was ten, I'd plastered myself against the glass of an enormous shark tank, and even promises of cotton candy couldn't lure me away. And the Aquarium down in Myrtle Beach, with the real live mermaids? Dang. Mom and I couldn't get enough. It didn't matter they were just women wearing tails. It was awesome with a capital A.

I smiled, wondering what Mom would think if she were here with me. Would she think all this was as cool as I did, or would she be scolding me, saying it was too dangerous? No—that would have been Dad. Mom was always the wild one of the pair. It was probably better that Dad had no idea where I was, because me being missing would be far less stressful than knowing I was deep-sea diving with my favorite alien.

The ship jerked. Crashing forward, I smashed against my part of the control panel, knocking the wind out of me.

Gasping, I flopped back in my seat. "Are we at the bottom?"

"No. We hit something," David said. "Something was there, and then it was gone."

"Is it another giant octopus?"

"No. This registered a lot more bone. Something more dense and much larger."

The darkness outside seemed all the more ominous. I wasn't quite so ready to splay myself against the glass as I was a few moments ago. What was it this time? A whale? Whales could go pretty deep, right? Nice big, cute, krill-eating whales?

We jolted to the right and I flew from my seat and thumped to the floor. A vertical tail the size of Wisconsin swam past the window. Pale. Ghostly. Definitely not a whale.

David clutched his seat, staring straight ahead. "Jess?"

"I'm okay."

I crawled up to my chair. David's gaze was still riveted to the dark water. "Did you see how big that was?"

I rubbed my sore skull. "Yeah, I saw it. Shouldn't we be trying to get away?"

"Probably, but which way do we go? It showed up a second before it hit us, now it's gone."

Lovely. A giant, aquatic ghost. How many humongous fish lived down here? Giant squid, frilled sharks, God knows what else. Hopefully whatever it was wasn't hungry.

A white speck shone in the distance. It got bigger, ominously reminiscent of the submarine. The glow winked out, as if something swam in front of it, before lighting again. And again.

The radiant dancer moved closer to the ship, like a lone Chinese lantern swaying in the breeze. But there wasn't a breeze out there. Was there even a current at this depth?

I swayed to the left as the orb shimmied in that direction, and to the right as it shimmied back. Everything was so beautiful in the sea. Tranquil. Peaceful. I wished I had a blanket so I could cuddle up and sleep under that light, have it watch over me, protect me from anything that might float by.

Sleep. That was what I needed. It had been a long day. I deserved it.

My lashes fluttered. Their weight hung, begging me to close them. Relax. Forget about the sea, and aliens, and … everything.

"What the … " David's voice jarred me back.

I squinted. The hypnotic brilliance had transformed into glaring, emotionless eyes and rows of needle-like teeth—if needles were the thickness of tree trunks. The windows filled with nothing but mouth.

A scream ripped through the ship and I realized it came from me. I jumped away from the windows while David shoved his fists into the liquid console. We throttled toward the teeth.

Toward?

I stumbled back onto my chair as the windows collided into the massive, snapping jaws. We rammed, jumped back, rammed, and jumped back again. What was this, a macho pissing contest or something?

"David!"

"Working on it!"

Oh, really. Was he working on it?

Giganto-Jaws lunged at us, teeth bared and throat open. The ship vibrated, a gurgling hum radiating from the walls as we swished back and forth. Holy heck! We were trapped in its jaws!

A spew of bubbles drifted past the window as the creature let go, and we seemed to float. Alone. In the dark. But where was Giganotosaurus Jaws?

David turned toward the ceiling. "Edgar! Thicken the outer shell. We need to dive. Now!"

A scaly tail the size of a caboose caught the light from our cabin just before smashing against the windows. We jolted, and I fell to the ground again. I tried to get up, but my cheek wouldn't leave the tiles. It felt as if a million unseen hands held me, squeezing me against the floor.

What was going on? Had we dove so deep only to be booted out of the park by Godzilla's goldfish?

We rattled, cascading and spinning. My sight blurred. My breakfast threatened a reappearance. I closed my eyes and prayed David and Edgar could bring us under control. The tiles rumbled beneath my cheek before we collided to a stop.

My body left the floor before slamming back down once again.

A deep sting sank into my cheek. The edges of the floor and wall blurred together.

What ... how?

I blinked until I could focus, and pushed myself from the floor. A few feet from me, David dangled from the side of his seat, motionless.

"David!" Dragging myself from the unforgiving tiles, I sat him back in his chair. His head lolled back, his mouth slightly open. "Oh, God. David, please wake up!"

Pressing my fingers against the side of his neck and his wrists,

I sought a pulse. I couldn't find one, but relief flooded me as his chest rose and fell in a shallow breath. I glanced over each shoulder, and toward the back of the ship, looking for what, I didn't know.

Why hadn't the seats come to life and protected us?

I pulled David from the chair and into my arms. "David?" I kissed him and ran my fingers along the side of his face. "David, please … "

I would have felt less empty if part of my chest had broken off and floated away into the abyss. I didn't care that we'd crash-landed again. I didn't care that the marine floor was probably more alien than the green planet we'd been marooned on. I didn't care that the pressure of an entire ocean weighed down on us. And I didn't care that he'd left me alone for two years.

He was here, now. And hurt. I fisted my hands and pushed with my mind. If he needed strength, maybe I could send it to him.

David, I'm here. I'm sorry I was such an ass. I'm an idiot. I wiped the hair from his eyes. *Please wake up. I don't know what to do.*

But maybe I did.

Lifting him higher, I held both palms beside his temples. I thought of warmth, home, strength, love, and friendship. Every positive thought I could come up with rolled through me and into him. It was a long shot, but if he could hear me, maybe he could feel me, too. Maybe I could strengthen him with all that was me, and all that was us.

His lashes fluttered. His eyes opened, but didn't seem to focus. "Jess?"

I gulped back a sob. "Yeah. I'm here."

He tried to sit up, but frowned and relaxed back into my arms. "Are we okay?"

"I don't know."

He winced. "Edgar?"

Oh crap. I'd nearly forgotten. "Edgar!"

The silent, barren walls mocked my call. I waited, praying that the *grassen* would pop out of the wall and dance toward us.

"Edgar!" I wiped the hair away from David's forehead. "He's not answering."

"The ship didn't change color? No flashing on the panels?"

"No."

David whispered a word in Erescopian. My imagination translated it to an English word that started with an F. He sat up on his own, rubbing his neck.

"Give yourself a second. You're hurt."

"If we lose cohesion, a sore neck isn't going to matter all that much."

Good point.

I helped him up to the console. The windows had closed, hiding the outer ocean from view.

"Can you tell how deep we are?" I asked.

He stared into the fading blue liquid. "About twenty-thousand feet. We're sitting on the ocean floor, just on the edge of the drop off."

The Abyssal Plain? Not like it really mattered. We were pretty much at the bottom of nowhere. Unless, I guess, you peered over the edge of the trench. "And how much further do we need to go?"

"About three more miles."

Crap. "Is the ship okay?"

He slid his arms out of the console and plopped to the floor. His gaze fixed on a point in the back of the ship before he sighed and rubbed his face.

"Is it really that bad?"

"I might have a chance with a *grassen*, but unless Edgar pops out, we're in big … "

A bright light shot out of the floor, glowing and pulsing like something out of a Star Trek movie. I stood, grabbing the back of David's seat as a shrill, screeching sound cut through the room.

A line etched through the decking. A yellow glow filled the

room with a sunny glow. But there was no sun at the bottom of the ocean. Whatever had caused this couldn't be natural.

David stood slowly, his gaze riveted to the growing line. The chill of fear trickled through our bond before morphing into terror as a hissing sound filled the chamber.

The glow separated, and cold, lashing water flooded the cabin.

I grabbed my backpack, tossed it onto my chair, and zipped my camera inside. David made a sound like a screeching child and hopped onto his own chair. Callous, biting cold slashed my ankles. My toes numbed. I couldn't blame him for crying out. These kinds of frigid temperatures could shut down his heat-hungry nervous system.

The fissure widened, and the sea crested in like a tidal wave, seizing and yanking me from my chair. I kicked and spluttered as the torrent slammed me to the ground and rolled me across the tiles. My hands flailed, my fingers grasping at the slick flooring without finding purchase.

"Jess!" David's voice faded into the bubbling fury around me. White froth slapped across my face as the deluge flipped me into the air and pulled me down through the punctured floor and out of the ship.

The frigid surge stung my lungs and I tried to cough, but icy splashes threatened to drown me. I tumbled over and over, lost in a world of bubbles and bitter cold fury pummeling me from all angles, dragging me through the sea. My fingers froze. My arms ached.

Until I thudded onto a solid, unforgiving surface. I lifted my head and spluttered in the continuing surge from above. Crawling as far as my frozen limbs would take me, I fell, rolling onto my back. The torrent gushed from a hole in the cavernous ceiling— drilling down and splashing on the rocky surface below. Steam rose from the ground, casting a foggy haze through the room as the deluge continued to thunder.

"David!" I squinted in the fog and blinked the water from my eyes. "David!"

Had he escaped the cyclone? Was he still in the ship?

"David!"

The endless roar of the waterfall gave me my only answer.

Catching my breath, I crawled out from under a dripping stalactite. My backpack bobbed in the swells about a yard from me. My camera! All the pictures from Columbia and the video of the octopus! I waded through the churning water and reached for my bag as a dark form fell through the hole above and thudded on the rocks.

"David!"

I chucked my backpack aside and scrambled toward him, dragging his unconscious form back and hauling his legs from the churning froth. Several bubbles erupted across the top of the water as my backpack succumbed to the draw of the sea. My heart sank with it. That camera had been by my side for the last four years. *Old Reliable.* My most valued possession.

But not more valued than David. I pried my eyes from the place where my camera disappeared and eased us onto the wet rocks. David's drenched frame hung like a weight in my arms. My muscles screamed from the strain.

"David?" I wiped the drenched hair from his forehead. His skin—so cold. "Please, David."

When we first met, he'd nearly died from a chilly forty-degree night. How much of these freezing temperatures could his body take?

He quaked, and my heart leapt. I cuddled him to my chest, giving him what warmth I could. But how could I really warm him when I was just as wet and cold as he was?

The raging torrent above stopped as if someone had turned off a faucet. A rounded shimmering disk hung in the ceiling, surrounded by long, striped stalagmites of different lengths. My reflection shone back at me, as if I were admiring myself in a mirror, or in a pond. But above me.

An upside-down pond?

The remaining water around us swept through a hole in the cave floor, emptying the chamber as quickly as it had filled. I lugged David into my lap and wrapped my legs around him, holding as tight as I could. A few feet away from me, the last of the swell swept into the hole in the floor, leaving my backpack dripping at the base of a boulder. Part of me drained away with the stream of seawater pooling beneath the stained leather.

I took a deep breath as the insanity settled. The camera could be replaced. I needed to worry about David—and getting us out of here.

A tidal pool nearly identical to the one above sloshed within the rocky surface, mirroring the roof of the cavern. How was any of this possible? A chamber beneath the sea, filled with air. No one would ever believe it.

I unconsciously reached for *Old Reliable*'s shoulder strap, but it wasn't there. My eyes trailed once more to my dripping pack. A photographer without a camera, in a world no one had seen before. It wasn't fair.

David groaned.

Priorities, Jess. Priorities. Forget about the friggin' camera!

My sneakers squished as I eased David down to the hard rock and snuggled beside him. My skin tingled and my muscles ached. Keeping him warm might be the least of my worries. We were twenty-thousand feet below sea level, without a way to get home. But for now, it was all I could do.

Steam rose around me, chasing the chill from my skin. At least I had that to be thankful for. Maybe we were inside some sort of a volcanic formation. I didn't know, and I barely cared as exhaustion stole the last of my strength, and the walls, the fog, and the swirling pond above glided into the darkness.

6

Sometime later, I lifted myself from the rocks. A tiny snore puffed from David beside me, reminiscent of the night he fell asleep in my closet, eons ago. I placed my hand on his brow—boiling hot, just as it should be. Thank God for our natural steam bath.

I rolled over and studied the stalactites above. White, sparkling glitter seemed to drip along each rocky blade—but maybe it wasn't a sparkle. They shone, stinging my eyes as if they glowed all on their own. Natural fluorescent lighting? Mother Nature would never cease to amaze me.

Dozens of similar formations poked out from different points in the ceiling, probably the only reason I could see. The rock surrounding them mocked me: solid across the entire chamber, except for another shiny surface on the far wall that reminded me of the giant mirror Grandma had hanging in her living room. It was like a prison. No way out, except up through the shiny disc in the ceiling, or down through the pond in the center of the room. Neither seemed a good or plausible choice.

My shoes squished as I shifted. Ugh. How long had I been laying there soaking wet? I yanked off my sneakers and poured water out of one of them. That couldn't be good. I wrung out my socks and left them near one of the tiny holes in the floor venting steam.

David groaned as I slipped off his shoes and socks. He blinked several times before he smiled.

Then he sprang to his feet, steadying himself on a stalagmite jutting up from the floor beside us. "Where are we?"

Setting his conservative, white socks next to my pink plaid, I focused my thoughts, sending him a Jessica-induced video representation of the wave sucking us through the hole in the base of the ship and spitting us onto the rough cave floor. He spun, surveying the top and bottom mirror-like exits. "This is impossible. It's environmentally infeasible."

"I know, right? But here it is."

He smoothed back his hair. "The pressure in here would have to be the same as outside. Why are we still alive?"

My jaw dropped. I hadn't thought of that. "Umm, I don't know, but I'm not complaining." Getting crushed to death? Definitely not on my top ten list of things to do today.

David stood on the edge of the circular pond and examined its identical twin above. "So our ship is up there?"

"Yeah, I guess. Unless it floated away."

His eyes darkened as he faced me. Not that I blamed him. No ship meant no escape. And that simply was not an option.

I straightened, forcing the pessimist in me away. "The ship was filling with water. It would sink, right?"

He nodded.

"If it's on the ocean floor, above us, there would be less chance of it drifting away." I looked into my reflection in the pool above. "We just need to figure out how to get to it." *And pump out all the water before we drown.* I grit my teeth. Optimism didn't always work when everything was against you.

"No," David said. "You're right. It has to be up there. We need to find a safe way out of this room." He continued his inspection of the cavern. "There are more openings over here." He walked to the far side of the chamber and touched the shimmering wall that looked like a mirror. He retracted his hand quickly, water dripping from his fingers. "Cold." He wiped the droplets on his jeans. "If that's the ocean, water should be flooding this room." He shook his head. "It's like a bubble where there shouldn't be a bubble. It makes no sense." He moved around the chamber, pressing against the walls. "Solid. Everywhere."

He said it like that was bad, but it was also kind of good. I wasn't too keen on the idea of any of those walls caving in on us. There was a gazillion pounds of freezing-cold ocean out there.

He walked over and slid to the rocky ground beside me, leaning against the stalagmite. "I wish you hadn't come. You were supposed to be safe on that island. Now you're stuck in this ... " He waved his arms in the air. "Whatever *this is* with me."

Regret coursed through our bond, swirling quickly into something else. Something warm. Inviting. He crossed his arms over his shoulders, hugging himself.

I inched closer. "It's okay to be glad I'm here."

His lips pursed. "I thought we weren't supposed to be reading each other's minds?"

"It's hard not to when you're flinging your emotions at me."

He smiled. "Touché."

I leaned against his shoulder. Funny thing was, I felt the same way. Something about being with David made everything all right, even though everything was very, very wrong.

My stomach grumbled. "Sorry. I haven't eaten in a while."

"Neither have I." He tugged me closer, tightening his grip. "I don't know what to do, Jess. It's not like either one of us can go outside and search for food."

"I know." I clung to him. "We'll find a way out of this. We always do."

"This isn't like the other times. Before I knew what we were dealing with. This time I think we're both hopelessly out of our league."

I closed the gap between our noses. "Maybe. But that doesn't change the fact that ... " A mass of green lay across the rock formations near the back wall beside the mirror. It hadn't been there when David inspected the phenomena before. "What is that?"

David rose to his feet and walked toward the wall. I stumbled behind him on still-tired legs. He picked up what looked like dripping, soaked, mossy leaves. Water trailed from his hand into a divot in the rocks below.

He stared at the limp plants, and then at the mirror. Sometimes I wish I could read his mind whenever I wanted, not just when he sent me thoughts.

Raising his hand, he nearly touched his reflection before pulling his fingers away. The leaves dropped from his grip as he staggered back, peering over both shoulders.

"What is it? What's wrong?"

His gaze centered on me. "It's food. We're being fed."

"What?"

"We're in a cage."

7

"What do you mean we're in a cage?"

"It's the only thing that makes sense."

"How does us being in a cage make sense? This has got to be some sort of natural formation that just hasn't been discovered yet."

"Then how do you explain the food? It shows up out of nowhere when we show signs of hunger. It's not naturally growing in here. The walls are completely dry, and those leaves are wet. That's a sea plant. Someone put it there."

"Do you know how crazy that sounds?"

"Insane. Completely insane, but even you thought that the ocean's depths haven't been completely explored. Anything can be down here. An entire civilization for all we know."

My eyes narrowed. "If you start spewing stuff about Atlantis I swear I'm going to crack you one."

"Then I'm really glad I have no idea what you're talking about."

My stomach grumbled again. We'd fallen asleep, so I wasn't sure how long we'd been down there, but my stomach told me long enough. My gaze trailed back to the seaweed. "Do you really think we can eat that?"

"It would be risky. We don't know what it is."

I picked up a fistful of the soggy leaves. They blurred as a feeling of light-headedness flushed over me. I grabbed the wall to keep from falling.

Like an idiot I'd skipped breakfast yesterday to meet up with Matt. How incredibly stupid. Would ten minutes really have made a difference?

I shook the fog from my head. I'd never gone more than twelve hours without eating, and that was sleeping all night for a blood test. I'd been ravenous the next morning.

"Jess." David's eyes told me he'd read my thoughts.

"If we're going to get out of here, we'll probably have to climb. We'll need our strength." And I, obviously, was running out of gas.

He reached for the plants. "It's not worth the risk. I can last another day without losing my faculties."

But I couldn't.

My hand trembled. Clear liquid dripped off the bubble-like pods covering the jagged leaves.

If we *were* in a cage, then someone went through a lot of trouble to create an air-filled habitat miles beneath the surface of the ocean. Why do that if they wanted to hurt us? I broke off a piece and slipped the salty pod into my mouth. I tensed, but held steady, managing not to hurl as I rolled the plant around on my tongue.

It reminded me of the peas Mom had grown in the garden when I was a kid. Pliable, but hard at the same time, and pretty much tasteless once my saliva drowned out the seawater. I bit into the pod and chilled liquid rolled over my tongue, exploding in a bitter tartness that ebbed into a sweet, syrupy soup.

"Omigosh!" I held the leaves up to David. "You have got to try this. It's delicious!"

He fingered the leaves, staring at the bubbles.

"Come on, plant boy. This is right up your alley."

He slid a wad of leaves into his mouth, chewed, and smiled.

"It is good."

He took another bite and handed me some more. I poked another leaf in my mouth and crunched the pod, whisking away the salty sea taste and replacing it with the sweet goodness of the plant.

David glanced at the mirror, and then to me. "That plant provided both sustenance and hydration. The thick outer shell must be adaptive to the pressure. Ingenious."

"Like I said. Earth. Full of surprises." I surveyed the water-filled ponds above and below us, wondering how many surprises lay in store for us that I hadn't even dreamed of outside fantasy novels.

David ran his fingers along the edge of the mirror. "Thank you," he whispered, staring into his reflection.

I hugged his arm. "Do you really think there is someone on the other side of that thing?"

"If there is, it wouldn't be someone. It would be more like some*thing*. This environment is like nothing we've experienced before. Our bodies would be crushed under the pressure out there. If they live in this, who knows what kind of form they would have."

The glossy sheen shimmered inside the mirror, glistening, waiting. Were we really in a cage? Were there things on the other side watching us, studying us, playing with us like hermit crabs in a terrarium? Would they give us toys next, see what we like to climb on? Give us exercise wheels? What? I covered my face, my brain not coming to terms with what David seemed to take for granted.

One thing I did know: there was no way I was going to live in this little room for the rest of my life.

I stepped up to the mirror. "Okay out there. Thanks for the food and all. We appreciate the hospitality, but we'd really like to go home, now."

David raised a brow, but our watery image didn't stir.

"Listen," I continued, "there is something pretty bad going on up on the surface. You see, these aliens are coming, and they're going to take over the planet. You're going to get new neighbors, whether you like it or not." I cringed, wondering if they'd think that was a bad thing. "I just want to go home. Can't you understand that?"

"Maybe."

David and I spun toward the voice behind us. A silvery-shaded boy popped out of the water and leaned both elbows on the edge of the pond. He glistened in the fluorescent-like lighting. My heart lodged in my throat.

"Who are you?" David asked.

"The more pertinent question is, who are you?" He pushed up and sat on the edge of the pond, leaving his feet dangling in the ocean depths.

Were there flippers under there? A giant tail? If he was a merman, and I didn't have a camera, there would be Hell to pay! I moved next to David, grabbing his arm. A tingle formed between us, easing some of my fear.

The boy flipped himself around and levitated, ascending on two very human-shaped legs. His body glimmered in that same silvery gray tone as his head and arms. His eyes seemed opaque, as if he didn't have eyeballs—like he was one solid sleek and shiny piece with no beginning and no end. I forced myself to breathe, not sure if I was in awe or terrified beyond belief. My trigger finger twitched, and I glanced at my backpack. To hell with being scared. I needed pictures. *Old Reliable* had been through worse. For all I know, he was in there, ready and waiting to take the photo of my lifetime.

David squeezed my arm before I could take a step toward my camera. Stupid, stinking, telepathic alien. This wasn't fair—any of it.

The creature walked toward David. "The female's species we are familiar with. They dwell above. But your make-up is unknown to us."

I tightened my own grip on David. "He's Erescopian. He's not from our planet."

The boy folded his arms, taking on a pose quite similar to what

I'd done earlier in the mirror. "I see. One can actually dwell off a planet?"

"Yes," David said. "In specialized ships." How was he staying so calm? We had no idea who this guy was and David was acting like they'd met on line at Starbucks.

"Very interesting." The boy circled us.

"Is that what we are in now," David asked, "some sort of specialized ship? Is that why the pressure isn't affecting us? Where is the air coming from?"

Always the scientist. I was more worried about whether or not this dude was going to eat us.

I tried not to move as the boy reached out and touched my shirt, rubbing the fabric between his fingers.

"This coating is not part of you," he said, ignoring David's questions.

"Umm, no. It's clothing. We wear it. It-it keeps us warm, and, you know, hides stuff."

Our gazes met. "Hides stuff?"

"Yeah, you know. Private stuff."

He stared at me before he turned back to David. "And why are you on this planet? You are from somewhere else, yet your pheromone markers are all over this native." He pointed at me.

Pheromone markers?

David blinked twice. "We're ... " He cleared his throat. "Close."

The silver guy leaned nearer to David, as if smelling him, and then did the same to me. "It seems that you are close quite often. Your essence is within each other."

David straightened. "We're connected."

Silver flinched. "But you are not the same. You aren't even compatible."

"I don't care, and it's none of your business."

Silver's eyeball-less eyes widened. "Interesting. Most interesting indeed. And your individual species have no problems with this?"

"We're just friends," I said. "I don't know what the big deal is." Okay, so maybe David and I were a little more than friends, but David was right. It was none of this guy's business. "How about you answer some of our questions. Like where are we? What is this place, and how the heck are you down here and no one topside knows about it?"

"The air-breathers know what we allow them to know. There is no need for them to know more." He pointed to the water-filled hole in the ceiling. "Your ship sunk and landed on the plateau above. We've tried to inspect it, but the security system has proven quite effective."

"Security system?" David asked.

"Yes. This." He raised a hand to the pond, and the sea rose in the center, bubbled, and dripped up like ice melting in reverse, forming a segmented build with ten long, creepy legs.

Edgar!

A wave of relief flowed through our bond. The little guy was okay and apparently giving our captors some holy hell. Good boy.

"As for this place … " He raised his hands and surveyed the room, " … we created this environment to mimic the pressure, gaseous combination, and temperature in the vessel that brought you here."

"So now what?" David asked. "Do you keep us here? Study us?"

The boy's solid face pinched where his mouth should be, forming a smile. "You seem to have high expectations of how interesting you might be." He glared at the mirror, and returned his attention to us. "We are wondering why you ventured to our depths. The air-breathers have already studied this section of the sea floor."

"We were looking for a source of kinetic energy. It originates at the base of the trench."

The boy arched his back in a very in-human way. "You seek to enter the rift?"

"Maybe. Do you know where the energy comes from?"

Silver's features wiped away, almost disappearing from his glossy skin. "Why do you seek this energy?"

David shifted his weight. "My people are trying to make a home on a neighboring planet. This energy isn't there. We need it."

"This is not something you can just—take."

"That was not my intention. I want to study the source, try to understand how it works so I can duplicate it for my own people. I'm not here to steal from you."

Silver nodded. "We can feel your sincerity, but you do not understand what you ask. And this power is not ours to explain, or to give."

The boy scrutinized his reflection in the giant, glassy mirror again. His hands drifted out to his sides, as if floating. The slight indent where his nose should have been pulsed.

Were the ones outside talking to him? Could they be telepathic, like David?

Silver jerked his attention back to us. "We cannot help you. You need to leave, before you cause more problems than you came here to stop."

"How do you expect us to … "

The boy took two backward steps and dropped back into the pond. The surface barely swelled as he disappeared into the sea.

David crouched on his haunches, holding the sides of his head.

I seated myself beside him. "So now what?"

"How would I know?"

"It was kind of a rhetorical question. I didn't really expect an answer."

He reached for me. "I know. I'm sorry."

We reclined on the hard stone. I cuddled onto David's chest, but the rock floor must have been killing him. "I guess we're back to: *how the heck do we get out of here?*"

He stared at the shimmering pond in the ceiling. "We don't

even know if our ship is still up there. They could have done anything with it." He shivered, and I pulled him closer to ward off the phantom chill.

Even if the ship was up there, David couldn't swim for it. Not at these frozen temperatures. I was pretty sure I wouldn't last long, either.

The illumination faded to a barely visible gray. David tensed and sat up.

Silence surrounded us. Not even a trickle came from the watery exits.

David's arm slipped around my shoulder. My eyes grew heavy as a sweet aroma tickled my nose.

Were they drugging us? I sat up. "David?"

"I feel it." He eased me back to the ground.

My chest fluttered. I shook, clutching his shirt.

What was in the air? Poison? Did they decide it was easier to just get rid of us? And then what? Would they set us out to sea? Feed us to the sharks?

Pressure built between my temples. Aching. Throbbing.

My vision blurred. We couldn't just give in. We had to do something. Anything. But what?

I folded myself against David, hiding in the safety of his arms until I relaxed and reveled in the sweet, syrupy smell. David's grip fell slack, and the room faded to nothing.

8

A drip echoed through the dim cavern, angering the throb in my temples. I blinked, but it did nothing to dispel the darkness.

The water beside us sloshed. David and I sprang up at the same time.

"Who's there?" David asked.

"Do not fear," a voice whispered. "It is me."

A bluish shine burst through the water, casting an eerie radiance throughout the room. The water fountained through the air and thickened, forming a human shape as the silver boy landed in a crouch beside the pond.

I wasn't sure if I was horrified or impressed. Was he actually made of water?

David slid his arm around me and drew me closer. "What do you want?"

Silver inched forward, still in his crouch. The light cast an ominous glow behind him. "They don't know I'm here."

They? The area where the food had appeared hung in complete darkness. I tightened my grip on David's shirt.

"I have questions for you," Silver said.

"All you do is ask questions," David replied.

"But the previous questions were not my own."

David's arm tensed around me. "You said you wanted us to leave. You need to give us our ship to do that."

"They left that matter for discussion after the tide changes. The others have all retired."

"And why haven't you retired?"

Silver's face tilted to the side. "As I said, I have questions." He inched closer. "What do you propose to do if you discover the secrets to the energy you seek?"

Anger sizzled through our bond. "I told you, I need that energy on another planet. To bring another world to life."

"Does this planet have an ocean?"

"Yes. It's not as big as Earth's, but parts of it are deeper than the trench."

"Sea life?"

David's expression slackened. "None yet. Our plan was to ask Earth to share some of its wildlife and plant life." He turned toward me. "Only to help quicken Mars's recovery once the precipitation problems are settled."

"Precipitation problems?" Silver asked.

"It doesn't rain."

Silver nodded. "The particles are not charged with the life power."

"You know where the power comes from, don't you?"

"Possibly, but like I said, it is not something you can understand. It is not something you can take with you."

David stood. "I don't have a choice. And I *will* figure this out. Too much depends on it."

Silver straightened. "You can't enter the rift. You will not be welcomed."

"There's something else down there." David's brow inched up.

"Something you're afraid of."

"The depth dwellers are not like us, although they are more like us than they care to admit. And they don't take kindly to those above them, either my people or hers." He pointed at me. "They will protect themselves viciously."

"I told you I don't want to steal anything. I just want to study the power source. Reconstruct it somehow."

"This cannot be done."

David leaned forward. "Is this why you came? To talk us out of going there?"

"No." Silver held his hand beside my face and ran it along my side. Close, but not touching. "This is of great interest—how your resonance mingles within hers."

David shoved Silver's hand away from me. Water splashed across the floor. "Why?"

"Because you are dissimilar. Contact with different kinds is frowned upon here. We are kept apart. Segregated. Same stays with same. I find it curious that two of different species are together."

"Well it's different on the surface," David said.

I cringed. *Not that different.* Dad had bribed me with eggs and extra bacon that morning when he'd tried to convince me that David wasn't coming back. And David's only Erescopian friend, Nematali's nose crunched up like she'd smelled rotten fish every time she saw David near me. Dad had come around a little bit, but in general, things weren't much different on the surface.

Silver stood. "The lesser levels of your ship are reinforced and water tight—as if the ship were designed with the purpose of transporting a large, seaborne cargo. I don't believe that you didn't intend to steal the power source, and neither will those below you."

David stood and faced Silver. I rose beside him. The muscles in his neck twitched. His hands trembled. Had he lied to me? Was he planning to steal it all along?

"That ship is designed for many functions," David said.

"Whatever it is that you are protecting, I swear, I won't take it."

"But you could," Silver said.

David nodded. "Yes, theoretically."

Silver stepped back and sloshed back into the sea. The lights dimmed, leaving us in darkness once again.

***

An amber glow filled the room, and I rubbed the weariness from my eyes. David sat beside me, slipping on his shoes.

"How long have I been asleep?"

"I'm not really sure." He handed me my socks and sneakers.

"No more visits in the dark?"

"None that I am aware of, but we need to get out of here. Who knows what's going on up on the surface."

My feet tingled as I forced them into my still-damp shoes. The windows remained dark, but another pile of seaweed lay on the rocky shelf. Not quite the breakfast of champions, but it would have to do. I handed a bunch to David. The cool sweetness of the pods didn't seem as satisfying as it had earlier.

The pond in the floor began to bubble. A spray shot up from the center and rained down around us before another geyser appeared, and another until a uniform, frothing column formed with the pond as the base and the hole in the ceiling as the topper.

Silver stepped out from beside the column. "You are free to go. But you must leave. Return to your world. Tell no one what you found here."

David stood. "I told you what our plans are."

"You must forgo any plans. Return to where you came from. Immediately." Silver moved close, and seemed to smell us again. He lowered his voice. "There is an aperture at the bottom of the crevice." His pupil-less eyed swirled toward me, then David. "Within that space is the source you seek."

"You're helping us?" I asked.

Silver took a big whiff of my shoulder. "In time, I hope we can help each other. Wait until the tides change." He stepped back and raised his voice. "You must return to the ship the way you came."

The column of frothing sea roared, the surge gaining in intensity.

He couldn't be serious. "But the water is cold," I said. "Can you warm it?"

"We cannot."

David balked and took a step back. What was cold for me equaled instant hypothermic shock to him.

I slipped my hand around his wrist. "We can do this. Together."

He nodded, but his eyes lightened to a frosty blue. A color I hadn't seen before.

This wasn't going to be easy, but I needed to be strong. If not for me, then for David. For us. "What do we need to do?"

"Step in," Silver said. "Let the tides take you."

Sure. Easy for him to say. But we needed to get home, and the first step, apparently, was to freeze our asses off.

I guess it wasn't all that much different than going down a log flume. You are warm from an afternoon at the amusement park, you get soaking wet and cold on the ride, and then you dry off. You just prayed that the wind didn't kick up afterward and ruin the rest of your day.

I grabbed my backpack and pulled out *Old Reliable*. The chances of him working were slim, but I had to try. I mean, seriously, who would ever believe all of this without proof?

I flipped the power switch, raised the lens, and pressed the shutter button, but no satisfying click rewarded me. The last shreds of hope sank and floated away. I slipped the camera back into my bag and closed the zipper.

David's eyes seemed apologetic before he gulped and looked back to our icy elevator.

I pulled the straps of my backpack over my shoulders, warding off the unbridled panic sizzling across our bond.

You can do this. No problem. I shoved the thoughts toward him, but he barely glanced at me. I guess I could understand. This ride wasn't going to be all that pleasant for me, either.

I took a deep breath and let it out in a puff. The best way to remove a Band-Aid was to just go ahead and rip it off, so I might as well start ripping.

One. Two. Three.

I sprang for the geyser, ignoring David screaming my name. The frigid water lashed my cheeks and the rest of me succumbed a second later. The bite dug into my skin, seared through my muscles, and probed deep into my bones. I coughed as the spray blasted my face, splashing and rolling me until I shot up through the hole and crashed onto the decking of our ship.

A screech filled the cabin and Edgar jumped on my back. He spun in circles, jabbering desperate sounding clicks and pops.

"I'm fine," I said, even though it was only partly true. I threw my backpack to the side. "But when David comes through, he's going to have hypothermia. We need heat. Lots of heat." I turned to the spout. *Come on, David. We're ready. I'm here.*

9

Edgar reared up and clicked at me. I could actually see anxiety in every one of his glossy, black eyes.

"Don't worry about me. I can take it. If it gets too hot, I'll let you know."

He jumped into the wall and the ship's illumination faded to a deep, ominous blue before brightening. A slight hum filled the room, and delicious warmth drifted down from above. But would that be enough to help a frozen alien?

The giant waterspout heaved, and David plummeted to the decking beside me. He curled into a ball, wet and shivering; his human skin tinged blue. I pulled him to me, blanketing him with my own body, but he didn't even feel cold to me. He didn't feel hot, either. How chilled were we?

The fountain flowing from the opening in the floor reared up over our heads like a demon cobra before it splashed back through the aperture and disappeared. I hugged David, trying to control his shiver as my own skin prickled.

Please, Lord, help me warm him up!

"J-Jessss."

"I'm here." I cuddled David closer. "Edgar is heating the ship. We're going to be all right."

The lighting took on a reddish glow, and the temperature rose. I rolled David to the floor, collapsed beside him, and let the warmth infuse me, bake me, bring me back from the frigid abyss. This was certainly more than I could do for David with what little body temperature I still had.

Blinding yellow brilliance erupted up from the hole in our floor. The ship creaked and moaned as the giant orifice zipped shut like closing a winter jacket. Bright sparkles shone through small fissures before the liquid metal finally filled in. I blinked away my surprise. A clean, unmarred floor lay before us as if nothing had ever happened.

It was over. We were safe in our ship. Free to go.

Steam drifted off our clothing as the humidity in the room heightened. I coughed, but a heavy weight still burned within my lungs.

David moaned and faced me. "Y-you're going to k-kill me y-you know that?"

I choked out a laugh. "I knew you'd follow if I jumped in. It's one of those things that you just have to get over with."

He flopped onto his back. "Why does everything always have to b-be so c-cold?"

Edgar slipped out of a wall and nestled himself between us.

David scratched behind the *grassen's* eyes. "Thank you, my friend."

"I can't believe they just let us go like that."

"I don't figure they really did." He got up and stumbled toward the console. "Let's hope Edgar was able to make repairs."

My little *grassen* lifted his front two legs in the air, waving his gray limb up and down.

The walls in front of the control panels shimmered and faded into clear glass. The ocean glowed artificially around us. A few yards from the ship huge, dark blobs hung in the sea. Some of the light filtered right through them. Some kind of jellyfish?

David eased into his seat and sunk his hands into the console. We ascended from the shelf.

"Good job, Dude." I patted Edgar's head.

The blobs swam with us, shadowing.

"What are those things?" I asked.

"I think those are our gracious hosts."

Huh? The globules convulsed and rolled over, rocking in the current of our ship. They seemed more like a waste product than a sentient animal.

"But Silver looked nearly human."

"I doubt that was really him. I think that was a form to make us comfortable. Just like this human-colored skin I'm wearing. It makes no sense for a creature with a land-dwelling form to be living under water."

I ran my fingers along the glass considering the creatures surrounding us. They were just big squishy globules floating in the sea. How could they be thinking, communicating beings? A smaller blob fidgeted and twitched behind the others as if it had an itch it couldn't scratch. Could that be Silver?

David tapped his lower lip. "Edgar, how did they cut a hole in a liquidic ship? How did they pull us out of here?"

A sense of unease trickled through our bond as Edgar scurried toward the panel. "Does it matter? We're okay now, right?"

David lowered his hand. "This is advanced technology, even for Erescopians. We should have been more protected. If I knew how they got in, I might be able to keep them out if they change their minds about letting us go."

Edgar sunk his legs into the console, and the walls flashed in an array of colors.

David raised a brow. "Ingenious. Impossible, but ingenious."

"What did he say?"

"They used the water like a knife to split and hold our hull open. They can control the ocean like a tool."

His gaze carried to the sea. That was a whole lot of water to use against us if they wanted to.

He sat back. "As soon as they took the knife out, our ship was able to reseal itself like nothing ever happened. I don't think they ever meant to hurt us. Maybe they really were just curious."

"Is there a way to fight them off if they get curious again?"

"Only if I can figure out how to control water in the next few minutes."

We rose, and the blobs continued to follow. David tapped the wall beside him.

"What are you doing?"

"The only thing I can do. Watch for the tides to change." The console flashed crimson. "Here it comes."

The globules seemed to crunch into themselves and darken. They froze, hanging stationary while we continued to ascend.

"What happened to them?" I asked.

"Changes in the current movement must affect them somehow. That's why Silver told us to watch the tides."

The darkened entities sank one at a time, disappearing into the depths below.

David leaned toward the console. "Here's our chance, Edgar. Let's dive."

A small beam of light shot out from the front of our ship as we scooted across the plain's surface. We passed several blobs that sunk and settled to the ocean floor like a littering of boulders on the sand. Darkness crept up before us, chilling me despite the heat inside the ship.

"There it is."

My heart rattled against my ribcage. Were we really going to do this? Whatever was down there scared Silver. He didn't think we should go. Maybe we should listen to him.

I reached for David's hand. His warmth didn't settle me the way it should have. He trembled. His mind raced through billions of emotions. He was just as afraid as I was.

We crested over the edge of the plateau and fell straight down like dropping from some sick, suicidal roller coaster. The darkness seemed to close in around us as we spiraled, sinking into depths man was never meant to intrude. The gloom pierced, devouring the searchlight. Deeper. And deeper

"We're nearly six miles down from the surface," David said.

Holy crap.

"The ship is holding. Not even a blip on the panel. We're doing fine."

My hair fell past my cheeks as gravity pulled me down with the ship. The seat held my waist, but I still fell forward toward the windows.

I couldn't wrench my gaze away from the murky haze outside. So dark. Vast. We shouldn't be here. Nature separated humanity from this place with miles of water and freezing temperatures for a reason.

The weight of it all pressed against my chest, like I was doing something really bad. Something God never intended me to do. Would He be ticked? Was this the part where nature fought back against man, like white blood cells lash out against a virus?

A blaze of illumination fanned along the walls.

David flinched. "That's not possible."

"What's not possible?"

The ship vibrated, then slipped back to silence. But we continued to fall.

"No!" David's hands fisted. He propped his knee on the front of the console to keep from falling forward and waved his hands manically over the swirling panel. "Edgar, where are you?"

My ears popped as we descended like a boulder. "What's happening?"

David's eyes flashed a deep human blue. "We lost propulsion. I can't control the ship."

"What?"

"We're sinking."

This, I knew. The searchlight continued to spiral through the darkness, cascading into a pit of doom.

David muttered something in his own language, and the tiles behind me hissed. The liquid-metal mottled, pinched, and formed a grid-like ladder. "I'll be right back." He spun out of his chair, gripped a rung, and climbed up the steps blanketing what used to be the floor that led to the rear of the ship.

I climbed over the back of my chair and followed. My sneakers sunk into each protrusion, like walking up padded steps. "Is there anything I can do to help?"

"If I can think of anything I'll let you know."

A handle-like-loop formed above David on the back wall. He gripped it, hauled himself up to the partition, and sunk one of his arms into the surface while clinging to the loop with the other. Somehow he managed not to dangle his feet down toward the front of the ship.

Edgar popped out of the panel on my left, scuttled across the floor, and dove into the same wall David hung from.

Man, what I wouldn't give to not have to worry about gravity like my ten-legged little friend. I felt so stinking helpless I couldn't stand it. There had to be something I could do. Knock on a door, hold up a sign, boil some water, something!

The arm David hung from started to shake. Concern tingled through our bond. He squinted at me before continuing whatever he was doing.

Then his thoughts blanked out, like the *David-ness* in the chamber disappeared. Was he blocking me on purpose? Why?

Oh, God. Whatever he was doing wasn't working. We were going to die, and he didn't want to scare me.

"David?"

He frowned and grunted as if straining himself.

Well, I couldn't fix the ship, but if support was all I could give, then dammit, I was going to be supportive. Even if it killed me.

I climbed up to the top rung, hoisted myself up, placed my hands on David's back, and pushed; holding him up.

The muscles in David's arm relaxed. "Thanks."

"Any time." I gritted my teeth, struggling against his weight and the wonderful force of gravity. "Do you know what … "

A deafening sound echoed through the chamber. David's arm dislodged and he smashed into me, knocking me off the ladder. I gasped as we tumbled along the floor and crashed against the front windows over the console.

David rolled off me. "Are you okay?"

I clutched my swimming head. "I think so."

The gravity shifted, and we hefted into the air, falling against the chairs before flinging back against the windows again. David grabbed me as the ship shifted, tumbled, and slammed until we settled with a thud. I untangled myself from David and stared at the floor above.

"Oh my God! We're upside down," I said.

David raised an eyebrow. I translated the gesture to "Obviously, you idiot." Not that he'd ever say that.

He rubbed his forehead and a deep, helpless dread slid along the invisible tether between us. A sense of finality coated his thoughts. Doom. End.

It scared the crap out of me.

I needed him. As much as I wanted to be independent, strong, and just like those super-ninja heroines I'd read about in books, I wasn't. I was average. A college student. A photographer. Not an adventurer, despite everything we'd been through together. I wasn't the hero. I was the sidekick. I was the one on the sidelines, more than happy to give the props to the guy doing the hard stuff.

It was probably all I'd ever be. Come to think of it, I wasn't really upset about that. The world needed support people. Support people, well ... supported.

And right now my hero needed me. Maybe more than ever.

I gathered my thoughts into a big ball and shoved with all my brain's little might. *We're going to be fine. We've gotten out of worse situations than this. We got this. We totally got this.*

I gnashed my teeth and imagined all the strength I had funneling through the air and injecting itself into David.

A thin smile graced his lips. He glanced up at me, his bangs shadowing his lashes. There was a power hidden in those eyes. Strength he wasn't even aware of.

He kissed my cheek. His lips lingered; his breath teased my skin, sending a quiver through my frame that had nothing to do with the frigid temperatures outside. Every muscle tensed. Pressure built inside me, like I needed to pop, and a bolt of energy circled my stomach and streamed along our bond. The uncertainty seething through the link withered away. Disintegrated.

Bold need took over. Forced. Demanded. But need for what? I gasped and leaned away.

His gaze carried over my lips before he blinked twice. The need dissipated into strength. Resolution. He turned to the front of the ship. "I need to see how bad the damage is."

Whoa. Holy intensity overload.

I inhaled, reeling in the explosion of emotion as David walked across the ceiling and peered up at the console. The fluids swirled and flickered with a bluish glow. It was like staring at a vat of blueberry Kool-Aid upside down. Why didn't it spill all over us? David reached up, but the console was about five feet from his hands.

"Want a boost?" I asked.

A wry grin settled over the left side of his mouth. "Don't worry. I got this."

He crouched and sprang into the air like an over-juiced Energizer Bunny. Grabbing on to the sides of his chair, he inverted himself.

The seat came to life, encompassing him. His hair hung toward me, but otherwise he showed no sign of being upside down while he sunk his arms into the goo. Show off.

"Everything seems fine," he said. "We just don't have propulsion."

Edgar popped out of the wall and scurried across the floor over my head. He stopped near David and turned toward me. He shrieked, spun around in circles, and jumped into my arms. Or maybe he fell.

He hid his mandibles in the crook of my arm before peeking up at David and chittering.

David looked down at us. "The way their equilibrium works, he probably didn't even know we were upside down until he saw you on the ceiling."

I nuzzled my favorite giant bug. "I'm okay, buddy. We're just in a bit of a pickle right now." I cringed as the odor of rotten eggs surrounded us. I stopped petting Edgar and waved the air around me. "What is that smell?"

"I don't smell anything." David drew his hands from the console. "Wait a minute. Now I do."

He waved his arms over the control panel and the spotlights lit up the sea in front of the windows. Tiny, floating, fluffy things darted away from the lights, leaving a clear view of row after row of volcano-like tubes spewing black smoke into the water.

"Is that what we're smelling?"

David nodded. "Extremely high concentrations of hydrogen sulfide."

"Is that bad?" I gagged.

"Poisonous. Explosive. Corrosive. Flammable. Yeah, I'd say that's bad."

My eyes stung and teared. "What do we do?"

David shifted, and his seat opened up. He did a somersault and somehow landed on his feet. Stinking ninja alien.

I rubbed my eyes. "It burns."

He grabbed the sides of my face. "Your scleras are all bloodshot. Close your eyes really tight."

He held my wrist and led me across the floor—or ceiling, I guess. The soft hum of the liquid walls effervesced from my left, followed by the soft slosh of someone manipulating the wall. I opened my eyes a crack to see a sheet of shiny black paper hop from David's hand and attached to my face. I pawed at the edges, struggling.

"No!" David said. "It's only a breathing mask. Just like the last time on the green planet. Let the fabric fit itself to your face."

Easy for him to say, but a second or two later the air started to flow.

He slipped his hands beside my cheeks. "Better?"

"Yeah. Thanks." I wiped the tears gathered beneath my mask. Dang, I was such a wuss.

"I have it set to give you pure oxygen. Hopefully that will help any damage."

"Damage?"

"You just inhaled poison, Jess."

Stuck at the bottom of the sea, breathing poison. What next? Couldn't David and I ever have a normal date?

He plucked another sheet from the cabinet and affixed it to his face. He didn't even flinch when it took hold.

The ground rumbled.

My breath hitched until it stopped. "Earthquake?"

"Sure felt like it." He jumped up and grasped the back of his chair. The liquid metal came to life once more, circling his ankles before he let go and hung from the base of the chair, reaching down for me. "Let me help you."

I stretched up and he lifted me like I weighed no more than a gallon of milk. As he hefted me to the other chair, it seized me. Spinning me into a sitting position and securing me upside down.

"What the heck?" I asked. "Why didn't it do that when we fell the first time?"

David laughed. "I wasn't connected to the ship. You don't expect it to act on its own, do you?"

Umm, maybe. The blood rushed into my skull. "Is there a reason we're upside down?"

"Technically, the ship is upside down." The floor rumbled again. David fiddled with the controls. "Definite seismic activity."

Great. Just great.

I tried to right myself, holding my chin to my chest. My brain stopped throbbing, but my neck started to burn. David worked away at the console, seeming oblivious to our upside-down-ness.

The ship jolted to the right. No rumble. Just a smash.

"Was that seismic activity?"

"I have no idea what that was." He waved his hand over the console, and three more spotlights lit up the sea outside the windows.

I gaped.

Long, white, finger-like tubes swayed around the base of what looked like miniature, smoking, black volcanoes. A red, feather-like plume jutted out from the tip of one, then another. Then an entire field of swaying ruby-red danced in the currents. Unbelievable.

And me with no camera. How freaking unfair was that?

David laughed.

"What?"

"You're funny."

"Why am I funny?"

"We're stranded at the bottom of the ocean, and all you can think about is your camera."

"You were supposed to stop reading my mind."

"I didn't. Sometimes I can read your face." He took my wrist and directed me over the console. A hazy, white octagon appeared on the glass before us. "Think of that shape like a lens. Maneuver it where you want, and think *still frame*."

Seriously? I giggled like a kid with a new toy. But still frame? That's an annoying way to say click.

A still picture of the plumes zoomed on the screen and disappeared. So cool! "Did I do that?"

"Yes. Do it again."

Awesome. *Click. Click. Click.* Picture after picture graced the screen. One even micro-zoomed, showing the fine fibers of the tiny red hands.

"Oh! I gotta get me one of these!" The ship joggled again, jolting us. "That *was not* an earthquake."

"Something's moving beneath us."

"What kind of something?"

My chair pulsated as a gargantuan, white elephant trunk-thing filled the screen on my side of the windows. It bent toward David, and a fluffy red plume the size of a Volkswagen shot out and bashed against his window.

"Oh my God!"

David sunk his arms into the controls and mumbled something in Erescopian. His gaze flew back to the screen as plantus-giganticus reared back again. "Hold on."

My seat immobilized my head, but my ears still rung from the shake as the thing outside smashed against our hull. The ship shifted back.

"Is it pushing us?"

"We probably landed on top of its nest or something. It's only trying to defend itself."

Swoosh. My backpack slid toward the rear of the ship. It didn't really matter whether or not this thing was only defending itself. It was beating us to a pulp. How much more could we take?

Bam.

The plumes filled the window again, and then another jolt came from the side, sloshing us to the left. Was there more than one?

The ship rose off the ground and spun through the water, righting itself. The plumes swayed around us as we drifted back toward the ground.

I grabbed my chair to steady myself, but my stomach and brain kept rolling. "Did you turn us over?" I asked.

"No. Those things did. Probably by accident." David peered into the console. "Oh, no."

"What's wrong?"

"The sensors say we haven't hit the bottom yet. We're only on a ledge of some sort."

We sunk back toward the sea floor. Our rear settled on something while our front continued to descend, tilting us downward. Our headlights pointed into another vast hole.

Ledge my right butt cheek. That looked more like the edge of the Grand Canyon!

Something hit us from behind. We skidded. Darkness sprawled below us. We jimmied. Slid.

"Oh, Shi—" A scream wrenched from my gut as we went over the edge for a second time.

10

We spiraled into eternity. David sat back in his chair. His features slackened, defeated. His lips edged into a straight line.

Oh, no you don't. "There has to be something we can do!"

He scrunched his lashes closed and pushed harder against the headrest.

So that was it? He was giving up? To Hell with that. I was not ready to be buried at sea. Not now. Not ever.

Release. I pushed the thought with all my might, and the chair loosened from my waist up.

"What are you doing?" David asked.

"Someone has to save our rear ends."

I stretched across him and shoved my hands into the dashboard. Warm, juicy goo rolled between my fingers. Blech.

Okay, ship. Slow us down ... Do something ... Anything ... Make us stop.

The searchlights continued to whirl through the darkness.

Umm, please? Pretty please?

The lights picked up something other than sea. An outline.

"What is that?" I asked.

David's eyes widened. "The bottom!"

His arm darted out, shoving me back to my seat. The chair seized and immobilized me with one movement. My heart ricocheted off my ribcage. This was it. The end.

The ship jolted and stopped with a heart-wrenching crunch. The chair gyrated around me, shaking my brain to a pulp.

The outside illumination had disappeared, leaving us with nothing but the soft glow surrounding the panels.

My temples throbbed. The deep, echoing sound of my breathing reverberated through the cabin.

"Is this the bottom?"

"Yes. Thirty-six thousand feet down. But … "

He looked out the window, squinting beneath his mask. Our interior illumination cast a blue haze over a solid rock wall.

"But what?"

He turned back toward the panel. "We're straddling some kind of fissure. I don't think this is the real bottom."

"It has to be. If we're thirty-six thousand feet down, that's the bottom."

"Are you sure?"

"I think so. I mean, I wrote a paper on it in school. I got an A, so I must have gotten the facts straight." The ship juddered. "Please tell me that's not another ticked-off plant."

"More seismic activity." He tapped the edge of the console. "Jess, there's still a lot of ocean below us."

The ground gyrated and a rock dislodged from the wall to the right and sunk right past the window. The trembling deepened as the ocean floor moaned and roared.

"What's going on?"

I braced myself against the dashboard and the seat. The cabin blurred as I gave up trying to focus. The shaking chattered my teeth.

"This is not happening," David whispered. "This is *not* happening!"

I screamed as we tilted forward into the widening fissure and slipped, rumbling deeper into the crevice and jolting to a stop, wedged between two giant rock walls with a vast void of sea beneath us.

With the front of our ship pointed straight down, I hung from my restraints, panting in the odd silence.

The pitch black looming in the depths below filled the window below me and threatened to soak through, penetrate, and consume us. The illumination within the ship brightened the cabin, but not the outside, as if light wasn't even possible at these depths.

"How far down are we now?" I asked.

"Thirty-six thousand eight hundred and sixty-two feet."

And the darkness promised so much more.

"This is a one way trip, isn't it? We're not getting out of here."

David's bindings released. "We will. I promise. I just need time to think."

He slipped down onto the console, straddling the liquid controls. Reaching up, he dragged his fingers along my cheek, bunching up the fabric in my mask. My hair fell from the sides of my face as if reaching for him.

"I'm scared," I said.

"I know, but I think we'll be okay."

He held my shoulders as my chair released me. I slipped from my seat down into his arms, my sneakers setting on the window below us.

"Can the glass hold my weight?"

He nodded. "It's not glass like you know it. It's made to withstand a lot more than your little frame."

I looked up, past our chairs to the far back of the ship. I suddenly felt small, like looking up at the ceiling of Notre Dame Cathedral. Why did the ship look so much larger up on its end than it did when it was horizontal?

David snickered.

"What?"

He bit back his grin. "I'm sorry. You just have the oddest thoughts sometimes."

I folded my arms. "You said you were going to stop ... "

A bright red beacon flashed in the depths below us, drifting in the darkness.

"What is that?" I asked.

"I don't know." He crouched down and shoved his hands back into the console beside our feet. "The instruments aren't picking up anything."

"Is it another one of those giant mouths with fins?"

"I don't think so. That thing registered a lot of mass and solid bone. I'm not detecting anything out there at all."

The flash returned, glowing longer before fading out. A bluish flicker glinted from the right, larger than the first.

I crouched closer to the glass. "Could it be submarines? Could they have sent someone to help us?"

David shook his head. "Like I said, there's no mass. Whatever it is, it's like it's not even there."

Another blue shimmer joined the blinking. They seemed larger with every flash. My hands trembled. So quiet. Like noise was as useless as the lights from our ship. I wanted to reach for a knob and turn up the volume, because there had to be some kind of sound. Anything. The silence, it was too much.

David's hand covered mine, but he didn't turn his gaze from the glowing spectacle before us. He whispered something in Erescopian, and released my hand. He made a wide, stroking movement over the console, and a loud boom echoed around the ship.

I covered my ears. "What are you doing?"

"Chances are these are the beings Silver was so worried about. Our best chance to get out of this is to make friends."

"With a loud obnoxious noise?"

David tapped the panel. "I'm hoping they'll realize we're trying to communicate."

Either that or you'll piss them off.

The lights continued to multiply. Oranges and pinks added their radiance to the display. They circled, twitched, and began to form patterns before drifting apart. Sometimes moving closer, other times backing away.

"Still no readings on the instruments. Have you ever seen anything like this?" David asked.

"No. I'm not sure what to make of it."

The reds and the oranges began to twirl in pairs. They brightened and drifted as one, like embers burning in the sea. My stomach fluttered and tears formed in my eyes. It seemed wrong that something so wonderful remained hidden far below the sea, where no one could appreciate it.

The embers winked out, leaving us in the soft bask of the remaining blue twinkles until they, too, faded into oblivion. I found myself reaching toward the glass, wishing I could bring them back, before my hand lowered back to my lap. Whatever that was could have been miles away, for all I knew.

The glowing beams from the ship searched the barren waters, lone beacons in the endless night. I shivered. It might not even be nighttime. We were too deep for daylight to penetrate. It could be noon up there for all I knew.

What could possibly be out there in a place that never saw the sun?

The ship jolted, and David's arm shot out and pressed me back into my chair. An ear shattering grinding noise echoed within the cabin.

Jesus, couldn't we have just a few seconds where we weren't in imminent peril?

We shook and rumbled, forced further through the fissure by

something I couldn't see.

My chair tightened, and David released his grip. Bubbles shot out around us, covering the windows, before my stomach bottomed out.

The grinding stopped. Free of the fissure, I closed my eyes, trying to keep from throwing up as we seemed to fall, spiraling faster than should be possible in water, propelled by God knows what.

The ship lurched forward, and I jolted as we stopped. A yellow glow filled the sea around us, like looking into the sun. My chair loosened as David reached over and grabbed my hand. His wide gaze heightened the fear already sizzling across our tether. Whatever had pushed us down here, we were at its mercy, and there wasn't a thing we could do about it.

A flood of red light erupted in the space above our heads. David cried out and my chair liquefied, dropping me hard onto the window. Crimson encompassed the entire ship … as if it *became* the ship. I fumbled to my right and found David's hand in the fuzzy redness. His voice echoed like it was in the distance and his hand twisted from my grip as if yanked away.

"David!" I tried to reach out to him, but air pressed against me on all sides, pinning me to the window.

A deep ripping sound resonated through the thick crimson blur. "David, where are you?"

The pressure released, and I jumped to my feet. The glass vibrated beneath my sneakers as the ripping sound escalated to a roar—the same roar that had riddled me at the base of Niagara Falls as a kid. And just like in my nightmares after that trip, water lapped around my feet. But this time it was real, flowing across and covering the window.

I stared, transfixed as the sea soaked my ankles. A white frothy torrent streamed into the compartment from somewhere in the back of the ship. I gulped back the simmering panic rising in my gut. If I didn't find a way to plug that hole, we were dead.

I turned to my left and to my right, combing my hands through the foggy, red cloud still obscuring my vision; unsure of what I looked for, but certain I hadn't found it.

The color deepened. I moved, but my sneakers splashed wherever I went. "David!" I pawed through the red veil around me, searching for something. Anything. "Edgar!"

The tepid sea met my hips. This was it. I was alone, and the sea had come to claim me. Had Edgar and David abandoned me? Left me to die?

Jess! David's voice raked through my mind, more a desperate plea than calling my name.

"David, where are you?" I turned toward where I though his seat had been, but my hands hit a solid, but soft wall of red that seemed to push me back as if it knew I was trying to get to him.

I panted in jagged gasps. My mask tightened around my cheeks. My next inhalation suctioned the plastic against my lips. Air. I needed air!

Slow, steady breaths, David had said.

The water rose above my head. I gasped and kicked my feet, treading. When David and I had crash-landed on the green planet, my mask had given out after I panicked and ran. I couldn't let myself collapse in a wheezing heap this time. The air purifiers weren't made for freaking-out college students. They were made for composed, rational Erescopians. I needed to stay calm. I had to control my breathing, but where was everyone?

A giant swell grabbed my helpless form, dunking me and forcing me back down toward the piloting station. I cried out and spluttered as the mask constricted. I thrashed until I came up into the air and panted as the rolling sea rose toward the back of the ship. The mask clung to my face, covering me like a plastic bag. Where was the air?

The material eased away from my nose, filling with oxygen. I took a deep breath, and another. My scalp hit the rear wall above, forcing me back into the murky, red depths. My mask sucked to my face again, useless.

It didn't work when it got wet!

I swam back up and inhaled when my mask filled. My brow grazed the rear wall again, leaving only a small space between the water and the highest point in the ship. I was running out of air! My heart thumped, wrung, and rattled, clawing out of my chest. I kicked and waved my arms, keeping my face aloft as the sea splashed around me. I needed to focus, to keep my cool. David was somewhere in here, and he needed air, too!

The roaring scream of the flood suddenly stopped, like someone turned off a faucet. The sound of my heartbeat seemed to echo within my mask. The water level remained at my chin. I took two breaths to calm myself in the reprieve.

"David!"

The silence tore through to the bottom of my soul. I'd seen *grassen* swim out in space. Edgar didn't need to breathe very often, but David did. I willed my panicked gasps to a steady, quiet pace. The sea swirled around me. Not cold, but temperate, like Bell's Lake in August. Comfortable. At least I wasn't going to freeze to death. Settled, I relaxed my mind and closed my eyes, opening myself up to the resonance of the world around me.

David, where are you? The grip of our tether grappled around my spine and yanked me under. I swam back up, gasping. The draw of our connection dissipated as if brushed away. Erased.

Oh, God! David!

I gasped again and plunged my face beneath the water. Near the bottom, David struggled in his chair, trying to swim up. He'd been beside me the entire time!

Heart thumping, I kicked off the rear wall and swam down to him. He wrestled with his ankles, as if something held him to the chair, but the only thing near him were a few floating instruments from the ship. I slipped my hands under his arms and pulled, but he barely budged. He shoved me away and pointed up. He knew I needed air. But I couldn't leave him there.

Dammit! Think, Jess!

My lungs screamed and I pushed off from the bottom. My mask stayed glued to my face as I broke into the air. I treaded, shaking as the soft fabric filled. Tiny lights sparkled in my line of sight, but disappeared as I inhaled. Oxygen never tasted so sweet. But I wasn't the only one who needed to breathe.

David thrashed beneath me. I needed to get him air. Dozens of movie scenarios flooded my mind. I could help him, but not with this mask. I clawed the plastic's edge and ripped the fabric away from my face. Soaked, it hung from my skin before I got the material completely off. I took in a deep breath. No rotten egg smell. Hopefully that meant the noxious fumes had cleared.

I took in two more mouthfuls of air, and plunged beneath the surge. The salinity stung my eyes. I scrunched them shut and stroked four times through the warm water until our bond told me I'd reached David. I cracked my eyelids, allowing the salt to burn as I reached for him.

David splayed his palms. *Stop. Get back to the surface. You need to breathe.*

I gripped his wrists, immobilizing him. *So do you.*

Violet tones pulsed through David's artificial human skin. The transparent mask skewed his features, except for a wide gaze betraying fear far deeper than the twisted, panicked emotion flooding through our bond.

I snatched his mask. The fabric squished in my hand and floated away. His expression slackened. His lips formed a straight line. *You need air. Just leave me.*

No way.

I cradled his face and brought my mouth to his; forcing what little breath I had into his lungs.

He struggled against me before his muscles relaxed. I grew

EMBERS IN THE SEA

dizzy. He grabbed my waist and heaved, shooting me back toward the surface.

Breaking into the air, I took a huge gulp for myself, and expelled it. The next one I held.

I swam back down. David reached for me, and accepted my gift.

With each rise to the surface and dive below, the link between us strengthened. Each time our lips met, a renewed energy surged through the contact. Not just air, but life. Love. Connection. I finally understood. We weren't two people anymore. We hadn't been for some time. That's why I'd been so lost for the past two years. Half of me was on Earth, and the other half had been on Mars. I wasn't just breathing life into David, I was breathing life into me, into my own soul.

But I couldn't do this forever. With the next gasp, I swam past him to the floor. I clutched his ankle and strained against a force I couldn't see. His foot barely moved. But why? There was nothing holding him. I gave him the rest of the air in my lungs. He grasped my waist and throttled me back up.

I gave myself two breaths and swam back down. His other foot was just as stuck. Did Erescopians sink or something?

Edgar floated beside me, his spindly legs kicking a mile a minute. He bit and gnashed at unseen objects around David. I shot back up.

When I returned, Edgar was spinning around David's right foot, chewing at the chair David seemed attached to.

Keep trying, buddy.

I released my air into David's lungs. Edgar swished up from the bottom and grappled with the sea as if the translucent fluids attacked him. Had the salinity driven him insane?

Then I felt it—the overbearing sense of a thousand eyes focused on me, scrutinizing, judging.

I reached for David, but the presence surged against me. The clear water turned red again and gelled. I held up my hands, but all I could see was deep, encompassing crimson. Something clicked in the back of my neck, and the red deepened, coating my eyes. I sunk toward the window, gently swaying in the passing tide ... basking in the embrace of—nothing.

I tried to move, but the goo squished past my arms. David's eyes widened before he spiraled upward, dragged by something I couldn't see, and disappeared.

"David!" Thick goo invaded my mouth as I screamed. A rope tangled around my right ankle. Then my left. I tumbled back and smashed my skull as someone or some*thing* drew me out of the ship and into the sea.

11

I squinted and sat up, sliding my blankets down to my waist. Sunlight trickled through my bedroom curtains, casting a brilliant sheen over the cover of this month's National Geographic.

Wait. Why did I wake up at home?

"David!"

Unease crept up my spine. My mother's old wind-up clock ticked three times from the top of my dresser. I jumped out of bed. My feet squished when I hit the carpet.

Eww. Why was I sleeping in soaking wet sneakers? I kicked off my Nikes and massaged the raised, red welts on my feet. *Ouch.* What the hell was going on?

"David!" I steadied myself as my head swam. The room shifted, rolling before becoming solid again. What was wrong with me?

My pink sweater lay across the chair by my desk, and the mug I forgot to wash still sat atop my desk blotter. Just as I'd left it, but just as I'd left it eons ago. The room faded into a haze and refocused. A deep hum vibrated through my mind.

I tried to shake away my fogginess. I'd been somewhere.

College. When did I get home?

"Dad!" I called.

Not that I expected an answer. He'd be at work during the day. No, wait.

David.

David had picked me up at college. We were under water—at the bottom of the ocean. Something attacked us.

"David!"

The handle on my door jiggled and swung open. Matt walked in.

"Matt? What are you doing here? What's going on?"

"What do you mean?" He closed the door behind him. "You've been asleep since you got home."

"Since I got home? What are you talking about? Where's David? What's going on?"

He splayed his hands. "It's okay. They said you might be a little disoriented."

I pushed him away. "Screw disoriented. This isn't real. This isn't my room." But then again, it was.

A sweet smell wafted in the window. Peanut butter.

Peanut butter?

The room swam again. I grabbed the edge of the bed as I lost my balance. The nutty smell intensified causing my head to throb before the pain began to fade away.

Home. I was home. Everything was fine.

Matt gripped my shoulders. "Let me help you sit back down."

I blinked until my eyes refocused on Matt's broad smile. "M-Matt? What are you doing here?"

"Your dad asked me to watch over you." He fluffed the pillows behind me and helped me to lie back on the bed. "Take it easy, Slugger. You've been through a lot."

"I have?"

His smile warmed me. "That's what they tell me. So, how was it?"

"How was what?"

"You know, the whole ocean thing."

Ocean? I straightened. David ... we'd been in the ocean. It was real.

"Everyone's talking about what you found. But I can't figure out what it was. Everyone is being so secretive."

Mariana's Trench. We dove, looking for ... "We found it?" I blinked the sting from my eyes. "That means David is okay?"

"Yeah, he's fine. He seems happy about it all."

Of course he'd be happy. He'd saved the world. Again. And now he was probably off and away to Mars. "Did he ask for me?"

"No. He's too busy with what you brought back."

Of course he wouldn't ask for me. Duty first, Jess second. But what was it that we'd found? I cuddled in to my pillows. Why couldn't I remember?

Matt kneeled beside the bed and leaned his elbows on my mattress. "What is it, anyway?"

Good question. "I guess we found whatever it is that makes rain."

"You want to make it rain? It rains all the time."

"Not on Mars. They don't have that the same kinetic energy Earth does."

He looked to the side. His bangs shifted across his brow. "He seeks the source?"

"Yeah, but I don't know what it is. I can't even remember finding it, or how I got home."

"He wants to bring the source to another planet?" Matt fingered his chin.

"Umm, if we took it with us, then, yeah, I guess so. I don't really know." I rubbed my temples. "How long have I been asleep?"

Matt's lips twisted into a sneer. "It doesn't matter what planet a land-dweller comes from. They are all the same."

Huh? "What are you talking about?"

"You take with no intention of giving in return."

Whoa. Hold the farm.

On top of my desk—the National Geographic—it was a few months old. Dad would have piled three or four more issues on top of it by now. And he never would have left that mug there if he saw it. Come to think of it, everything seemed the same. Exactly the same. This wasn't my room. It was the *memory of* my room.

I stood. "Who are you? Where am I?"

A smile crossed his lips. The same cheesy smile from Matt's senior-year portraits. "This is where you sleep, isn't it?"

I reeled in the desire to slap the smile from that fake face. "Where. Am. I? And where's David?"

"Demanding. Unreasonable." His eyes darkened. "You should be released into the sea. Exterminated."

A mound formed in my chest and hung inside me as Not-Matt backed to the door and opened it.

"Wait!" I ran for him as he stepped out, but Not-Matt slammed the door in my face. I banged on the frame. "Where am I? What did you do to David?"

The tangy twist of grape jelly added to the peanut-buttery smell hanging in the air, so thick the stench clogged my lungs. I choked, slipping to the floor. Mom's clock ticked, the sound echoing between my ears. Tired. So tired.

My vision blurred as I leaned my head back.

Jess!

The door behind me buckled. Invisible hands fisted my insides and pulled me toward the bowed woodwork. The tether!

"David!" I scrabbled to my feet. Another slam bent the frame. "I'm here!"

The pull inside me slipped away as the wood arched and cracked before shattering. The pieces dissipated in the air like a fog.

David stepped through, huffing.

I jumped into his arms. "I can't believe it! When I saw you

dragging through the water I thought you were dead."

"It's me, but we're not alone. Anyone else you see is a mirage."

I nodded. "I saw Matt Samuels."

"I saw my father." David grimaced as the door reappeared behind him. "That was a little too real. I thought I was home."

The silence seeping through my replicated walls pressed in on us. How could they have built these rooms so quickly? How long had we been unconscious?

"The last thing I remember was … " I shivered, recounting David trapped beneath the water, and our little ten-legged friend struggling to help him "Edgar! Have you seen him?"

"I only saw the creature who I thought was my father." Worry lines creased his brow before he turned his face away.

For some reason I didn't think he was concerned about Edgar. Something trickled across our bond—a feeling between shame and terror. The resonance of Sabbotaruo hung in the air between us, as if seeing someone disguised as his father had dredged up feelings he'd managed to keep down. Until now.

But as far as I knew everything was okay between them. Something must have happened between him and his dad while David was on Mars. Something horrible.

David returned his gaze to mine. "The man who came to my living space was trying to get information—find out why we were here. I did admit we were searching for something before I realized it wasn't really Sabbotaruo."

I gulped. "I kinda spilled the beans. I told him about the source and needing rain on Mars. He didn't sound all that happy with the idea."

David eased me into the crook of his neck and stroked the back of my hair. "It's all right. I don't think them knowing what's going on is going to change our situation."

"Do you think Edgar is walled up in a room like this somewhere, thinking he's home?"

"Doubtful. With his sensory perception he'd have to know something wasn't right."

"Do you think he's okay?"

"If anyone can take care of themselves, he can."

The curtains shifted as if taken by a soft breeze, even though there was nothing on the other side. It all looked so real. The technology behind all this might even match David's.

"Do you think these are the people Silver warned us about?"

"Yes, but I'm not so sure they are as terrible as he made them out to be." He waved his hand around my room. "Why would someone who wanted to kill us recreate all this?"

He had a point, but a creeping sensation slithered up my spine. "Wait, why are you so calm? And why do you seem so ready to trust someone who's lying and pumping us for information?" *Please tell me I didn't just hug a big jellyfish in disguise!*

"I'm not. I'm just trying to figure things out. We shouldn't blindly trust Silver just because we met him first."

Sweat beaded on my forehead, and I took a step back. I'd felt the tether when he was breaking down the door, but it had stopped suddenly, as if erased, only seconds before he broke through.

David's brow furrowed. "What's wrong?"

I hugged my shoulders. All of it—everything around me, it was way too real. It smelled real. Felt real. Too good to be true.

This wasn't home. I knew that, despite my surroundings. I couldn't trust anything I saw.

My gaze dropped over David. Perfect as always. Maybe too perfect.

I pointed to his feet. "You're still wearing your shoes."

"What?"

"You have to be just as soaked as I was. Why don't your feet hurt?"

His brow twisted before he pulled off his sneakers and socks. Eight perfect, bronzed toes settled into my carpeting. Not a mark on him.

David perused my fetid feet. "Your toes are all pink."

"Yeah, I noticed. Why aren't yours?"

"I don't know. It's not real skin, remember?"

I resisted the urge to tear out my hair and scream. "How do I know you're really David?"

"Can't you feel me?" The colors lightened in his eyes. "I knew it was you the second I passed through the door."

I hugged my waist. "Yeah, well, I'm a little confused right now, and I'm not really sure of anything."

David leaned down, bringing his lips to mine. Heat tingled my skin. I drank him in, allowing the essence of everything that was David to infuse me, soften me from the inside out. Tiny, loving fingers breezed through every cell, seeking out my fears and whisking them away, then infusing me with certainty. Strength. Love.

A sigh drifted from my lips as I cuddled to his chest. Whoever created this place may be able to look like anyone they chose, but I doubted they'd be able to replicate *that*. My guard retreated, and I allowed my skin the luxury of his touch. But only for a moment. We were still trapped in some sort of imaginary world, and the real world still needed saving.

"I'm sorry. I guess I'm just scared."

"I know. It's all right."

I leaned away from him. "So where do you think we really are?"

"Still eight hundred-plus feet below the bottom of the trench, I'd imagine." He picked up a magazine. "They went through a lot of trouble to make us think we weren't at the bottom of the sea."

David walked to my window and tapped on the frame. "It's sealed."

I opened my closet. A smile crossed my face as the heater fell out, along with the sleeping bag David had rolled himself up in the night he hid in my room. That was years ago, but I still thought of him every time I went near that closet.

"I guess there's no way out of here." I turned and faced the door. Could it be as simple as just walking out? "Is it safe to assume my upstairs hallway is not on the other side?"

"I walked right out of my own living space into yours. When I first woke up I thought I was back on my father's military cruiser."

I inched toward the door. "Do you think your room is still there?" How idiotic was it that I wanted to see his home when we were trapped at the bottom of the ocean with God knows what going on between the humans and Erescopians up above? But I knew so little about David. How did he live? What was his life like before he came to Earth?

David turned the handle. The door opened, just like it would have in my real room. He stuck his head out. "It's still there. Do you want to see?"

I followed him through the door. My damp, pruned feet tapped onto shimmering black tiles. David picked up a silver oblong plate holding something like celery stalks, and grabbed a tall, narrow cylinder. A window opened in the wall to his right, and he placed the dishes inside.

"You didn't have to clean up for me."

He shrugged. "I never had a girl over before. I didn't feel right to leave the table a mess."

The table—the only piece of furniture in the room. Not even any chairs. "Do you guys stand when you eat?"

"Sometimes. Do you want to sit?" He held up his hand, and the floor pinched. A chair rose, as if melting in reverse. So cool.

"Thanks, but I'm okay." I slipped my hands in my pockets. "Where do you sleep?"

He sank his fingers into the wall and a small archway appeared.

I walked through and stopped. A long, narrow slit cut through the wall ahead of me with a stark, bare shelf beneath it. "This is where you sleep?"

He set his hand on the slit. "Yes, in here."

I leaned closer and ran my hand along the smooth, hard slab inside. "How do you get in?"

"You just slide through the opening."

Okaaaay. I squeezed through the slit, gliding my palms across the cold, hard bed before I laid down.

The gray, stark walls oppressed, mocked, and closed in toward me, but I forced myself to keep my eyes open.

My breath hitched. I bit my lips.

The pressure, the lack of air, it was only an illusion. I could handle this. If I concentrated hard enough I'd be able to stay here; imagine what it would be like to live on a spaceship, to spend a few moments living as David did his entire life.

My heart pummeled as nightmares of being buried alive consumed me. The rest of the air sucked out of the small space, and I gasped as David dragged me back through the narrow slit into the not much larger alcove.

We fell to our knees and I flopped into his arms. Sweat drenched the hair at my temples.

"Your heartbeat increased," he said. "Are you all right?"

My hand shook on his chest. "You actually sleep in there?"

"Yes. It's safe, confining."

Confining? Bile pooled at the bottom of my throat. My heartbeat rattled. "I can't be closed in like that."

"I never asked you to be." He lifted me to my feet. Disappointment radiated from his eyes. Had he hoped I'd like it in the miniature coffin?

"I know you didn't make me go in there. I guess I thought I could … " What? See if I had what it took to be a space ranger? I pressed my hand against my chest and exhaled. "I don't know what I thought."

The rest of the room seemed to shrink. I hid my face in his soft cotton shirt. How could anyone live like this?

David scooted me back out toward the door. "How about we

go back to your room?"

Yes, yes. Back to the nice, normal, human space.

I breathed in the sweet, familiar aroma of the flowers in Mrs. Miller's garden as soon as we stepped out of David's jail-like, antiseptic quarters. I shuddered as a sense of relief eased the ache from my muscles.

The smell of the flowers wasn't real. The window wasn't even open, but the sensations still comforted me, just like my real room would. I cringed when David shut the door behind him. How awful his life must have been, living in that ungodly, claustrophobic space every day. No wonder his people were so desperate to find a planet.

David sat me on the edge of my bed. "We can stay in here. I don't mind."

"Thanks." Everything around me, so real, so comforting. But it wasn't real. None of it. "We're going to have to figure a way out of this. You know, find the source and all."

"Yeah, I know." He blinked, scanning the room. "I don't think there is much we can do, though, until they start talking. I mean, we can't even try to break through the barriers, because for all we know the sea is on the other side."

Good point. "But we can't just sit here." I walked to the wall beside my window and pushed. The sheetrock didn't give at all. None of it did, no matter where I shoved.

"I tried that in my living spaces already. There's no way out."

"There has to be. Maybe there are some of those liquid doors like on your spaceships."

"If there are; they aren't coded to our DNA." He took my hands. "When I seek out intelligent thoughts, I feel warmth beyond our walls. I don't think these beings want to hurt us."

"Well, the one that looked like Matt didn't seem all warm and fuzzy. He sounded like he was waving pompoms for team kill-the-humans."

David glanced over his shoulder, toward the door. "Yeah, I

didn't get a comforting vibe there, either, but the ones watching us now seem more—I don't know, interested and perplexed."

"They're watching us?"

"It would make sense. Can't you feel them—a presence?"

I closed my eyes and reached out. Something crept toward me, as if the air compacted against my ears. I fluttered my lashes, and the sensation ebbed away. "I feel something. I don't know. It's weird. It's almost like … " A sharp pain lanced my shoulder. I stumbled closer to David. "Oww!"

"What happened?"

I spun, backing into him. "It felt like someone stabbed me with a pencil."

He circled around me. I could sense his gaze scanning the room. "There's nothing there."

But there had been. "For nothing, it sure hurt." I rubbed my shoulder.

David stared at the far corner of the room.

"What's up?"

He paled. "Do you smell anything?"

"Just the roses in Mrs. Miller's garden."

He took a step backward and winced. "Oww."

"Pencil?"

He nodded. The indent of whatever poked him marred his cotton tee-shirt, but the mark disappeared as he turned toward the door. Cautiously, he took another step away from me and grabbed his shoulder again. "Gah!"

He glared at me, and I didn't have to ask to know he'd been poked again. "Why are they doing this to us?"

"I'm guessing they want us in close proximity to each other." He released his arm. "I feel like the spores we gather on developing planets. Like we're under a microscope and being studied for our reactions to stimuli."

The lights dimmed slightly, and I clutched David's arm,

waiting for something to jump out and grab us. When it didn't, I loosened my grip, but only a little. "I hope that means show time is over. Maybe they'll leave us alone now." His skin quaked under my grasp. "Are you okay?"

"The smell is just … I don't know."

"You mean the roses?"

He shifted me from his arms. "Maybe I should go back to my room." He took two steps away. "Oww!"

"Phantom pencil?"

"Yeah." He rubbed his arm. "I guess we're staying here, tonight. Whether we want to or not."

"It's okay. It's not like we haven't slept together." My cheeks heated. "I mean, well, we haven't slept together, but we've, umm, you know what I mean, right?" Yeah, Jess, he knows you're an idiot.

He laughed. "I can sleep on the floor if you want."

A knot formed in my chest. That wasn't what I wanted at all.

I'd spent two years trying to forget how I felt about him, but David had always been there, in the back of my mind: present, even in his absence.

When he was trapped underwater, and I brought him air, the depth of our connection finally hit me. We really were part of each other. There was no denying that anymore.

"I don't want you to stay on the floor." I slipped my hand in his. "I've missed you. Can't we fall asleep holding each other, just like we did in the woods?"

His smile caught what little illumination remained in the room. "You know I'd love to stay with you. But I wasn't sure if *you* wanted that. You weren't exactly happy to see me when I stepped off my ship."

No, I suppose I wasn't. "I'm sorry. I guess I freaked a little." Or a lot.

Poor Matt. I just left him there.

The scent of the roses heightened, whisking thoughts of Matt away. David stared at me, his eyes wide, beautiful, and hopeful. I reached for him. "Stay with me tonight. Please?" I tugged him toward my bed.

He didn't put up much of a fight. "All right. That would be nice."

Reaching the edge of the mattress, I turned toward him, running my fingers up the center of his chest. Every second I spent with him we seemed to grow closer, as if part of me was meshing with him. But at the same time he felt like a stranger. He had this whole other life away from Earth, away from me, like he was a different person.

Then again, he was a different person, wasn't he?

"You know, it never occurred to me that I should call you Tirran."

He twitched under my fingers. The set of his eyes changed, as if he'd been slashed with a knife.

"I'm sorry. I meant Tirran Coud. I didn't mean to drop your mother's name. I didn't mean any disrespect."

He grabbed my wrist, pulling my hand away from his chest. "There's no disrespect when you are as close as we are. But you can continue to call me David."

I shook my head. "But that's wrong. It's just a name you plucked out of my head. It's ... "

"My name now." His voice—so tense. He closed his eyes and took a deep breath before opening them. "I prefer who I am with you. Tirran Coud is ..." He closed his eyes again. "The name David gives me peace, helps me to ... " He looked up at the ceiling.

What was it? What was he so desperately trying *not* to tell me?

His gaze returned to mine. "David is the name you gave me. This might be hard to understand, but it's precious to me. Please don't take it away."

Take it away? That's not what I meant. That wasn't it at all. I shook my head. "Okay. David it is."

His eyes still swirled unnaturally, as if there was far more to it than a name. Maybe someday he'd be comfortable enough to explain, but that obviously wasn't right now.

And it wasn't really the worst of our worries at the moment. I shook the odd fog from my head, realizing that this wasn't really my room; and we should be terrified, not having a conversation about names, and …

My muscles slackened, easing away my stress and concern over … what?

I rolled my sore shoulder as I sat on the mattress. "I know I woke up just a little while ago, but I'm tired, like I haven't slept at all."

"I don't think we actually slept. Everything has been manipulated since we got here." He stretched his neck. "From the lack of regeneration in my muscles, I'd have to guess we've been awake since we left Silver's people. About three hours."

Only three hours? I narrowed my eyes. "You can tell how long you've been awake by how much your neck hurts?"

He turned to me. "Can't you?"

"No." I rolled my shoulder. My neck did hurt a little, come to think of it. "How long do you think we've been underwater?"

"A little over a day, at most."

I yawned. My bed whispered, begging me to cuddle my favorite pillow. I rubbed my eyes and blinked the feeling away. Maybe they lowered the lights for a reason. If we fell asleep, who knew what they would do to us? "Maybe we shouldn't sleep."

"I still don't feel any malice. Just interest."

He eased beside me and jumped when I placed my hand on his shoulder.

"I'm sorry. What's wrong?"

"Nothing." He flopped onto the bed. His eyes seemed puffy, even in the low light. "We should just try to get some sleep." He turned onto his side and perched himself on the edge of the mattress, giving me more than enough room.

"Are you okay?"

"I'm just ... I'm sorry. I'm ... "

I tugged gently on his shoulder, laying him back on the bed. "What is it?"

He shifted his weight. "This is extremely awkward."

"Why?"

He turned away again.

"Please tell me what's wrong." I reached over him and slid my fingers down his torso.

He stopped my hand at the base of his ribcage. "Are you sure all you smell is roses?"

I took a whiff of the air. "I guess so. I really don't even smell it anymore."

"That's what I'm worried about." He kept his back to me.

"I still have no idea what you're talking about."

"We're being manipulated. They want to see what we'll do."

"About what?"

He blurred in the low lighting, and in one swoop of the sheets, we were sitting, facing each other. He held my wrists near my shoulders. "They are pumping pheromones into this room."

"Pheromones? Why?"

His hands shook on my wrists, his gaze lingering on my lips before returning to my eyes.

Oh. That's why. "They can't possibly think we'll ... can they?"

His face didn't change. He barely seemed to breathe.

The scent of the flowers heightened, relaxing me. My room was a haven. The one place on Earth where I was truly at ease. Safe. I nuzzled David's neck, taking in his earthy smell.

"Jeeessssss ... " He leaned away.

I smiled as the turquoise in his irises swirled toward a deep gray before returning to blue. "I don't need pheromones to want to be with you, David." I twisted one wrist free and ran my fingertips along the edge of his cheek. "I've missed you so much."

"I-I've missed you too."

I trailed soft kisses along his neck. His grip on my other wrist slackened. "Jess, I don't think we should … "

"I'm not asking for anything we haven't done already." His pulse thumped beneath my lips. "This isn't the pheromones. It's just you—" *kiss*, "and—" *kiss*, "me."

He grabbed my shoulders and stared, as if memorizing the lines in my face. His grip tightened and slackened. "Maybe you're right. Everything should be fine." He shook his head to clear it. "Wait. No. It will not be fine. I can't. We can't."

"Why not?"

"You don't understand. I'm getting older now. Things are different."

I kissed him gently on the upper lip. "They don't have to be. I forgive you for being away so long."

He trembled beneath my touch—just the reaction I wanted … needed. It had been far too long since I'd touched him.

I slid my hands behind his neck and combed them through his disheveled locks. The sensation of the soft fibers running between my fingers sent a shiver down my spine. This hair and skin wasn't his. It was a costume. Protection from Earth's cooler temperatures and protection for me, so his touch didn't burn. The last time we'd seen each other, he'd gone through the horrible pain of infusing this human skin onto his own just so he could hold me. No one had ever sacrificed themselves like that for me. Ever. I loved what his human façade symbolized, but I really wanted what was beneath— the flawless violescent skin—the real David.

I formed a vision of him holding me with pearly lilac hands, imagined my palms rolling over his bare scalp, soaking in the heat emanating from his perfection. I opened my thoughts, thrusting them toward him. His eyes widened and his grip on me tightened.

I'd lied to him. I wanted so much more than stolen kisses in the woods. I wanted all of him. Now.

Our foreheads grazed. "I'm ready. I want to."

His lower lip trembled and fell into a gape. "I-I, we-we can't. I'm afraid I'd … "

"Don't be afraid." I dragged my fingers along his back, over the soft cotton. I kissed the soft space on his temple. "All that matters now is us. What feels right. What feels good."

A flash of uncertainty raced across his features—the same hesitation I saw when we started getting intimate in the shelter he built for us on the green planet.

I slipped my hands to either side of his face. "I don't care what anyone else thinks. I don't care about Nematali, or my father, or any other human or Erescopian. This feels too right—you and me, *it is* right."

He kissed the inside of my hand. "It would be incredibly selfish of me not to point out that everything you just said might be because of the pheromones."

I gathered all my strength, all my need, all my desire—packaged it up in a little ball and flung it into his psyche. He shuddered, leaning back and breathing heavily.

A smile crossed my lips. "Was that pheromones?"

His nose flared. "No." Flashes of green, blue, and purple swirled into his irises, as if the natural colors that made up his eyes separated and fought to become one again. He grabbed my hips and pulled me closer. "I've been waiting a long time for this."

I wrapped my legs around his waist. "Then you should have come home sooner, because this is all I've been thinking about."

A growl erupted from deep within his throat. He lifted me with one hand, pressing me against his stomach. "*Volo tamier estmale esse cuin medio tui, est,*" he whispered, trailing his warm breath along the side of my face.

The words held a cadence that settled over me, stroking me from within. "What does that mean?"

"Mea est." He ran his tongue along the soft space just below my ear. A light groan tickled from his lips. Needy. Demanding.

Screw it. I'd find out what it meant later.

Energy surged through our tether. David sought out, found, and caressed each cell within me, sending a charge of pressure and tension riddling back to the surface. Deep folds of need coursed across my skin, darted within, and exploded in an eruption of tingling, scorching sparkles burning and cooling from the inside and bursting out like a megaton bomb. The sensations whirled together, too many to comprehend. I clung to him, panting as the shockwave subsided.

The hairs on my arms stood out as I stretched back with a sigh.

He didn't need to be physically inside me. He was already there.

Shutting my eyes, I tugged at the hem of his shirt, sliding it over his head. The warm material dropped from my fingers and dripped beside my waist like melted butter.

I ran my hands along the back of his shoulders, envisioning the deep scars left from the scourge. Not ugly, but beautiful—a tangible sign of his love for me—a constant reminder that he was willing to die to keep me safe.

I settled my mouth over his, and the heat of his tongue overcame me. A gentle suction gave him what he wanted and a low moan tickled my lips. Sparks burst and fluttered down my throat, into my chest, and exploded out to worship every inch of me. I cried out, and he eased me closer, shaking.

His hands glided beneath my shirt and smoothed up my sides as he rested his cheek against my chest. "I could stay like this forever," he said.

I kissed the top of his hair. "No one's stopping you."

David's smile emblazoned my soul as he parted my lips with another kiss. Deep, driving need coursed through our bond. Pounding, demanding.

My arms quaked, my skin seethed, writhing with this flood of new, intoxicating energy. His muscles tensed, drawing me closer. I rocked my hips, driving myself against him. He growled and spoke several Erescopian words through clenched teeth. The beauty of his language withered into a desperate, staccato phrase. I slipped my hands across his chest. His muscles flexed, twinged, and rolled beneath my fingers, as if his body reached for me—yearned as much as I did. My fingers passed his ribs, and I sketched a line with my thumb across his—

I gasped and leaned away.

David cried out.

"What is … " I brought my hands back to his abs and drew my fingers along a ridge of bony protrusions running down the left side of his stomach.

Sweat glistened on David's chest. He winced as another row appeared on his right side.

His breathing came in short gasps. "I'm sorry, I'm trying to force it back."

"Force it back? What is it?"

David hunched his shoulders. "When you wrapped around me, it was too much." He gulped and pressed his arms to his stomach. "My body tried to engage you. I'm sorry."

The two bumpy ridges grew beneath his grasp, spiking along the sides of his abdomen.

"I don't know what that means. What are those?"

He turned his face away. A blue tinge flared across his cheek.

Why did he seem so ashamed? I pushed his arm away and ran my hand over his navel, between the two protrusions. "Is this where your sexual organs are?"

David turned away as he nodded. "You, the pheromones; it was just too much." He took in a deep breath, quivering like it hurt. "Just give me a second." He wrapped both his arms around his stomach again, covering himself.

Wow.

I knew he was different. I guess I just didn't expect the alien side of him to be so—alien. I moved alongside him and ran my fingers across his cheek. "Never be ashamed of who you are."

A half-hearted laugh puffed from his lips. "I could have hurt you." He ran his left hand over my stomach. "Your skin is so soft, so fragile."

The fear in his gaze sent a dull ache down to my heart. I stroked the arm still clinging to his stomach. "What do those bumps do?"

"My people aren't intimate for the sake of intimacy. We only embrace like this when we mate." He shivered. "It's not like it was in the woods. I'm older now, and my body is built to react. I don't even want to think about … "

His silence cast a deafening shroud through the air between us. "What would have happened?"

His gaze returned to mine. "Our bodies attach while mating." He massaged the ridges in his abdomen. "My human covering stopped them from manifesting. We got lucky." He sighed. "Your frame isn't built for this. It would have been horrible."

Sweat beaded my brow. "Attach?"

"As in impossible to separate until the act is done."

My hands twitched. "The act?"

He closed his eyes and turned away.

Oh. *That* act.

David grabbed his shirt and pulled it back over his head. "I think I better keep this on from now on."

Ice ran through my veins as the white fabric skated over the bumpy protrusions.

So, we couldn't hold each other anymore?

His eyes saddened as he slid his hands over my cheeks. "You've opened me to sensations I never knew existed. I don't want to stop touching you. Ever." He traced his thumb over my bottom lip: tentative, unsure. "We just need to be careful. I'm not human, no matter what I look like. And I would die if I ever hurt you by accident."

I nodded, choking back a sob. David kissed me—a normal, human-like kiss. No jolt of electricity, no insane injection of sensations that melted every bone inside me.

How awful was it that the alien energy that gave me so much pleasure could also fuel something in David that could hurt me.

For the first time, I actually feared our differences.

David flinched.

Crap. He's empathic, you idiot. "I'm sorry. It was just a stray thought. We need to be careful. I understand."

He brushed his brow to mine. "Please don't be afraid of me. *Never* be afraid of me."

"But she should be afraid." The corner of the mattress shifted as a mop of golden curls leaned into the light.

"Maggie?"

12

Maggie blinked twice. "Why didn't you finish what you started? We were quite interested in the outcome."

David skidded me across the sheets, gripping my shoulder as he moved between us. "Who are you?"

"We do not designate ourselves like air-breathers."

Holy cow. First Matt, and now Maggie? Her golden curls sparkled, almost like they were made of water.

"What do you want with us?" I asked.

"Want? We want you to finish procreating. You accomplished nothing."

David's grip on me tightened. "I won't hurt her."

"Which is why we were interested. Every scenario we came up with left you undamaged, but her dead. We've seen many females destroy males while mating, but not the other way around."

Destroy? Could it have come down to that? Were we really so different that he could kill me just by being so close? I shivered. Even though the Erescopians had been in our solar system for more than two years now, we hardly knew anything about them.

I knew I loved David, no matter how hard I tried not to. But maybe she was right. Maybe they were all right. No matter how hard we wanted to ignore the truth, we were from different planets. Different species.

The realization cut a deep gash in my chest, spilling my little girl fantasies onto the floor. It was time to grow up. Time to face the facts. "I'm not his mate," I admitted.

And I never would be.

Not-Maggie narrowed her eyes. "Was that not a mating entanglement you just instigated?"

"We were just fooling around."

One of her perfectly plucked eyebrows rose. "Interesting. Very, very interesting." Her gaze trailed back to David, her eyes unnaturally wide. She blinked and returned her attention to me. "I am unfamiliar with these kinds of games, but you should take caution. The male is very young and does not have the control you think he does. In time, your *fooling around* may leave you unnaturally compromised."

Unnaturally compromised … as in ripped apart. Bleeding. Dead. David hadn't come out and said it, but his reaction told the story. Humans weren't built to be *engaged*—or whatever he called it. I wouldn't survive. Period.

"The male knows coupling would harm you, yet he continued. You should consider the possibility he is not as trustworthy as your simple mind believes he is."

My hands fisted. "You don't know anything about us."

"Untrue. We know a great deal about land dwellers. We have gathered knowledge on your kind for centuries. In fact, we've become quite bored with the pursuit." She perused the nails on her right hand. "There was mild interest in the male's new species, but after initial examination, our only question was how two incompatible species would circumvent the coupling incongruity."

I cringed. *Incongruity* as in wrong, not meant to be.

David's grip on me tightened. "We have some questions of our own."

He hadn't flinched while my thoughts centered on our incompatibility. Either he was giving me the privacy he promised, or he had come to the same conclusion. I'd have felt better if he'd appeared upset, but the set of his jaw and the furrow in his brow screamed determination, and that resolve had nothing to do with our relationship. He didn't even look at me.

It was better this way, but that didn't make it any easier to bear.

I dug my nails into my palms, hoping they'd bleed and distract from the lances thrashing through my heart. When it didn't work I dug harder.

Not-Maggie rested her hands on her lap. "Questions are to be expected."

"Where are we, *really*?" David asked.

"We created this space to simulate the gaseous atmosphere and sparse pressure on the surface. You are approximately forty-one pulls below where we found your ship lodged in our cavern ceiling."

David wove his fingers into mine, his stare fixed on the Maggie-clone. "There was another creature in our ship. Dark. Ten legs. Where are you holding him?"

She tilted her head to the side. "We have no knowledge of the creature you speak of."

"Liar!" I yanked out of David's grasp. "What did you do to him?"

David drew me back. "There's no sense of dishonesty. I think she's telling the truth."

She shrugged. "I have no reason to lie to you."

So they hadn't found Edgar. Maybe that was our ace in the hole. "Is our ship still okay?"

"It is as we left it."

"Filled with water?" David asked.

"Of course. Water overtakes all here. To get you out, we had to let the water in."

So it was flooded? I pawed David's shoulder. "How long can Edgar go without breathing?"

"A long time if he's prepared, but I don't know if he filled his oxygen pouches recently." David turned to Not-Maggie. "You're sure there was no one else in the ship?"

Her expression didn't change. "There were no other life forms when we extracted you."

Those lances cutting into me broke in two and shredded what was left of my chest. It wasn't possible. *Grassen* could swim in outer space. Water should be no problem for them. He had to be somewhere.

Not-Maggie settled further on the bed, crossing her legs. Well, she didn't actually cross them. All of a sudden, they were just crossed—like her body oozed from one position into the next.

"How many of your kind are watching us?" David asked.

"The others have lost interest," she said.

David glanced about the room. "I doubt that. If they are scientist-types I'm sure they have more poking and prodding to do."

"Do not overestimate how curious your two species might be to us. You were interesting only because we could not figure out how you would attempt to mate. Now that you have disengaged the copulation, there is nothing more we can learn from you."

"We only stopped a few minutes ago. You're not going to make me believe that they are all gone but you."

"Then you think too highly of yourself. There are many things to do in the ocean. Wasting time is not one of them." She blinked twice. It seemed almost robotic. "If they are discussing you at all, it is probably whether or not to jettison you into the sea."

A blue sheen tainted David's cheek. "You can't do that."

"They can, and they most likely will. As I said, you have no value to us."

"But we have value to each other," David said. "You are a sentient race, maybe even more so than the air-breathers. I can feel your respect for life—for this planet and everything on it."

"But you are not from this planet, are you? You are an outsider. Worse than she is. Both of you are meaningless in the depths."

David leaned toward her. "You're lying. In fact, you're not even really here. You're behind me, aren't you?" He jumped off the bed and walked to my window. "You're on the other side of this wall, watching us. Your emotions are flooding through this partition. What's out there? You? The ocean? How many of you are watching?"

She lowered her gaze. "At the moment, only me. As I said, the others have lost interest, and I fear we are losing time before they allow the sea to flood this compartment."

His eyes flared as he walked toward Not-Maggie. "But you don't want that. I can feel it. And you're afraid. Do the others even know you're here?"

She shifted her weight. "I led them to believe I left the area when they did."

My mind swirled, lost. I couldn't feel a darn thing. Was David right? Was she some kind of projection? Was she really swimming around outside and watching us like fish in a tank, but in reverse?

"Show yourself," David said.

Not-Maggie nodded. The wall and window behind David rolled as the colors faded and disappeared. The sea hung before us like a shifting liquid curtain. My equilibrium waggled, and I caught the edge of the bed.

You were supposed to gaze down into a pool, not have one hanging like a giant mural on your wall. I turned away to steady myself. When I returned my attention to the oddity, a sheen of bubbles flowed from the floor to the ceiling before dissipating, just like peering through the glass at the aquarium. But in this case, I knew there was no glass.

David stepped back as a red radiance filled the sea. I gasped and shielded my eyes from the brilliance. Thousands of red, glowing, worm-like protrusions twice the length of my legs waved in the gentle current, cradling thicker, suction-cupped, octopus-like arms. Each tendril trailed to a round center bob the size of the Baker's picnic table before bursting out the opposite side, shedding blinding red opalescence through the ocean and my room. The creature resembled a sun drifting in the sea. Breathtaking, yet terrible all at the same time.

"Bio-luminescence." David squinted. "That would make sense at these depths. I wonder if this is the one that ramrodded a hole into our ship."

"That was not me," Not-Maggie said, standing beside me. "I came only when I heard of your existence. By that time, you were already in these alcoves."

"Can you tone down the lights?" David asked.

The wall reappeared. I turned to the girl that looked so much like Maggie. "You're beautiful. Absolutely amazing, like a sparkling ruby necklace floating in the sea."

"Thank you. I've been told so before. Reds are coveted here."

"Your voice sounds sad when you say that," I said.

"Being red is not always an amicable classification." She stepped toward the window. "From the day I was born, I've had my every move watched. I've been treated like a delicate shell waiting to be broken. It is only recently that I've been able to swim on my own, to see some of the wonders our world holds."

Wow. It sounded a lot like growing up on a military base.

"They don't watch you anymore?"

"Not if I stay within our borders. They don't allow anyone to venture outside."

"Why not?"

"They fear those above us."

"Humans?"

She snorted out a sound that may have been a laugh. "No.

Humanity is barely recognized as a species. They are so few, and clustered on the landmasses like barnacles on the hide of a host. And I suppose fear is not the correct word. My people despise those above."

"Are you talking about the round bodied creatures? The beings living above the rift we fell through?" David asked.

"The Uptiders. The separation between us and our dull, symmetrical neighbors has been going on longer than our oldest can remember. They are forbidden to come here. Abominations. Weak. Small."

"You don't like them because they are smaller than you?" I asked.

"Uptiders are considered vile. Plain. Non-luminary. Any creature that cannot create light is considered secondary to those that can. They are treated like lower beings, even though they carry almost every attribute we do."

David stepped closer. "You say they are considered vile and secondary, but from the tone of your voice, it seems you don't agree."

His eyes narrowed, and a slight tingle prickled across our bond. David turned and faced the window, his concentration focused not on the simulated glass, but on the spectacular red creature hidden on the other side.

Not-Maggie raised her chin as David approached the window.

"You need something from us," he said. "Your mind is whirling in fear and anticipation. What is it? What do you want?"

The apparition faded, folding its arms and rubbing its shoulders. "I can give you the source you seek."

David and I straightened at the same time. "What?"

"I've been told that you can pressurize your ship, that you can carry large amounts of water."

"Theoretically," David said. "How did you know that?"

The walls around us faded as if erased, then reappeared.

A disembodied voice echoed through the cavern. "I told her."

13

I stood as the sheetrock beside my window waved like a flag in the breeze, pinching out and forming a long, vertical tube. The manifestation rolled and swirled, forming two legs, two arms, and a head before the color settled into a shiny, metallic gray.

How was that even possible? "Silver?"

His pupil-less eyes turned toward me and nodded.

"But you're one of those Uptiders," David said. "I thought it was forbidden for your kind to be here."

"It is." Silver stepped beside Not-Maggie. "Some time ago, I saw a bright red glow deep in the chasm below. When the seniors weren't watching, I drifted down further than I have ever been, and found an incredible creature wedged in a rift in the ocean floor."

"It was amazing," Not-Maggie said. "He could hear my thoughts, just like I was speaking to my own people. And it wasn't muted and simplistic like your thoughts. It was clear, intelligent. He had no problem understanding that I was trapped."

Silver nodded. "I realized she was from below, but I couldn't leave something so wondrous for the crabs to devour. So I helped her, even though contact between our species is forbidden."

How crazy that must have been, seeing a glowing creature when he'd become used to darkness. She must have shined like a ruby in the sand.

Ruby. That kinda worked for her. Better than constantly thinking of Maggie every time she looked at me.

"Is there a reason you're telling us all of this?" David pointed at Ruby. "She's terrified. Every word out of your mouth frightens her more. Like she's waiting for ... "

David gawked as Silver stepped closer to Ruby, placed his arm around her waist, and pulled her closer. She hunched her shoulders and dropped her gaze.

No. Way.

"Oh," David said.

Ruby kept her face down. "I continued to travel through the rift any chance I could, and he was always there. He's taught me so much."

"And I have learned not to fear those who dwell below us."

David folded his arms. "You want something from us. I can feel it from both of you. What?"

They took each other's hands. The area where Silver's eyes should have been twitched. "Take us with you."

"What?" David and I said in unison.

"Your ship can hold water. Take us from these seas. Bring us to where no one judges you or fears you just because you are different."

I held up my palms. "I hate to pop your bubble, but that's not what it's like up there. I mean, we're not all that different from you in that respect."

"Yet the two of you are together. You share a connection. Surely if both your species allow this there must be ... "

"No one allowed this," David said. "What happened between the two of us was an accident."

Ouch. That hurt.

David's face paled. "I mean, not an accident, but it's not something that should have happened. It's complicated, and the few who know have not made it easy on us."

"You keep your relationship a secret just as we do?" Silver asked.

David sighed. "Yes, I suppose we do. No one seems to understand."

"Then help us," Silver said. "We don't care where we go. We no longer want to be separated by miles of sea."

"But you can't live without water," David said. "Besides, there's about to be a huge fight on the surface. You don't want to be anywhere near there when my people come."

Ruby raised her eyes. "And that is why you need the source?"

David nodded. "If I can bring kinetic energy to Mars, my people might agree to leave Earth alone. I have to give them a viable planet, or they're going to take this one."

She turned to Silver. "This sounds like a cause that would behoove our people as well."

"You can't be serious," Silver said. "We discussed traveling higher—evading both our species. Not—"

She took a step toward David. "You told my friend that your new planet has oceans almost as vast as our great sea. Take us there."

"I can't just take you there. Aren't you listening? My people are coming. I need to make it rain."

Ruby stood taller. "I can make it rain for you. I am the source you seek."

14

I gaped. "Hold the farm. What? What do you mean you are the source? I thought we were searching for energy?"

"Kinetic energy," Ruby said. "It is part of our biological process. I've given off the life energy only once, but I can do it again."

"What?" David stepped forward. "That's impossible. The energy is like an explosion. It shoots out through hydrogen and oxygen molecules."

She nodded. "Gaining in intensity during its journey. We are told that the energy travels to the place where the ocean touches the air, and gives the water mobility, sustaining life for all." She folded her hands and lowered her gaze. "I can do this for you."

David flinched. "I thought I was searching for some kind of manifestation in the planet's crust—volcanic or something. I never dreamed ... " He rubbed his face. "I can't take you to Mars. The ocean's salinity isn't the same. The PH could wreak havoc on your bodies. There are just too many variables. I have no idea how that will affect you."

Silver caught Ruby's gaze. She nodded, and Silver turned back to David. "This is a risk we are willing to take. We are tired of hiding. And if you need the energy to stop a war, the only way to manifest the power is through a rift dweller."

David held out his hands. "Did you catch the part about you maybe dying? And I don't even know if I can keep the pressure in the ship long enough to get all the way to Mars. What you're asking hasn't been done before."

Ruby tilted her head to the side. "Interesting, that you are not grabbing quickly when offered what you seek. This is unlike a land dweller."

David closed his eyes and took a deep breath. "I need to make sure you understand the danger."

"We appreciate your concern." Silver wove his fingers between hers. "We are willing to take the risk."

"Do you think we can do it?" I asked David. "I mean, all that water would make the ship a lot heavier, right?"

"We'd probably lose some maneuverability until we reach open space. As long as no one is chasing us, we'll probably be fine."

As long as no one was chasing us? Had he forgotten that someone was *always* chasing us?

Silver appeared beside us. As in *poof* all of the sudden he was there. I jumped, grabbing my chest.

"Sorry for startling you." He turned to David. "May I speak to you, privately?"

David squeezed my shoulder before he and Silver moved toward my dresser.

I sat on my bed and massaged my temples. How crazy was this? We came all the way down here, and ended up getting captured by the very energy source we were searching for. How stinking convenient was that? Maybe too convenient.

Ruby settled beside me. "I regret not being forthright from the beginning. I was not here when they captured you. I was with the one you call Silver when my people took you from your vessel. He told me what had transpired between you. I needed to trust you before I offered myself."

Her golden curls wound in perfect ringlets beside her face, covering that small scar on her temple from the one and only time Maggie tried riding her bike with no hands. This girl really was Maggie to the very finest detail.

I perused the soda stain on the carpet. "I don't know why you trust us so much. Not that you shouldn't trust us, but … " *Yeah, I'm just an idiot.* "You know what I mean."

A soft smile crossed her lips. "When I look inside you, I see an incredible devotion to the one you call David. This is beyond the link that seems to bind you."

I shrugged. "Yeah, well, I really lov … l-like him." I balked at my hesitation. All I wanted was to let my emotions flower and burst and scream to the world. But I couldn't. No one would understand.

"You deny your feelings. You lie, even to yourself. Why?"

I was starting to hate being surrounded by all these telepathic people … aliens … fish … *Whatever.*

"I'm not really denying it, but we're from different planets, and he keeps going home. We're never together, and when he's gone—" I shook my head. "It just hurts too much."

"Does it hurt so much that it outweighs the pleasure he gives you when he is near?"

Did it?

Years of agony. Waiting. Disappointment.

When he'd finally come back, I was happy for the first few seconds, but then all the pent-up frustration came out in a giant fist-flinging ball of rage. Damn, I was mad at him. He didn't even seem to understand that he'd been gone for a long time. It would happen again. I was sure of it.

David leaned close to Silver. He nodded, his eyes focused, his expression hard. He was going to save Earth. Again. I had every confidence in him. Two extra passengers and a million gallons of water wouldn't stop him. And the only reason—the real reason, was me.

If we hadn't met, Earth would have been toast by now. He'd given up so much, toiled so long—just to save my home.

Well, not just to save my home—to save me. David and I shared something more powerful than anyone could understand. I'd tried to fight it, tried to forget him, but how do you forget someone that's already part of you? And the more I was with him, the less I could lie to myself.

This wasn't the mental mojo everyone thought it was. I loved him. I needed him. And no matter how much he frustrated me, I wouldn't be able to escape the pulsing energy that drew us together. We were linked. What had he called it?

Connected.

And I never wanted to cut the string.

A trickle of exhilaration flashed away from me before I could reel in the joy I felt from simply looking at him. Across the room, David's eyes widened. He smiled and a mischievous glint sparkled in his gaze. I could sense something building within him, and I shivered. Part of me ventured out and ran invisible fingers over the shimmering twines connecting us.

My breath hitched as the energy I'd sent to David returned to me in a super-charged flood. Our tether heated, burning my stomach for a second, until the spinning warmth shot out, swirling and sparkling, inserting pure delight into every part of me that could feel. I took several struggled gasps of air, each one harder than the last. The burning bordered on painful, before easing back and blanketing me in a comforting pressure that surrounded me in waves.

Holy Hell. How could he inject something inside me like that, and so easily, like it was nothing? He glanced back to me, ignoring Silver's whispers. His smile broadened, seeming almost smug—or was it satisfied?

When I thought of how much I loved him, had I sent him the same jolt? Could I possibly make him feel the same crazy sensations he sent to me?

My heart skipped a beat. More than anything, I wanted to make him happy.

"You most definitely did," Ruby said.

My cheeks heated. I lowered my eyes.

"Why does this embarrass you?" Ruby asked. "You are already connected. There is no reason you should not be together."

Easy for her to say. Her father wasn't in the Army, or in charge of a fleet of spaceships Hell-bent on making Earth their own. It just wasn't that simple, no matter how hard I wanted it to be true. God, I wanted the fairytale—for it all to iron out easily like in the books. But it wasn't going to happen, and the sooner I believed that, the better.

Time to deflect. "So, what makes being red so special that they're treating you like a china doll?"

She shifted her weight. The mattress moved beneath me, just like it would if we were really back in my room. Star Trek's holodeck didn't seem so out of this world anymore.

"Reds are larger and bear more heavily than the other colors."

"Bear more heavily?"

"Reds bear three to five young at a time while the other colors normally bare only one."

"Oh." I had the feeling she was young—maybe younger than me. It could be that my brain thought I was talking to Maggie, but her whole vibe screamed kid. But that didn't stop her people from looking at her like a baby machine. No wonder she wandered away. I would have, too.

"My mother is red. I have dozens of brothers and sisters in many wonderful colors. So far, I am the only *lucky one*." Her lips tightened. "Our species is dying out in this sector of the ocean. Fewer and fewer are born every season. It is my responsibility as one of the few remaining reds to even our odds of survival."

Whoa. My dad only wanted me to go to West Point, not breed my own little army. That was way too much pressure to place on one girl.

She closed her eyes, and her lips trembled. She was her family's crown jewel. The only one born to privilege. It sounded so much like a princess story—Jasmine all locked up in her palace, dreaming to get away from her suffocating life and falling in love with a beggar boy in the market. I highly doubted her people would be all too happy about their precious prize hooking up with one of their blobby neighbors from above.

Ruby folded her arms, hugging herself. "Eight of my siblings were like Silver. Plain, round, and uncolored. Two of these abominations came from my own birth brood."

"Wait, what? Are you saying Silver and you are the same species?"

She nodded. "Nearly half of our births hold the defect. They're sent away, up through the rift with the Uptiders, before they can spread their repulsiveness further."

"So, half your babies are pretty and colorful, and half are plain—and you get rid of the plain ones?"

A jagged pain sliced from the base of my throat to my stomach. I had taken a tour of a goldfish farm when I was a kid. When the babies were large enough to see their colors, they were divided between the pretty ones and the ugly ones. The pretty ones were moved to large tanks so they could get bigger. They never said what happened to the ugly ones.

That wasn't natural selection or survival of the fittest. It was just … wrong.

"That would explain why you and Silver could speak telepathically. You're the same species." I glanced at the guys. "They can't do that. I mean, just because they're not pretty? It's cruel. It's horrible."

"I never thought so, but the more time I spend with Silver, the more I wonder." She shifted closer to me. "He makes me—*feel things.*"

"What do you mean?"

She hunched her shoulders. "A few moments ago, when you and David looked at each other, it was stimulating to you. Pleasant."

Pleasant really didn't cover it, but, yeah.

She peered in the guys' direction, and back to me. "The one time I gave off the life power, he ... did something to me." She folded her hands and stared at them. "We were conversing, and I enjoyed the sensation of letting my tendrils slide over his form." A smile lifted her lips. "He quaked when I touched him. I think he liked it, too." She paused, sucking in her lips and biting. I wondered what she was doing in her real body. "That's when he *did it.*"

The tiniest part of me didn't want to know. Her confession felt like a total invasion of privacy. But hey, she was doing the talking. I was just listening. No harm in that, right? "What happened?"

"My center, where my coils meet ... opened ... like I had a void within me." Her apparition faded before darkening again. "I was frightened at first, but something about Silver's presence made it all seem so right." She stared past me, as if a million miles away. "He twisted himself into something like a cylinder and ... slid into me."

Okay, yeah, this was waaay too personal. It almost sounded like they were having ... Eww. I turned away from her.

"Is this upsetting you?" she asked. "I don't want to offend, but I thought you would understand."

Wow. She guilt-tripped better than Dad. But who else would she talk to?

I smiled. "I'm okay. So when did the energy-thing happen?"

"When he was inside me he relaxed and his form tried to spring back to his normal shape. It hurt at first, very much so."

I bet it did.

"But then I felt—I'm not sure how to explain it, but there was all this pressure and it kept building, and all of the sudden the life energy flared around us like an explosion of yellow light." Her hands swayed at her sides. "It was horrible, terrible, and wonderful all at the same time. It burned, but in a good way. Does that make sense?"

I nodded. "It makes perfect sense."

"But it was too much. The power kept exploding, over and over. I couldn't stop it." She hunched her shoulders. "The truth is I didn't want to stop. It felt so good, like nothing I'd ever experienced before. But Silver ripped away from me, caught in the energy surging from my core. I reached for him, but everything went black."

My eyes widened. "Seriously?"

"We woke up floating next to each other. I don't know how long we were dormant."

Wow. It seemed like they were attracted, and acted on instinct, like any guy and girl would. Maybe this was natural, maybe this was just how they did things ... but if they got rid of all the round ones, how would they ... Holy. Crap.

I inched closer. "Can I ask how you would normally let out the power? I mean, you sounded like everything that happened between the two of you was strange."

"It was. The release of the life energy is part of the reproductive process. The power never should release at another time."

My stomach twisted. "And what, exactly is the reproductive process?"

"It takes a great deal of energy. When my time comes, I will need to alter half of my organs to a new form so I can impregnate myself."

"Impregnate *yourself?*"

She nodded.

Oh, God—like frogs changing sex in a single sex environment.

Her kind threw out their males, and over time, they adapted so they could still reproduce. Like Amazons of the deep. Freaking creepy.

Jess, David's voice exploded in my mind. *You won't believe what Silver and I just figured out.*

I straightened. *Maybe I would. She's a girl, and he's a boy, and they're from the same species.*

Confusion and excitement trickled through our bond. *Does she know?*

I don't think so. Ruby shifted her weight, twirling her fingers in and out of one another. *It doesn't seem like she's reading my thoughts.*

The air in front of us shimmered with a million droplets of water, like rain frozen mid-fall. They glinted before smashing together, forming Silver. He fumbled for Ruby's hands. "We need to talk."

She nodded, and their forms wavered before slipping to the floor as if they sank right through the carpet. I covered my eyes. "This is pretty major."

David trailed his fingers down the center of my back. "I've never seen anything like it. They compromised their own species for so long, but nature kept giving them what they really needed: more males. And they just kept throwing them away."

Heat soaked through my cheek as I cuddled against his chest. I could have held him like that forever. I sniffed and rubbed a tear from my eye.

"What's wrong?"

I eased away from him. "It's stupid. I kinda felt like she and I had something in common, but we don't. She fell in love with someone from her own race, even though neither of them realized it. It's nothing like what we're going through."

He traced his fingers beneath my chin. "You know I don't care about that, right? I've made my sacrifice, and I have no regrets."

Where the hell did that come from? Sacrifice? Seriously? Is that how he really felt?

I pushed him away, but he drew me back. "That's not what I meant, and you know it."

A painful ball formed in my throat. "Then why do you always leave me?"

"We both need to make concessions to make this work. I want to be with you, but my people need me." He released my arm and combed his fingers through his bangs. "Don't you think I'd rather be with you, holding you, soaking you in?" The colors in his eyes separated again. "I was one hundred and eighty million miles away, and I could still feel your pain. I tried to send you comfort, but I suppose that's just another failure to add to my excruciatingly long list."

"You knew it bothered me last time when you didn't call. I can't believe you went another two years and didn't contact me again."

Defeat melted the expression from his face. "If I sent a transmission, it would have been monitored. What we've done, this connection we have ... " He shook his head. "My father is capable of many things, and not all of them are honorable." His gaze scanned my face. Remorse pinched his features. "Don't you know how badly I wanted to come back and hold you, let you know everything was all right?"

"Then why didn't you? You couldn't take a day off? Sightsee on Earth or something? That's what spaceships are for, right?"

"It takes nearly a week to get here in a civilian transport. Even if I could find passage on a military ship, the journey would have been at least two days."

"And the little Earth girl wasn't worth the effort." I waved my palms in the air. "I think I understand, now."

He grabbed my shoulders. Blue fire burned through our tether. "Excuse me for trying to build a new planet. By myself. Don't you understand? By. My. *Self*." I cringed, trembling under his grip. "None of my people have the knowledge needed to do this. They need me. I can't be so selfish to go and do what I want when my entire race is counting on me!"

He folded his arms and turned away, shaking beneath his tight cotton tee-shirt. Confliction coursed through our bond—the deep desire to be with me, but the need to help his people.

Here I was concerned about the pressure Ruby was under, not even recognizing what David was battling every day. What was wrong with me? He wasn't the one being selfish. I was. How could I still have all these egocentric feelings after all he'd done to save my planet? What kind of idiot was I?

"You're not an idiot," he whispered.

"And you're not supposed to be listening to my thoughts."

He hunched, still staring at the wall. "I'm sorry, but I just yelled at you. I don't like yelling at you. I was afraid you'd be mad again."

I moved behind him, placing my hand on his back. "There's really no one else who can do this?"

"I was the only eco-biologist to survive the experiments that created the mustard powder."

I cringed. The mustard powder—the nasty stuff that I found on his ship two years ago. What had he called it? A biological weapon. One that David had accidently invented. And Earth nearly paid dearly for his mistake.

"I'm trying to teach as many new minds as I can, but they're just not knowledgeable enough yet." He finally turned. "As much as it hurts to leave you, I need to go back."

"But all your work, and they're still coming to take Earth."

"Not while I'm still breathing. We have a perfect chance now with these two beings."

"Can we just take them to Mars, though? Isn't that kidnapping?"

"I know it's bad to say this, but I don't really care. If they can live in the seas I've created, and Ruby can have as many babies as Silver thinks she can, she can populate Mars with hundreds of little rain-makers. Her offspring can sustain Mars forever."

"But what about her family here? They're going to freak."

His features hardened. "Not my problem. There are billions of human and Erescopian lives at stake. I can't worry about our people and the rift dwellers too."

Whoa. I stepped back.

"Don't look at me like that. I've faced failure way too many times, and now your planet is more at risk than ever." He grabbed my arms. "Don't you understand? I won't have to build anything or make anything grow. She can make it rain right away. Maybe not on the entire planet, but at least in a large enough area that I can prove it will work. We might not have to lose *any* of Earth."

I yanked out of his grip. "Wait, what? What do you mean? I thought you were trying to stop the attack on Earth completely."

A little part of me died when he didn't immediately answer.

He closed his eyes and took a steadying breath. "There was never any chance to completely stop them, Jess. I thought you understood that. That's why I wanted to get you and your father safely to that island." He lowered his eyes. "My people were preparing for the return to Earth when I left, and we've been gone for too long. The scourge may have already started, and I still need to get these beings to Mars."

A leaden weight formed in my chest. "B-but, my dad. Maggie. Matt."

"I have no idea what's happening on the surface." He brushed his cheek to mine. "I'm sorry."

15

The walls blanched, fading to a translucent sheen. Our new friends hovered in the sea outside, basking in the red glow emanating from Ruby's soft, floating tendrils.

The liquid curtain pinched, and Ruby and Silver walked right out of the simulated partition before it became my window again. Ruby pawed for my hands, but they splashed across my skin. Omigosh! They actually were made of water! Well, at least their fake-selves were.

"We need to go," Silver said.

A miniature wave rolled over the carpet, washing my shoes away from the bed. "What's going on?"

"They've decided they have no more use for you."

The flood bubbled up from recesses behind the floorboards and soaked my knees. David splashed toward me, his eyes wide.

"Can you swim?" I asked.

He grimaced. "Before I filled the oceans on Mars I'd never seen more than a few hundred gallons of water in one place." The sea level reached his hands. "At least it's not cold, but ... "

"The volcanic fissures keep our environment warm," Ruby said, like the reason for the warmth mattered when a gazillion gallons of ocean were rushing in on us.

She and Silver shifted lackadaisically as if standing at the beach watching the waves come in. Probably because they weren't really there. Unlike David and me, who were stuck with nowhere to go.

David waded through the surge and pounded against the walls.

"Don't," Ruby said. "These caves are in balance, even when flooded. If you damage the outer layers of compression facing, the weight of the ocean will crush you." She pointed at the window, which started to flicker as if the image was shorting out. "They have released this wall completely. I am holding the barrier in place to keep the room from imploding, but I can't do so for long."

He backed away from the window. His brow arched, probably discerning the feasibility of naturally-occurring pressure-free caves so deep in the ocean.

Our warm, comforting surroundings fizzled from existence. My ceiling fan faded into a huge, white, glowing stalagmite above, illuminating the solid, foreboding, brown stone walls that had replaced my bedroom.

The wall with my window shimmered back into the water-curtain holding out the sea. The real Ruby and Silver zigged and zagged on the other side, not gentle and floating like before, but anxious and frantic. Silver skidded upward and out of sight. Ruby twitched. Was she just going to float there and watch? See how long it took us to drown? And this far beneath the sea, we probably would, and quickly. When she lost her grip on that last barrier, we were in deep—

"We're going to die." David shuddered, staring at the curtain. "We came so close ... so close."

"We are not going to die."

His gaze remained fixed on the curtain, and the swaying bright red fluttering beacon on the other side. "I can't swim, Jess. Even if I could breathe ... "

"Look at me." His attention darted to me before whipping back to the liquid wall. "Look at me!"

He froze. His gaze trailed to mine. His lower lip quivered, and his irises lightened to a silvery blue. My stomach twisted. I'd seen David scared before, but nothing like this. "You might not be able to swim, but I can. I'll get you through this."

His shoulders stiffened. "How?"

The apparitions of Ruby and Silver melted away to nothing. I was on my own on this one. "I haven't figured that out yet."

The deluge breached our shoulders. I kicked off from the floor. There was a hole in the rocky ceiling. Small, but it was there. No leaks or drips clung to the edges, which meant there must be air above it. At least I hoped that was what it meant.

I pulled David up as the water bettered his chin. "Kick your feet!"

His shoulders twisted in my grip, so I could tell he was trying, but it didn't help him much as the sea drew him down.

"Keep air in your lungs! It will help you float."

"I can't!"

"You can, dammit!" I moved to his back and slipped my arm around his chest—just like the lifeguards always do in the movies. I kicked furiously to keep him afloat.

The sea surged, propelling us upward. Had the curtain given way?

I sucked in what I could of the last bubble of air. *David, once the sea is over your head, don't breathe. No matter how bad your body screams for oxygen, don't do it. That's how you drown!*

Terror gnashed at our bond. I wished I could shut him out. I needed to focus. Not so easy to do when the person you're connected to is convinced he's about to die.

What illumination still lit the chamber winked out. A merciless pressure trounced me from all sides. The wall must have given away!

David slipped from my grip before the pressure suddenly ceased.

I splashed frantically, searching for him, until the ocean flashed in a dazzling red fury. Soft, slimy tendrils slicked through the sea, pushing David into my arms and driving us up toward the hole in the ceiling.

Ruby!

The salinity burned my eyes, but I couldn't close them. Grabbing David's wrist I kicked with all my might, centering my thoughts on the shimmer coming from the hole. There was air up there. There had to be. We weren't going to die. Not here. No way. I got this. I totally got this.

My lungs burned. I tightened my jaw as my mouth tried to open. Air. I needed air.

I became dizzy.

Just open your mouth, a voice within whispered. *Inhale. It will all be okay.*

Bubbles trickled from my lips before I could clamp them shut again.

No!

I kicked harder, tangling in Ruby's tendrils. Twisting to free myself, I only got tangled worse. She was dragging me down! Was she doing it on purpose? Maybe it wasn't even her!

David went slack beside me. His mouth opened and four bubbles rolled from his face. My pulse throbbed within my temples as his dark locks waved through the water around his peaceful, closed eyes. His head lolled to the side, shifting in the current.

No! This can't be happening!

A last, smaller bubble escaped his lips. I bit back the scream simmering in my chest. My eyes widened, increasing the burn. Pressure built in the back of my throat, elevating and spreading into my temples.

No! No! No! No! No! No!

His frame's weight tugged me down. I kicked, clutching his tee-shirt and hoisted. My shoulders burned, my legs ached. If I didn't get oxygen I was going to—

My face broke the surface and I sucked in sweet, wonderful air.

David's arm started to slip through his shirt. I shoved one wrist under his shoulder and lifted. How long could he stay submerged? Was I already too late?

His skull slammed against the rock when the current hit us. We couldn't both fit through the hole at the same time!

A fountain shot past us, splashing on a bed of slimy, black goo before taking Silver's form.

"Let go," he shouted. "Climb out!"

"I can't. He'll sink."

Silver leaned forward. "I am beneath you. I will hold him up."

Oh, God.

Oh, God. Oh, God. Oh, God. Oh, God. Oh, God!

"You need to trust me," Silver said.

How was I supposed to trust him? How could I trust anyone down here?

David's weight lessened. I paused, barely breathing. He wasn't sinking anymore.

"I have him." Silver crouched beside the opening, his arms folded across his chest. "Now climb out."

My mind struggled with the idea of talking to Silver up here, while his body was below David, holding him up. But what if he let David go?

Out of options, I gulped down my fear. I had to trust him. I whispered a speed prayer and released my grip. David didn't go under.

I scrambled out of the hole, spun, and sunk my arms back into the warm sea. "Can you boost him up?" I asked.

"I'll do my best."

David's face broke the surface. Water ran from his soaked tresses and sheened the side of his face. I slipped my hands beneath his shoulders and heaved. He barely moved. "I can't lift him. He weighs too much."

EMBERS IN THE SEA

Silver held the sides of his shiny, bare skull. "I'm too small. I can't carry him any further."

The purple hue of David's real skin tainted a circle around his lips. But was that good, or bad? I'd seen his natural color flash before, but on dry land, when he was breathing. I needed to get him out of that hole so I could do CPR or something.

I heaved again. David rose, but my grip slipped, and he slid back to Silver, hovering like a dark blob just below the surface.

How many times had David saved my life? I couldn't let him down. Not now.

Dammit! Why couldn't I be stronger!

Silver turned toward the water. "Wait. She's coming."

The opening lit up with fiery red brilliance. Three or four glowing crimson octopus legs flapped near David's face. What if Ruby pulled him under, just like she nearly did to me?

I tightened my grip. There was no way I was letting go.

David's body bolted up through my arms and over my head. He landed on the slippery black goo, and Ruby's mammoth red form splatted beside him.

Silver jumped back. "She's on dry rocks!"

"I see that!"

Red gook oozed across the chamber floor. The five or so legs still in the water swayed manically, maybe the only part of her that could move. The rest of Ruby flattened across the stone floor as if she'd melted.

Oh, Crap.

16

Silver's pupil-less eyes widened. His mouth gaped. "Help her! Please, help her!" He sprinted to Ruby and his apparition disappeared, splashing water across the larger creature's prone frame. His plump figure bobbed just below the surface. Ruby's tendrils grasped for him, but his rounded body gave her nothing to hold on to.

I tried to grab one of Ruby's arms, but my fingers sunk into her flesh. Her entire gelatinous bulk quaked.

Silver appeared again. "You're hurting her!"

I drew my hands away. "I don't know what to do! She's like a big jellyfish!"

David lay several feet away, his chest motionless. My psyche screamed to split myself in two, one to help Ruby, and one to help David.

Lord, please help me!

Silver deconstructed himself again, splashing over Ruby. At least that would keep her wet.

I scrambled to David, rolled him onto his back, and settled my ear to his chest. No heartbeat.

He had a heartbeat, right? I mentally slapped myself. Of course he had a heartbeat! How many times had I fallen asleep on his chest, lulled by its gentle rhythm?

He wasn't breathing, either.

No. He wasn't dead. He couldn't be. Not on my watch.

I took a deep breath. *Focus, Jess. Keep yourself together. David needs you.*

Silver splashed his liquid form across the floor behind me, soaking my bare ankles as well as Ruby's drying skin.

Okay—CPR. How the heck do you do CPR?

I placed one hand over the other and pressed the heel of my palm against David's chest.

Push. Push. Push.

I pinched David's nose, tilted his head back, and puffed air into his mouth.

Twenty more presses to his chest. Breathe.

Another splash from Silver wet my ankles.

We couldn't keep doing this forever, but I knew neither of us would stop. Too much was at stake. I wouldn't give up on David. Ever.

Push. Push. Push … *Come on, David. Come back to me.* I placed my lips over his mouth. His skin—so cold. I choked back a sob and blew more air into his lungs.

Splash. Silver continued his dance behind me, but was it a fruitless effort? Were either of us doing anything?

I combed back my hair, squinting from the sting of saltwater and burning tears. I'd only seen CPR done in movies and television. I wasn't even sure I was doing it right. But I couldn't just sit there.

Push. Push. Push. Twenty repetitions. I could do this. Breathe. Splash. Repeat. Repeat. Repeat.

I slapped my palms to the floor on either side of David's face. "Dammit, breathe! Don't you dare leave me down here! Don't you dare!"

A serenity coated David's features, like he was sleeping. I could just cuddle up beside him. Keep him warm, like in the woods so long ago. Was that too much to ask, to go back in time,—back to a day before we climbed onto that ship on the beach and splashed into this death trap of an ocean?

I wiped my eyes. He'd travelled billions of miles, only to drown trying to save Earth.

How was this fair? How was any of this right? This couldn't be fate. This couldn't be the end of our story.

I gulped and turned to the rocky ceiling. The larger, white stalagmites shimmered, casting a dull glow throughout the chamber. Ethereal. Otherworldly. Their oppressive mass made me feel small and insignificant, as I had so many times before.

God, why are you letting this happen? Please help me. Please give me the strength to—

David's frame twitched, and he coughed. Water ran down his chin.

"Omigosh!" I pitched him onto his side as he coughed again. Holding back a sob, I fell on my rear when he inhaled on his own. I rubbed his back. "Just breathe. You're going to be okay." At least I hoped so. This was the part where they faded to black on television and you always assumed the half-drowned person lived a long and wonderful life.

I stood and turned toward Ruby's gelatinous mass. Parts of her back—or whatever that was, had darkened and lost its luster, as if her skin was drying. Where was Silver?

Dropping to my knees, I leaned over the hole in the floor. Silver's oval form spun and poked at the faded, floating tendrils.

"What are you doing?" I shouted, and cringed as my voice echoed between the stone walls.

A funnel splashed up out of the water and morphed in the air, forming Silver.

He landed in a crouch beside me. "Her lungs are collapsing.

She can't respire!" He dashed toward her and separated, splashing back over her drying form before rematerializing beside me. "You have to help her. Please, do something!"

"How can I help?"

"I don't know. You're a land dweller. Don't you know how to move something without water?"

Sure, if it's not made of melting JELL-O.

I steeled myself. *Get your head in the game, Martinez. You can do this.* I glanced at David and nodded. Yes. I could do this.

No. I *would* do this.

I turned back to Silver. "How long can she survive out of the water?"

Silver's real body bobbed up and down before slipping back into the sea. Fabricated Silver didn't even flinch. "We're told that if we ever get caught in a vent, we need to get out within … " His head jerked from side to side as if calculating. "About nine hundred and thirty-five of your heartbeats."

Yikes. If I remembered correctly from health class, that was probably about eleven minutes. And who even knew if that was accurate. She'd been on those rocks at least five minutes already.

She was out of time. Maybe we all were.

David hoisted himself to a sitting position. He glanced at me, holding his chest and breathing heavily.

Yeah, that salinity in his lungs had to burn bad. I was on my own. At least for now.

I swiped my hair behind my ears, wishing I had a rubber band, and faced Silver. "Okay. Help me out. What is this room? Why is there oxygen here?"

"There are volcanic vents below us. They super heat the sea, forcing it to turn to gas."

And thus the warmth. Interesting.

"Over the millennia, these ducts and chambers developed naturally, holding the air until released to flow through the oceans."

Silver held out his arms over Ruby. They dissolved into sparkling droplets and fell over her. I marveled as the liquid at his shoulders bubbled and pinched, growing back into arms. He seemed to shrink a little though.

He lowered his newly-grown arms. "We have the same chambers where I come from above. We use them to cultivate food plants that will not grow underwater."

I walked toward him. "Wait. What? You grow food in these things? How do you harvest them if you guys turn into piles of goop in the air?"

"They are flooded to allow entrance, and immediately harvested before the plants die. The air seals let the water in slowly so the crop is not destroyed. That is how they began flooding your chamber below; before they dropped the artificial viewing pane to euthanize you in a humane manner rather than having you drown slowly."

How considerate of them.

I shook away the thought. The artificial viewing pane—he must have meant the wall that became clear so we could see out to the sea. "Is there a viewing pane in this room?"

"No. This is an upper chamber. They are solid except for the main seal above that holds the air in."

I scanned the ceiling as Silver splashed more water over Ruby. "So how exactly does it work?"

"The air seal is loosened to allow the gasses to escape the first chamber into the compartment above. The movement of the gas forces the water out of the compartment above, and fills the lower compartment with water."

I scrambled around the room, searching for anything that might not be permanent. "What would one look like?"

He held his hands to his head, mimicking me. "I don't know. We don't have time for this. Please help me get her back into the sea."

If the air escaped, it would go up. Makes sense. So the next chamber would have to be high. My gaze drew upward to the rocky fissures about ten feet above.

"I don't see any ... wait a minute. What's that?" To the right of a stalactite the rock-face glistened, not dry like the rest. The material trembled, like a curtain stretched tight against a breeze. "That's got to be it!"

Silver folded his arms. "Maybe, but you can't just open them. We use the power of the tides. You'd need to be incredibly strong."

"I'm working on that." First, I had to get up there. But how? I'd need a ladder, climbing gear—

David tried to drag himself up from the floor.

—or a ninja alien agile enough to jump atop a twelve-foot security fence and strong enough to knock a helicopter out of the sky.

Oh, guess what? I actually had me one of those.

I scrambled to David's side. "Are you all right?"

He flopped onto his back. "We *are not* going up there."

One good thing about telepathy is you can cut right to the chase. "We have to."

"We're not flooding this chamber." He stood and blinked as if clearing a fog from his sight before striding to Ruby. "There has to be a better way." He slid his palms beneath her and lifted, but her bulk oozed like gelatin between his fingers.

Silver splashed over her and reappeared from the pond again. "She's not conscious anymore." He moved closer to David. "Please don't let her die."

David's gaze shifted to the fluctuating colors on the right half of the ceiling. A clear bead of moisture dripped down his temple, but I doubted it came from his damp hair.

"You can jump that high," I reminded him.

I swear the swirling colors in his eyes formed tiny daggers.

"I can't do this," he hissed.

"I know you can."

"The water will come in." He grasped my shoulder, his hand shaking. "No more water. You don't understand."

But I did. He almost drowned. We both did. But like it or not, we were miles below sea level. Chances are we'd have to get wet again to get to our ship one way or another.

"Ruby risked her life to save you. Are you telling me you're going to let her die?"

His gaze darted to the sagging blob of red flesh on the floor. His lip quivered.

"I know you're scared. But we all just proved that we're going to do everything in our power to make sure we all get out of this together, and right now she's drowning in the air." I pointed to Ruby just as Silver splashed over her again. "Are you still the guy I fell in love with? Are you going to let this happen just because you're afraid?"

He took a step back, scanned the ceiling, and gulped. His expression hardened. "How fast will the water come in?"

"I don't know," Silver said. "I'm not a farmer, but I would expect the chamber to fill at the same rate as the one below us."

I ran my palm across David's back. "We don't have a choice."

David nodded, but his hands shook. He walked beneath the shimmering part of the ceiling, setting his feet carefully on the uneven floor. I wished I could take away his fear, but I was just as scared.

The speed of the deluge and possibility of the water being freezing cold were also a factor. I didn't mention it though. We had enough to worry about.

He looked in my direction and grimaced.

Shoot. Please tell me he hadn't been reading my mind!

I'm sorry, stray thoughts and all ... I can't stop thinking, can I?

He returned his gaze to the ceiling. Maybe he hadn't been listening. He crouched and jumped. His fingers skidded across the top of the ceiling before he hit the ground.

"It's soft," he said, "but thick, like a hide of some kind."

"Can you get it open?"

His irises churned as he considered Ruby's quaking form. "I'll try."

Silver splayed moisture across her as David jumped toward the ceiling once again.

David scraped and scratched at the edges of the seal repeatedly with no luck.

"No!" Silver screamed.

We spun toward him. Huge red, blue, orange, and yellow tentacles elevated from the hole in the floor, waving and flapping against Silver's bobbing, cylindrical shape. His apparition gaped, faced us, and splashed to the ground beside Ruby as his real body succumbed to the flailing tentacles of larger rift dwellers.

They'd found him.

17

Silver's rounded frame sunk from view.

I ran to the opening. "Let him go!"

Several dripping, blue, waving tentacles rushed from the opening and flopped onto Ruby's back. The flattened tendrils jerked before slipping back into the sea.

I leaned over the hole. "Silver!" Not that he could hear me, or even answer. But I had to do something!

Swirling appendages wrapped around Ruby's dangling tentacles. Her bulk shifted toward the hole, leaving a dark red, bloody scrape on the ground.

"Stop!" I screamed. "You're hurting her!"

Another tug brought her an inch closer to the edge. Red fluids oozed into small puddles in the rock floor.

"I said stop!"

I punched through the surface, knuckles sinking into thick, lukewarm goo. I yanked my fist out and tried to stand, but a bright blue tendril slapped my cheek. I reared back, but not before the suction-cup-covered appendage shot out, wrapping around my wrist and dragging me toward the hole.

My feet slipped out from under me. I hit the rocky edge, huffing the air from my lungs before a forceful tug drew my face and shoulders into the water.

I clamped my jaw shut. Saltwater lanced the inside of my nose, as a fishy tang spread across my tongue and pooled at the back of my throat. I thrashed, pulling against the cephalopod's tendrils, until a firm grip latched onto my hips, pulling me back to the surface.

I have you, David's voice boomed through my mind.

But that didn't stop the giant blue octopus-thing from yanking me down further.

The sea stung my eyes. Two ginormous yellow and orange glowy monsters smothered Silver's dwarfed cylindrical frame before they sunk out of sight.

My shoulder burned and a submersed *pop* resounded in my ears. Fire raked through the rest of my arm. I screamed, bubbles flowing from my throat. *The burn. The taste!* I gagged, allowing the sea access.

David, help me! My heartbeat thumped in my head as I thrashed and punched at my captor with my good arm. The grip on my waist tightened, but I still seemed to drop deeper into the sea. Bright blue light from the monster below obscured everything as my vision started to fade.

Stay awake, Jess. Stay awake and stay alive!

I punched with the last of my strength, and a deep calm overcame my will to fight. It wasn't really all that bad. The water was warm, relaxing. A nice long nap might be nice. Yes, I definitely needed a nice … long …

A splash of bubbles perforated the silence, and someone tugged the tendril attached to my arm. They seemed to struggle, swirling the sea around us.

Dark fluids muddied the ocean as I flipped over. The illumination above seemed distant, like a tunnel beckoning entrance. My sight clouded, until a strong hand gripped my wrist and hoisted me up through the shimmering circle above.

I broke into the air with a gasp. Droplets streamed down my face as a blurry form carried me from the edge of the hole.

Sleep. Still needed sleep.

Someone scampered around me, and jostled me onto my side. I coughed, cringing at the burn surging up my throat and the throbbing agony in my shoulder. My stomach churned, and I opened my mouth, ejecting salt and sea. A warm hand slapped my cheek. A voice sounded in the distance. The hold, so warm. So strong.

The blur around me focused to a blue deeper than the sea.

David nestled my cheek to his chest. "I thought I lost you."

A fit of coughing riddled me before I retched. The ache in my stomach increased, and I heaved again. *Ouch.*

My jeans squished as I shifted my weight. Why was I sitting in a foot of water?

I rubbed the salt from my eyes. My fog slowly cleared, and David grabbed my cheeks.

A lance stabbed through my shoulder as he eased me closer, our noses nearly touching. "Please tell me you're in there."

"Yeah. What—"

The sea rose, now not far from my waist. I gaped as the malleable hatch that had once sealed in our oxygen jostled and flapped against the rock formations above.

"You got it open."

David kissed my temple. "Yes. Just before that thing grabbed you."

Forcing down my need to vomit again, I scrambled to Ruby's side. Brilliant flashes traveled across her back and along her tentacles, but the swells only lapped her midriff. I splashed over the top of her with my right hand. My left hung useless at my side.

David flanked me. "I appreciate us still trying to save her, but at some point we're going to have to do that swim thing."

The hole in the roof mocked me. Getting through probably wouldn't be the problem. It was getting an alien that couldn't swim all the way up to the ceiling. Especially if I was down an arm. I continued to splash over my new friend's trembling form. *Come on, Ruby. I'm going to need your help here.*

I gasped and spun as a miniature funnel bubbled up out of the pond behind us. A glowing green tentacle darted out of the hole in the floor and whizzed toward Ruby. David lunged for the creature, tackling and twisting the flailing member. Something snapped, and dark fluids ran along the creature's spotted emerald flesh and stained the nearby rock formation before the limb whisked back through the opening.

"Nothing's going to keep them out when the water gets higher," David said.

I clenched my teeth. Once David and I were treading, Ruby's people would have the upper hand. I was a strong swimmer, but could I fend them off *and* keep David afloat? Not likely. Not like this.

"I need help with my arm. I think it's dislocated."

"Again?"

I gritted my teeth. "So sorry. I've been fine for two years. Something about hanging out with you makes my arm randomly pop out of the socket."

His palm pressed against my good shoulder. My feet left the ground and the room became a blur. I'd barely gasped when my hurt shoulder slammed against the rock wall. Shards of exploding pain shot through my arm and lights flashed before my eyes as we slipped together to the floor.

"Freaking warn a girl next time!"

David stood. "It's over, how about we focus on the positive?"

The water licked my chin. There wasn't much positive to look at here. I stood, massaging my arm. The sea splashed against my thigh. How high would it need to be before the rift dwellers could get in?

Ruby swished and wiggled, turning her bulk completely around. I wasn't sure if she was facing toward the hole in the floor or away.

Thick, blue tendrils fumbled for her, but she lurched back. A pointed white beak jutted out from her center, snapping and catching one of her attacker's appendages, slicing the soft flesh in half. Blood fogged the sea as the injured creature withdrew through the hole.

Dang.

The swells now buffeted my shoulders. David moved closer, his gaze trained on the ceiling, his breaths deep and labored. The sea swirled and pinched between us, fountained, and formed Maggie's face—and nothing else—as if her head floated with no body to hold it up.

"I will hold them away as long as I can," Ruby said through Maggie's lips.

"Wait, you've been out of the water. Can you fight?"

"Not well, but I can give you more time. There is no doubt they will get past me. You need to get to the next level as soon as possible."

My feet left the floor and I kicked to stay afloat. We whipped toward the hole in the ceiling. "What do we do when we get to the top?"

"I will come," she said.

David glanced at me, gaping. I didn't need a tether to read his thoughts. We were in deep trouble.

Maggie's face dissolved back into the sea. David tilted his nose up as our pocket of oxygen continued to shrink.

"Remember to kick your feet," I said. "And keep air in your lungs. It will help you to float."

He nodded and I grabbed his hands. Ruby's red glow swayed within the swells as green, blue, and yellow brilliance joined hers. At least three more rift dwellers had slipped through the hole in the floor.

We were out of time.

18

One hand on David, I reached up with my good arm and tried to grasp the flap above. I kicked, lifting myself as high as I could, but my fingertips barely brushed the edges. David slipped beneath the water and I dropped down, shoving my hand under his arms and raising him to the surface.

He coughed. "It's too hard."

"It's not. And you aren't giving up."

A flash of blue light surrounded us. I spun; praying for a sign of red, but green joined the blue.

David cried out before he disappeared beneath the surge.

"No!"

Something squishy wrapped around my ankle before tightening and yanking down. A green glow seared my pupils. The salinity stung, but I couldn't close my eyes. I bent my knee and floundered in the water, clawing at the flashing green tentacle drawing me further and further away from the air. The creature furled around my torso, constricting. I had to break free. But how?

A shiny black disc on the side of the creature passed near my face, the circle pulsed, centering on me. A pupil? I punched the dark shape with what energy I had left. The monster reeled back, its grip loosening, and I managed one kick upward before she dragged me back down again.

To my right, David and the blue creature rolled, sinking to the ground. David kicked and thrashed against hundreds of pin-like protrusions and blue octopus tentacles. A blow to the rift dweller's center sent a piercing shriek echoing through the depths before the creature let go. The beast's gazillion tentacles waved peacefully as the motionless rift dweller drifted away.

Wrestling the tangle of limbs from his legs, David looked up just as my attacker's tentacles wrapped around my throat. I clawed at the slimy appendage and kicked. I had to be able to hit this thing somehow!

The creature arched its slimy frame and rolled me through the sea. I grunted, thrashed, and punched. I was not going to be something's dinner!

The waters around me dimmed and faded. I hung upside down, clawing at my neck and kicking madly. I was losing. What chance did a human being have against an animal the size of a car and totally in their element?

David crouched on the rocky floor and pushed up from the bottom, hurling himself toward me like a bullet. I ducked as his fists throttled over my head and bashed into Green Goon's center. The animal buckled and released me.

My vision cleared, and I grappled for David, twisting my fingers in his shirt, but I slipped as Green Goon seized me again.

David grasped my waist. His fingers dug into my skin as we both sunk back toward the beast below us.

Air. Need. Air.

My hip banged against the rocks, and David gripped my face, bringing his lips to mine. I tensed, before he forced a puff of oxygen into my lungs. How did he still have extra air?

A few bubbles escaped his nose as he spun and snatched the tentacle wrapped around my ankle. A shriek blasted through the ocean as David ripped the tendril in two. Green Goon retreated through the hole with a dark cloud fouling the sea behind her amputated member.

David cast the limb to the side. The severed tentacle drifted to the rocks as he grabbed my hand. We swam up from the bottom, but David lost momentum halfway to the top.

No. No way. We were not going to drown after all of that!

I slipped my arms around his chest, clenched my teeth against the blazing sting in my injured shoulder, locked my fingers, and kicked with all my might. My temples throbbed. My chest burned. Kick. Kick.

Help me, David. Kick your feet!

He kicked. How could someone with such long legs have absolutely no propulsion underwater?

We broke into the air. I inhaled, choking on the salty tang that ran into my mouth. Every inch of me ached. My toes tingled. I'd never take oxygen for granted again.

"Get out!" Standing on the edge of the water above, David reached down to me.

I stared up at him like a blithering idiot.

When did he get up there?

I raised my good arm and he hoisted me from the sea like an oversized fish on a hook. The swells sloshed along the edges of the rocky floor before shimmering to a still brilliance, perfectly mirroring the illuminating sparkles of the stalactites above. I took four labored breaths, waiting for the water to flare with green or blue light, and for monstrous limbs to lunge out and tug us back into the sea. Thankfully, I was disappointed.

A leathery flap buckled above—once again, our only defense against the pressure of the ocean. I flopped onto my back. We'd escaped one prison only to land in an identical one hiding above it.

And what was beyond this new flap, another chamber like this, or seven miles of frigid sea waiting to crush us?

David wrung a stream of clear droplets from the hem of his shirt before slipping his arm around my shoulder. A tingle soaked into my skin from beneath his hand, tickling and embracing me from within.

Was he serious? I gave him a mental slap, forcing him out of my psyche. "I'm not really feeling all that affectionate at the moment. A giant calamari just tried to rip my head off."

He puffed out a laugh. "I wasn't suggesting the kissing thing. I just thought it would be better if we could keep each other at ease."

At ease? He'd spent waaaay too much time with Dad before he left for Mars two years ago. But maybe he was right. God, I was tired.

I cuddled into the soaked cotton covering his chest. "I'm sorry. I didn't mean to be a jerk."

His fingers wove through my hair, and for a fraction of a second, we were back in the woods. I felt safe, just like I had then, even though the army was chasing us.

Wait. What? Safe?

I lifted my face. "Did you just do that ... give me the safe-feely thing?"

"Not intentionally, but does that mean you're okay?"

"I don't know if anything is ever going to be okay." I smoothed back my dripping hair. "We lost Silver, and now Ruby. We don't have a ship. We're stuck in another cave, and God knows what's going on in the real world." A painful ball formed in my throat. I swallowed it down. "I've never felt so helpless in all my life."

David squeezed me tighter. "We're going to get out of this. We always do."

That was true, but as the damp, foreboding stone walls shimmered around us, I had to wonder if that luck had finally run out.

Leaning against his shoulder, I closed my eyes. Maybe if we

could rest a moment, we'd be able to get our bearings and come up with a plan.

David's david-ness soaked through me, easing the throb in my shoulder and erasing some of the worry. A deep fog settled over my thoughts, easing me into a vacant stupor.

Until the soothing, artificial calm shattered with a crash. My eyes sprang open, and my pulse slid into the familiar vein of overdrive. The roar of rushing water echoed through the chamber, bolting me upright.

David jumped to his feet. "Jess!"

I grabbed his hand. Water funneled through the hole in the ceiling and seeped through fissures within the walls. My bare feet splashed as I took a step.

We were in a perpetual loop. Run, rest, run. But never really enough time to rest in between. Why we both hadn't lost out minds by now, was a miracle.

David's grip on my hand tightened. His head turned from left, to right, and up. He stared at the deluge falling from above.

Goddammit, sometimes I hated it when I was right.

His gaze lowered to me. I wished I could strip away the terror hidden within his eyes. He deserved better than this. Maybe we both did. But stewing over what could have been wouldn't change anything. We were both going to die.

19

His hands shot to the sides of my face, and his lips covered mine. A taint of salt melted to sweet, undeniable perfection. A kiss goodbye?

David's grip on me tightened. A swirling, desperate anger channeled through our bond, pulsing before softening as his tongue parted my lips.

The swell lapping my ankles seemed distant, unobtrusive. Did it even exist? Did *we* exist?

The roar of the flood echoed off the walls in a deafening thunder.

Yes, it all existed, but melting into David ceded the horrors to the background, blocked them from the now, and shoved them into the later.

I twisted my fingers through the hair behind David's neck and pulled him closer. A pressure inside me grew, squeezing out the rumble of the torrent beside us and the soaking sting of the water nearing our knees. *We* mattered. Nothing else.

David drew away. His kiss still tingled the edge of my lip as his eyes darkened. "We are not going to die."

I blinked. Of course not. We were getting out of here. Just like always. I squinted, checking the base of the column of water rushing in from the ceiling. Maybe when the chamber filled we could swim through, just like last time—as long as there was another chamber up there.

Dread slicked over my newfound confidence. Confidence I probably wouldn't have had unless... I turned to David. Had he just manipulated me?

"Don't," he said. "We need to keep positive if we're going to have any chance of surviving."

I shook my head. I knew that. And deep down I also knew we would get out. Failing was not an option. Too much depended on us.

A glossy, glass-like figurine stepped out of the bubbling column, shimmered, and became Maggie. Well, Ruby looking like Maggie.

"They let the water in," I said.

Idiot. Way to state the obvious.

Ruby walked toward me. "They didn't release your air. I did."

David and I froze, agape.

"We need to leave quickly. They are below, not expecting you to move further up."

"Why wouldn't they expect that?" David asked.

"Because this is the last chamber."

David's expression didn't change. I needed to hire him as a poker partner, because I nearly peed myself.

"You mean if we leave this room we'll be out in the open sea?"

"Yes, until we swim to your ship. I am waiting above to assist you."

But how far away was our ship? And wasn't it filled with water?

"We'll drown." Okay—stating the obvious again, but stoic-boy just stood there. One of us had to say something.

David's face finally paled. He shifted his weight as he stared at the rising water. For a second I regretted being so blunt. His passive stare was easier to take than the hint of fear now trickling through our bond.

"We will deal with drowning momentarily," Ruby said. "It won't take them long to realize someone is helping you. It would be foolish of them to backtrack through the chambers below. They will wait for this hollow to fill and come for you as soon as the water is deep enough to support them." She pointed to the hole in the floor. "We need to cover the aperture so my people don't enter when the sea has gained a safe height."

Cover a hole the size of a Volkswagen. Sure. I'll just sit on it.

David sloshed toward a glistening column. "This pillar is cracked along the ceiling."

Yeah, and?

He flicked his gaze to me. Had I thought that aloud?

"We're going to push it over."

My brow furrowed. "That thing must weigh a ton. Ten tons. We can't—"

David threw his weight against the column. The edges ground across the floor, revealing a second crack along the base. Okay, maybe we *could* do this. Or, umm, maybe *he* could do this and I could stand right over here and cheer him on.

The ocean soaked through the denim at my hips.

"It is only shifting," Ruby said. "You need to work faster."

"A little help would be nice," David said.

She held up her hands. "I'm made of water."

I guess that left me. I pressed my hands against the cold alabaster and pushed. Pain knifed through my shoulder. I was barely any help with two good arms. How could I help with only one?

"Don't think that," he said. "That actually did help."

But maybe not enough. A blue glow shimmered up from the hole, illuminating the water around the opening like some sort of attack beacon.

"They are coming," Ruby said.

One hand still on the pillar, David stared at the glowing opening. Sweat beaded his brow. *We need to find another way.*

Yeah, I figured, but what?

He peered up and smiled. *There.*

There what?

David propped his feet against the wall and held his hands against the column. Lifting himself, he spider-crawled straight up, poised between the pillar and the wall.

What are you doing?

The column leaned toward the wall closer to the ceiling, leaving David in a crouch. He grunted as he heaved, and the column started to teeter. Another shove and the gargantuan mass splashed down about two feet from covering the hole. Dangit.

My ninja alien dropped to the floor, landing on his feet with a splash.

Show off.

I jumped back as a glowing blue tentacle flounced through the air above the opening.

David darted toward the column. "Help me roll it!"

Turning my injured shoulder away, I threw all my weight against the column. David grunted beside me. It didn't seem possible, but the column began to roll. Damn, maybe he *had* yanked those helicopters out of the sky two years ago.

The area above the opening began to stir. The lights grew brighter.

"You must hurry!" Ruby walked across the top of the water. "The sea has attained the correct depth!"

A swirling emerald glow overtook the blue, as if Green Goon whacked the blue rift dweller out of the way. Someone must have been itching for payback.

"David?"

"I see him."

Or her, technically.

We shoved, pushed, and rolled. The swells lapped my chest. I started to float. "I can't get any more traction."

David growled and the pillar rolled another few inches, settling over the hole.

We did it!

But the flood surrounding us still flashed a brilliant green.

One had gotten through.

20

David gasped as a tentacle swirled around his waist and pulled him beneath the surge. The splash slapped my cheeks.

This wasn't happening. At least not if I didn't let it.

I took a deep breath and dove. The salt barely stung, but a haze of dark particles mottled the green glow beneath the water, swirling in infinite circles that masked the creature's light.

I lurched back as a foot flailed past my face. Bubbles rolled from David's clenched teeth as he held back the twelve-inch, snapping beak gnashing at him from Green Goon's core.

Dang, that thing was huge!

Springing up from the bottom, I breached the surface and took a gulp of air. I nearly choked when Maggie's face appeared before me.

"There are rocks on the floor," she said.

"Yeah, so?"

"A hard blow to the top of her mouth will be enough to stun her. It will be some time before she regains consciousness."

Her mouth? The beak, I guess. Could it be that easy?

"That is why we keep our mouths internal, unless needed for defense or feeding. They are our hardest extremity, but our weakest point if we are struck."

"Good tip. Thanks."

I dove once more. A bulky stone lay just below my feet. I grasped and hefted with both hands, but goliath-stone barely budged.

How about something a little smaller?

Swimming up to take another breath, I noted two grapefruit-sized rocks near the wall on the other side of David. I grit my teeth and mustered up an image of banging Green Goon on her beak and the creature sinking to the floor. I curled the thought into a mental ball and flung it at David.

He spun to the side and tried to hold her back while scrabbling for one of the stones. She snapped, and David flinched. Dark fluid ribboned through the sea in a continuing trail from his biceps.

He snatched a stone, shoved with his injured arm, and hurled his burden with the other. Green Goon sucked in her beak and the rock sunk to the ground.

He missed.

How the heck did he miss?

Goon's tentacles whipped out, wrapping around David's arms and legs. He struggled. The skin around his mouth darkened as he looked up toward the water's surface.

Crap. He was out of air.

I shot up and inhaled before darting down again. Green Goon had grown a few extra hundred tentacles, and most of them wrapped around David, driving him closer to her ivory beak.

Okay: rocks.

I swam down and grabbed the stone that David had thrown. I kicked, angling myself around until I hovered behind the thrashing creature.

Boulder to the beak … like hitting someone on the head. Just like in the movies.

You're okay. You got this. You totally got this.

I angled my legs up, turning myself into a sinking torpedo and kicked to gain momentum. Swishing around five tentacles, I curled toward the blazing green behemoth. I reeled back, ready to fling the rock, but a tentacle twirled around my waist, hoisting me backward.

She lifted me high in the water, away from the fight. I smacked the tentacle with the rock, but Green Goon didn't even flinch. Below, David thrashed and twisted in her grip.

No. No way. We weren't being taken out by a Technicolor squid!

I bent my knee, bringing part of the tentacle holding me closer, then proceeded to beat the green flashing member repeatedly with the rock. Frustrated, I grasped the soft flesh with my free hand, shoved it into my mouth, and bit. Revolting, fishy goo oozed over my tongue. I spit as the creature thrashed and dropped me.

Holding the rock straight down and kicking, I drove myself back into the fight below. Another tentacle wrapped around my waist.

I grunted and slammed the stone toward Green Goon's beak while my hips lurched backward. David tore away one of the tentacles on his wrist.

The rock crashed against the beak and Green Goon reared back, releasing me. The glistening stalagmites above shimmered, beckoning me toward the air, but David didn't have any time. I swam down, slipped my good arm around his chest, and kicked upward. The glow dissipated as the creature floated away, motionless.

We popped back into the air pocket and nearly crowned ourselves on the ceiling. David coughed, and I tried to keep him afloat.

Maggie's face appeared, floating atop the water again. "Your ship is seventeen strokes from here. Once you are in the open sea, you will need to swim," Ruby said.

David gulped before returning his attention to Ruby. "The pressure is over eight tons per square inch out there. We'll be crushed."

Ruby raised a brow. Did she even understand what he meant, having lived in a high-pressure atmosphere all her life?

"Is there a way to not-crush?" she asked.

David's gaze dropped to the swells sloshing around his shoulders. "That much ocean pressing down on us—I don't know." He sighed. "I don't think there is a way."

Crap.

Crap. Crap. Crap. Crap. Crap.

Okay. Okay. Think Jess. Your planet. What do you know about it?

I clenched my fists.

Dangit! Absolutely nothing!

Wait.

"The pressure doesn't smash the bubbles, right?"

"They are always round, if that is what you mean."

"Maybe if we can hold the air in our lungs the entire time it won't crush us?"

David held his hand on the ceiling. "That might help our lungs, but our eyes will probably implode."

Well, that didn't sound like fun.

I bumped my scalp on the rocks above. What did we have left, minutes? Seconds?

"Do you trust me?" Ruby's voice echoed through what little of the chamber remained unsubmerged.

Did we have a choice?

I took a deep breath. My heart throbbed in my ears as David hugged me with one arm and covered my eyes with his free hand. Would that be enough to save my sight?

A distant sense erupted in my mind, the awareness of David's voice, but the roar of my own quickening pulse blocked out everything. Blind, I pawed my palms up his chest, neck, and found his eyes. It might not help, but I covered them. At least neither one of us would have to see what happened to the other.

I kicked toward the sensation of the moving water. A scraping along my back told me we'd breached the exit from the chamber.

The pressure hit my head first. My ears pounded, like death itself had reached inside and tried to pull out my brain.

Holding tight to David's eyes, I glued my other hand over one of my ears. He skimmed up my back and covered my other ear. A muffled oblivion took over as a million bands of elastic wove around me and constricted. I willed my skin to fight against the onslaught of pressure, tensing against the will of nature to see me dead.

Seventeen strokes. That's all that separated us from our ship. But in which direction?

One of us needed to be able to see. There wasn't a choice. We needed to know which way to swim. If I pushed David's hand away, how long before the sea took my vision? Would I have enough time to find the ship and direct us to safety?

A chill rattled me to the core. Blindness. What kind of photographer could I be if I couldn't see? Was the risk worth it? Could I take the chance?

I had to. I was the only one of us who could swim. My sight was a small price to pay to get David to that ship. If he didn't fly Ruby to Mars, Earth, Dad, and everything I knew and loved would be gone. I gritted my teeth against a sob as my dreams drifted away in the currents. Real heroes don't always have a happy ending.

Please, God. Don't let it hurt.

I took my palm off my ear and fumbled for the warm, alien hand covering my eyes.

21

A thick, warm goop slapped against my back and coated me. David released me and drew my face into the crook of his shoulder. I kept my lashes scrunched closed, clutching him as we sank into warm, soaked mush. Where were we?

Trickles of soft ribbons wafted through the sea about my ankles. Were we moving?

Trust.

Trust? I slid my hand through the thick, gelatinous goo cloaking us. The material quivered.

Alive.

Oh. Crap. We were inside Ruby! Did she swallow us?

Trust.

Trust. Okay. Okay. Yup. Trust. Got this. No problem.

Oh, sweet Lord I'm inside a giant talking jellyfish!

My torso jarred as if we'd hit something and I collided against David.

My mind whirled, lost in blackness and struggling not to breathe.

David released me, and the goo slid between us, squeezing. A deep throb filled my eardrums, adding to the resonance of my own erratic heartbeat.

I thrashed. *David!*

Jess, you're fine, she won't hurt you.

Don't leave me!

His essence slipped away.

Alone, inside a … what exactly was I inside? My arms flailed. I thrashed. I had to get out. I couldn't stay here!

The goo sloshed against my cheek. Gentle, consoling.

A flash of red pulsed through my closed eyelids. Blinding, like when Ruby had shown us her real form swimming outside the boundaries of my fake bedroom.

I'm scared.

Trust.

I gulped back my tears. I really didn't have a choice in the matter, but more than anything else, I needed to breathe. My head pounded. Maybe if I opened my mouth just a tad, I could get a little bit of air. It's H_2O, right? If I breathed in a little water, maybe I could get a little bit of that O?

"*Don't do it.*" Mom's voice filled my ears. "*Hold on, sweetheart.*"

"Mom?" The word slipped from my mouth before I'd realized what I'd done. Liquid salt, then soft, fishy goop poured into my mouth. I gagged and slapped my hand over my nose and lips. My chest stung. Salinity from my tears mixed with the sea.

I coughed into my hand, forcing my palm against my lips to keep more ocean from filling my lungs. My vision fogged over.

Jess! A warm hand gripped my shoulder. *I got you!*

The squishy goo around me released, and I swirled into the cooler sea. The pressure squeezed my temples for four booming heartbeats before releasing me into soft, tepid, unpressurized waters.

David released me. *Open your eyes.*

I coughed into my hand again. David pushed off the ground and floated away. *Where are you going?*

We need oxygen.

My sight sparkled and blurred before a tiled floor focused below me.

The ship. We'd made it! But it was still filled with water!

I kicked back from the gaping hole beside me that led into the sea, propelling myself away, but that was the last bit of energy I had to give.

Air: such a simple concept. Invisible. You don't even think about it. But I'd never take it for granted again—not that I would have much longer to regret as my lungs burned, begging for a breath.

The sea tickled and hummed around me. Lights flashed, dimmed, and evened out.

The tether between David and me tingled. *Swim up.*

I tried to lift my arms, to propel myself up, but my body refused to respond.

The illumination dulled to gray. My head tilted back as the need to sleep encompassed me.

A hand pressed over my mouth and nose. *Kick your feet, Jess. You need to kick your feet.*

Everything shimmered and sparkled, creating a world all my own. I kicked, spiraling in a realm of lost, drifting nothing. I angled my back as I floated toward the surface.

Beside me, Dad blew some bubbles from his regulator and pointed at a school of yellow striped fish as Mom chased them through the warm Caribbean Sea just off the beach in Jamaica. Our one and only big splurge vacation.

Love. Family. Home.

The sweet essence of Mom's touch enveloped me. A hug from beyond. So long, too long since I'd felt her love.

"*It's okay,*" her voice shimmered through the sea. "*I'm here.*"

Whiteness flashed around me as my eyes shot open.

"It's okay, Jess, I'm here!" David screamed, holding my jaw above the churning sea.

I coughed, struggling in the few inches of oxygen drifting along the ceiling of the ship. The ease of Mom's presence shrank into a panicked flailing of my arms.

"Breathe," David shouted. "Just breathe. We're going to be okay."

Air. Beautiful, sweet air. But how?

"It's from the emergency oxygen stores. I'm using everything we've got to force the ocean out of the ship."

"But-but, the pressure. There's still a hole in the ship. How?"

"Ruby pushed me ahead to stabilize the ship, but I needed to leave the hole open to get the water out. Believe me, the ship is not happy about what I'm making it do."

I puffed, treading until the water level dropped and my feet hit something—the back of my chair. The molten metal stretched and flattened into a stand. A solid surface never felt so good.

David stepped from the platform atop his chair to mine and swaddled me in his arms. Warm air wafted through the room; sweet, delicious heat. The damp hairs on my arms lifted as my skin covered in bumps. My hands trembled. My body quaked.

"I have you," David whispered. "We're okay."

Were we?

The ocean receded below the front window. Ruby flittered in the sea, casting a red glow in the room.

"Do we leave her?" I asked.

"Like hell." He jumped down from the back of my chair, splashing in the water that still covered his seat.

"But they took Silver. We can't expect her to leave him behind." I coughed and rubbed the burn within my chest.

David sunk his hands into the gelatinous console. "One problem at a time. I'm not even sure if I can get the ship running. We sank here, remember?"

No.

Well, yes, but I'd forgotten. Getting back to the ship had been our only focus. The thought of still being trapped hadn't even crossed my mind. "You mean we're stuck?"

He swirled his arms through the console. "Nothing's working. I have less power now than when we first got here."

I climbed down into my chair. "There has to be something—"

My bare heel slipped on the back of my seat and splashed into the foot-deep wading pool that used to be the deck. I stumbled toward David and into the console. My right hand sank into the dull goop as I tried to break my fall.

The walls shimmered. The lights throughout the room brightened.

David's eyes widened. "What did you do?"

I shook the goo off my hand. "What does it look like? I fell."

"Power, propulsion, secondary energy stores … we've got it all!" He helped me back to my seat. "I think your little friend rigged the ship."

"What?"

"It appears he wanted to make sure I didn't leave without you." He pointed to the glowing corner of the console. "A bio-synced lock. When you manipulated the interface everything came on."

"But how?"

"Edgar."

My heart fluttered. He was okay! "Where is he?"

David tapped the wall. "He's not on the ship. He must have realigned all the systems, and then he took off."

The water between our seats rose into the air, gyrated, and bubbled into Maggie's form.

"We must depart," Ruby said.

"No," I said. "Not without Edgar. He's probably out there searching for us."

"But my people are coming."

Stupid bad guys. Why couldn't anything ever be easy? One thing for sure, I wasn't leaving my little buddy behind. "But what about Silver? Are you just going to abandon him?"

Ruby's apparition shrunk and looked away. "He's dead."

"What?" David and I asked in unison.

"They send away the babies because they are innocent. Returning is a death warrant. We are not allowed to intermingle. At all." She lowered her gaze. "I just hope it was quick."

I reached for her shoulder, but my hand sank right through her liquid form. "You're going to leave all by yourself? But you'll be all alone on Mars."

I cringed as the words left my mouth. Earth's fate depended on her coming with us. I should be trying to convince her, not telling her to stay. But I couldn't imagine leaving everything I knew behind to live on a world where I'd be totally alone. The isolation. It would be like torture.

"You don't understand," she said. "I hate them. I hate all of them. They lied to us and kept us apart, and then they took away the one being who made living in this ocean sufferable." She hugged her shoulders. "I want to get as far away from here as I can."

I guess I couldn't argue with that.

David waved his hands over the console. A drip ran from the edge of his wet bangs down the side of his face. Watching him and soaking in the determined set of his features made me feel safe. Real. Alive. What would I do if anyone took him from me?

A hum vibrated through the ship. I leaned over the back of my chair as the last of the water leaked through the hole in the floor. The tiles pinched, flexed, and elongated. The two sides twisted together before laying out flat and re-tiling as if nothing ever happened.

I'd never get tired of watching alien technology. But I'd wasted enough time, already. "What about Ruby?"

David ignored the vision of Maggie beside him and stared through the glass. The real Ruby pulsed, glowing a soft pink around her shimmering red center.

"I'm opening the lower hatch. I think you can get through."

Maggie's face remained stoic beside me as Ruby's form drifted below the window.

"Did you remember to leave water in there?" I asked.

He nodded. "This is the only compartment that isn't flooded, except for a few necessary systems that need to stay dry. I didn't have enough oxygen for the rest of the ship."

In other words, no emergency supply if something happens to our air. Great. The way our luck was running, we had about thirty minutes to live.

Maggie's face animated beside me. "I am within," Ruby said. "The sea outside is trembling with the energy of my people. Many of them. We need to go. Now."

I grabbed David's arm. "Edgar."

He stared at me before turning away. He gulped and closed his eyes. "I'm sorry."

He lifted his hands and the ship shot straight up.

22

A long strand of green, bulbous seaweed slapped against the window and fluttered before breaking free. I tried to remember the surface: the danger we faced, and how an entire planet's existence counted on us, but it didn't stop the burn building in my chest.

Edgar had booby-trapped the ship—made sure I was aboard before David left. The little guy loved me, and how did I repay him? I left him for dead. What kind of friend was I?

The ship slowed.

"We've got company," David said.

Dozens of beacons loomed above us, sparkling in green, blue, yellow, and orange. The glow breached the cabin, basking us in their radiance. Spectacular—if they weren't a bunch of homicidal squid with a taste for landlubbers.

"Can't we just go around them?"

"Not if we want to get through that rift. There's only one way out to the open sea."

The ocean to our right brightened as five more creatures appeared. Then the left became alight with more glowing rift dwellers.

The muscles in David's neck tensed. The bottom left of the console pulsed in a shade of fuchsia I hadn't seen on an Erescopian ship.

"What is that?" I asked.

David sucked in his lips and then let them slip free. "A gift from Edgar." He ran his hand above the pinkish glow as if testing the heat of a fire. "He found a way to syphon about ten gallons of water into the cyclers, and then expulse them at atom-enhanced speed."

"I don't know what that means."

He glanced at me. "Do you know what a gun is?"

I gaped, and my gaze darted back to the encroaching luminaries. So beautiful. I wanted to get home, but did I want to get away that bad? "Will it kill them?"

David grimaced. "I don't know."

The beings distorted and blasted toward us, like staring through a camera lens and zooming in at high speed.

Ruby turned away from the screen. "They are never going to let me go."

David's hand hovered over the fuchsia brilliance. Our tether thickened. Pulsed. His thoughts riveted through me in a jumbled mess: *billions of people. Jess's father. Mars. Failure. My fault.*

Multicolored beacons blared through the room. I shielded my eyes and leaned closer to the glass. Something moved behind the lights. Something smaller. Dull. Maybe a lot of somethings. One spun within the shifting tendrils, a blue glow highlighting its watermelon-shaped form.

No. Way.

David's hand wavered over the pink goo in the panel.

"Wait!" I grabbed his wrist. "They're not going to hurt us."

"What are you talking about?"

I pointed to the window. "Look. They're right on top of us, but they haven't attacked."

Ruby spun back toward the glass. "She is right. Why haven't they … " She covered her face with her hands.

"What's going on?" I asked her.

"So many," she whispered. "So many."

One of the dull somethings glided to the front. It wafted close to the window, hovering like a clear, floating oval.

I jumped from my seat. "Silver!"

Ruby cast her gaze downward. "No. Another male." She brought her attention back to the sea, focusing deeply on the Uptider hovering before her. A smile burst across her face. "Do you know this creature?" She held out her hand and the liquid bubbled from her palm and formed a ten-legged spider.

"Edgar!"

The vision disappeared, the water molecules melting back into her hand. He was okay, though. That's what was important.

"Apparently your small friend communicates better than you do. News of your departure, and ability to carry a portion of our ocean, has spread."

But most of these creatures would be ticked off by that news. He better be careful, wherever he was.

Another clear watermelon swam out from behind a larger female, and another.

Pairs. Dozens and dozens of pairs. Had Edgar figured out the secret of the kinetic energy? Had he been rallying recruits to our cause?

"Apparently you weren't the only one that has been sneaking through the rift." David said.

"They want to go with us," Ruby said.

David rubbed his face. "With that many, we could make it rain everywhere on the planet."

"But what about this planet? Don't we need to keep it raining here on Earth?"

Ruby turned to me. "The numbers are not too great to hurt our world, and remember, this is not the only place in the ocean deep enough to be a home for my kind."

I guess that made sense.

"There's a little problem though," David said. "I was worried about two of you living in the lower section comfortably. There's no way to fit all of you."

She straightened. "Discomfort is a small price to pay for freedom."

"There's just no way," David said, "unless you can shrink yourselves."

Maggie's image became still. The creatures outside fluttered, their lights pulsing. The males entwined themselves among the long tendrils of the females as the larger creatures circled like some strange aquatic animal show at Sea World. After six complete revolutions from the group, several pairs drifted back.

Maggie jerked up. "Eighteen have agreed to stay behind. They will try to foster peace between our kinds and communicate the truth."

I shivered. That probably wasn't going to go over too well. Better them than me.

Ruby's people broke their formation.

"There's still too many," David said.

"We will make do," Ruby whispered.

The last of the glowing creatures floated from sight, sinking beneath the ship.

David continued to check the console. "Let me know when everyone is inside." *Or you can't fit anymore.* His hesitation scurried across our bond: the weight of the water, pressure containment, and his ability to keep them alive once we got them to Mars … *if* we got them to Mars.

But we needed to focus on the now. We had more pressing problems to deal with.

"Is anyone else worried about why the ones chasing us haven't followed?" I kneaded my shoulders. "I mean, they were pretty adamant about drowning us before."

"That is why we can waste no more time," Ruby said.

Several blue, a few green, and a yellow creature swam away from the ship, along with their ovoid partners.

Ruby lowered her gaze. "They were unable to fit into the ship. They will return with the others."

David stretched across the panel, and the windows before us flickered and turned into video monitors. The screens focused on a swarm of glowing colors twisted together like bright scarves squashed into a box four times too small.

He turned to Ruby. "You can barely move in there."

"Let us worry about ourselves," Ruby said.

The pictures faded back into the windows. Beams of white light shot out from both sides of our ship, the only illumination to guide us through the depth's obscurity.

"Thank you," Ruby whispered, "for giving them a chance."

My heart clenched. *Them*, not *us*. Maybe it was worse for her, now, surrounded by her own kind—all pairs seeking the same freedom to love that she and Silver had hoped for.

Instead of being alone by herself, she now had to deal with being alone among others. Happy others—a constant reminder of her loss.

I reached over to hold her hand, but as usual my fingers went right through hers. I held them where her hand would be, even though she probably couldn't feel me. I wish I could coax a smile from her. Anything.

I knew how hard it was, losing someone. After my mom died, the emptiness had twisted inside me for months before receding to the background as a dull, ever-present specter. It changed me. I couldn't imagine the pain of losing someone you'd chosen to give your heart to. What was going through her head? How did she stay sane?

"We're here," David said.

The lights grazed across the rocky ceiling and then vanished within the small fissure that had brought us here. David swayed his palm over the panel, and the walls around us buckled and brightened before dulling to a pale gray.

"What happened?" I asked.

"I'm changing the shape of the ship so we can fit through

without getting stuck again."

The illumination reflected off the shiny rock walls as we approached the crevice. I leaned forward, marveling at how easily we passed through when the ship had the power to flex at will.

Tiny, spider-like creatures flittered from the beams, some leaving an inky trail behind them. Thistles of tangled plant life swayed, while others sucked into their foundations as we approached.

Despite pointing straight up, I clutched the arms of my chair and pushed back. My heart thumped as if we were breaching the top of a roller coaster. My hands dampened like we were banking a turn, and I didn't know where the car might go next.

The unknown ate away at me. My world lay up there, waiting. But we didn't just have to get to the surface. We had to get all the way to Mars and then, hopefully, Ruby and her friends could make it rain. There were no positives in any of this plan. Only hopes. For now, that was all I could hold on to.

"We're almost out," David said. "But it looks like something big is following us into the rift."

"How big?" Ruby asked.

"Big enough to make a disruption cloud for our sensors to pick up."

"Can we go faster?" I asked.

"We can, but whatever is down there keeps matching our speed." He sank back into his chair. "Here comes the top of the rift."

We exploded out of the dark into a blinding array of color. David muttered something in his own language, banking the ship to the right, away from the brilliance.

We lurched forward and jolted as if hitting something, before shifting into reverse. I crashed back onto the headrest as we stalled. David sprang to his feet, but didn't manipulate the console.

"What's wrong?" I asked.

He turned to me, the crease in his brow mirroring the fear already bubbling through our tether. "We're surrounded."

23

The glare surrounding us stung my eyes. I held up my hand, blocking enough of the glow to see the long, scrawling tendrils drifting together, burning like embers in the sea. This was why they hadn't chased us. They'd been waiting here all along.

Ruby's hands splayed, her gaze fixed on the windows. "Run through them."

"There are too many, and they've secured the rift behind us. We can't go up, and we can't go back down." David flopped back to his chair.

A green creature swam closer, its bulk taking up the entire window. Several of its tendrils hung loosely below her main frame. The edges of two tentacles swayed limply in the current, rough and darkened along their edges as if recently severed.

Green Goon. It had to be.

The walls and ceiling vibrated. Clear water droplets flew through our cabin, swirling and joining into a larger, malleable form that settled over the console.

My wet hair lifted and drew forward. The moisture swished

from my bangs toward the front of the ship and splashed into the larger form. The deluge continued, forming a translucent column that rolled, pinched, and elongated. Arms and legs oozed from the main form before a beautiful, friendly face appeared. Matt Samuels. Our visitor reclined on the console, eerily reminiscent of Matt lounging on Columbia's Alma Mater steps just before David's ship arrived.

But this being was not Matt Samuels. I knew better.

The warm smile that always graced Matt's face faded to a scowl as he leaned toward David. "You said you didn't come here to steal, yet you have stolen."

"We've taken nothing. They asked to come with us."

"But leaving is not their right. You have taken what is not yours. Drop your cargo."

"Never," Ruby spat. "You have imprisoned us. Lied to us. You have done unspeakable things."

Not-Matt pointed at Ruby. "And you will be dealt with most harshly. A Red, with all your responsibility … " His lip twisted. "Appalling."

"We're only taking the few who asked to leave." David stood and circumvented his chair. "You need to understand that the fate of the surface depends on this."

Goon waved Matt's hand. "I care not for matters of the air-breathers. I care only for my own kind, and every one of them is precious. They stay here. There is no more discussion."

David's hands fisted. "No."

Not-Matt reeled up from the console, inhumanly sliding to the floor and meeting David's rigid gaze. "Drop. Your. Cargo."

They stared at each other, David trembling slightly. I sensed apprehension and fear flooding through our bond. A bead of sweat shined atop his brow.

His voice boomed through my mind. *Not real. Not real. Not real.*

What wasn't real?

I cringed. The last time this creature manifested in our world, I'd seen Matt, but David had seen his father. Was that his struggle? Did he see Sabbotaruo? What could have happened between David and his father in the past two years to make David terrified to even stand in his presence?

A deep seeded anxiety trickled across our bond, a fear that hadn't been there the last time David and I had been together. If Goon had the ability to poke around in our heads, and something *had* happened between David and Sabbotaruo, I couldn't take the chance that Goon had taken the perfect form to force David to give her what she wanted.

"Lay off, jerk!" I shoved Not-Matt out of the way.

Well, I tried to, anyway. There was nothing to shove, and I stumbled through the creature's liquid form.

Not-Matt splashed to the floor, drenching me, then rematerialized next to David. His watery nose flared. This overgrown octopus was seriously getting on my nerves, and we were running out of time.

I shook the drops from my arms. "We're not giving up, and you and all your friends are going to swim your asses out of the way so we can leave."

Not-Matt's blank stare turned toward me. I struggled not to close my eyes or turn from the vicious scrutiny, before the left side of his lips turned up in a satisfied grin.

The glow around us heightened. "I tire of this," Green Goon said. "Release my people, or we will tear this vessel apart to free them ourselves." Something thumped on the side of the ship, followed by a lot of somethings.

David gripped the back of his chair. "You're bluffing."

Not-Matt drew his finger across the edge of the console. "Your technology is fragile. At this depth, all we need is a small tear. The pressure will take care of the rest."

The adrenaline running through my veins melted to a frigid frost. They *had* ripped us from this ship once already. What would stop them from doing it again?

"The bodies of your people are even more fragile," David said. "The force of the ocean rushing into the artificial pressure in this ship will rip apart everyone in the cargo hold."

Not-Matt sneered. "You are lying."

David leaned toward him. "Then go ahead and try it. Let's see how many of them die."

Ho-lee-crap. *Please tell me you're the one bluffing.*

No answer. Yikes.

Not-Matt turned to Ruby. "Are you ready to take the blame for the death of your friends?"

Her gaze darted between Green Goon and David.

"Not enough influence, I see. Maybe a different creature's execution will encourage you."

Matt's face turned to the windows, where a blue and a yellow creature floated into view, their colors flashed, creating an eerie emerald glow between them. Their largest tendrils curled and poked into the clear, quivering hide of a smooth, translucent oval creature held between them.

Ruby gaped. Her hands fell to her sides.

Holy cow. That had to be Silver.

Not-Matt's eyes narrowed. "Don't worry. I will make sure his death is excruciating." Matt's form froze as Green Goon moved her green bulk away from the ship.

Silver whirled and tugged against his captors as she approached. The larger creature extended one of its tentacles and lanced Silver, jabbing until the tendril poked straight through the other side.

"No!" Ruby screamed.

"Leave him alone!" I tried to punch the simulated Goon standing beside me in the face. My knuckles flew right through Matt's liquid head. When was I going to learn?

The blue creature jabbed Silver from the other side. Shimmering fluids mixed about them and dissipated in the sea.

"Stop!" Ruby fell to her knees. "Let the others go. I will stay. Just please, stop hurting him."

Matt's apparition laughed: a simple, melodic sound. I shivered. It wasn't right, seeing Matt's face on someone who'd done something so horrible.

He walked toward Ruby and folded his arms. "I want them all."

Ruby blinked her glossy eyes. "You don't need them. I can bear more than all of them combined. Let them go. I will come freely."

An orange rift dweller swam toward the ones holding Silver, and stiffened one of her legs to a point.

"Nooo!" Ruby lunged toward the window.

I moved forward, hitting the console. How could they …

The orange creature baulked, rotated, and retracted its sharpened leg before it was able to penetrate Silver's trembling hide. The creature thrashed as if covered by ants.

David punched the fuchsia corner of the console. A *whomp* echoed through the ship and a line of bubbles shot out past the window, bashing the yellow creature holding Silver and forcing it back. Its arm retracted from Silver's puckered frame before the yellow bulk curled in on itself and floated away.

The orange creature, still struggling as if the water burned her, darted to the left and out of sight. The blue rift dweller holding Silver twitched and jittered back before releasing her captive.

Goon hissed through Matt's lips and splashed into a puddle at David's feet. Her real body out in the sea spiraled like a dog trying to itch its back. She withdrew her lance arm and whipped it through the water as if fighting off a phantom attack.

Silver drifted, moving only as the current from the thrashing animals jostled his lifeless form.

One after another, the creatures that remained shimmered and pulsed. David pressed the fuchsia button again. The *whomp* took out a yellow reaching for Silver.

Green Goon somersaulted through the ocean. A dark shape blasted through the glow, then disappeared. Goon flailed her tendrils as if trying to catch the fleeting figure.

The blue that had been holding Silver retreated, leaving only Green Goon to face the spectral attacker. The black mass centered on her, driving the creature closer to the ship. How could anything that small threaten such a behemoth? Unless …

The phantom spun, slamming against the larger creature before ten spindly legs jutted out from the round, hairy subdivisions and sunk deep into green flesh.

"It's Edgar!"

Ruby's glistening hand reached toward the glass, toward the bent and broken oval hanging motionless behind his would-be arachnid savior and his executioner.

My stomach twisted. *Come on, Silver, move.*

Edgar's three long, white fangs caught the ship's illumination before disappearing into Green Goon's flesh. Green lights flashed and gyrated before she convulsed and scurried from sight, leaving a long, trailing stream of darkened sea behind her. Edgar moved to follow.

David leaned over the console. "Edgar, that's all we needed. Let's get out of here!"

The giant spider turned and sliced through the water toward us. He stopped by Silver's drifting, limp form and moved his nose over the Uptider's prone bulk.

Sweet Lord, please tell me he's not going to eat him!

All ten of Edgar's legs sprang out as if he'd been petrified and flattened like a pancake. He hovered over Silver before he clasped down, smothering the limp Uptider.

24

Edgar flexed his back segment, propelling his body through the water and dragging Silver's lifeless form toward the ship.

Ruby held her hands to her lips, her gaze fixed on Edgar's precious burden. Silver had been tortured and stabbed. What chance could he possibly have?

Edgar ducked below the ship and out of sight.

"How will we know when they are on board?" I asked.

The image of Maggie beside me splashed to the floor leaving a puddle running toward the back of the ship. The walls flashed yellow four times.

"Like that." David smiled. "Nice to have you back, Edgar."

David swirled his hands over the console. Twin beams of light cut through the dark as we ascended. I took a deep breath and released it. Now to get all these creatures safely to Mars. No biggie. Just a ride through outer space.

A dark, wet mass wiggled up out of the tiled floor. Edgar shook himself off, jumped into my lap, and cuddled into my arms.

"Dude, I was so worried about you."

He warbled as his prickly hairs nuzzled my cheek.

I pulled him back to my lap and faced David. "How long will it take to get us to Mars?"

"Us?" David pointed to his chest. "I'm going to Mars. You're staying on Earth."

My chest tightened. "Why?"

"Do you have any idea how hot it is there?"

"So, what? I can take it."

"It's over a hundred degrees on the surface. Worse than the lower levels of the ambassador's ship."

I started to sweat, remembering the long, sweltering alien halls. "But—"

He placed his finger against my lips. Edgar snapped at him, but David didn't flinch.

"I'm getting readings from above. The salinity is distorting sensors, but it doesn't seem like the scourge has started. We're going to fly to your house, pick up your dad, and I'm taking you both to that island."

Part of me had forgotten the scourge, or just blanked it out of my mind. Save the world? I was all over that. But now it all seemed just a little too real. "What about Maggie. Matt. Their families?"

I set Edgar on the floor. He sank through the tiles and disappeared.

David's lips tightened. "We'll pick up whoever is at your house. We don't have time to search for anyone."

"If your people are coming to take over the planet, my dad isn't going to be home. He'll be out with the rest of the military trying to stop you."

David's sigh tore a hole through my soul. "Your archaic technology will be useless. He has to know that."

"It doesn't mean he won't try. That's what humans do. We fight. We're not just going to roll over and die."

His eyes darkened. "As I said, we won't have time to search for him."

The tiniest piece of me wanted to argue with David ... to plead humanity's right to survive. But I didn't have to prove that to him. This was out of his hands. But could I convince Dad to come with us? Would he leave everyone else behind to die?

Probably not, but I had to try. I'd already lost one parent. I wasn't ready to be an orphan. Even if I was technically an adult, I would always be a little girl inside.

"Can we call him?"

David peeked through disheveled bangs. "Yes. What is the frequency of his portable communicator?"

Huh? "Oh, his cell phone? You mean the number?"

Crap. He was number two on my favorites list. No one knows anyone's actual numbers!

My phone.

I jumped from my seat and ran to the back of the compartment. Debris and pieces of seaweed littered the tiles, still damp from being submerged. I rummaged through a pile of mushy goo and found my backpack beneath.

About a gallon of water splashed across the floor when I opened it. My heart sank as I picked up *Old Reliable* and eased him back into the pack. I doubted anything could save a camera after it had been submerged for so long. But would the phone be any different?

Finding the small, pink case, I pushed the power button. Nothing. So much for being waterproof.

Slinging by backpack over my shoulder, I ran up front to David. "My phone is dead. Can you get any information out of it?"

His brow crinkled as a dribble pooled along the edge of my phone case and dripped to the floor. "You'll need to dry it out."

Duh. I'm not an idiot.

I never said you were.

Gah! Stinking telepath!

David smiled and tapped the wall to his left. A yellow square appeared in the panel a few feet behind us and opened up.

"Put it in there. Either it will dry, or the components will melt, but you won't be any worse off than you are now."

I nodded. A deep chill stung my wrist as I passed my hand through the wall, but inside the chamber scorched like an oven. I dropped my phone inside and pulled my hand free. "Will this work for my camera too?"

He lifted his shoulders. "It will either dry it or melt it. Same as the phone."

Dropping my backpack on the floor, I added *Old Reliable* to the opening.

Please let this work. Please, please, please let this work.

I sat back beside David. "How long will my phone take to dry?"

"I'm not sure. Try it again in a few minutes."

The water on the floor pooled then funneled into the air. The droplets swirled like a mini cyclone as a long, solid cylinder appeared within. Silver stepped out of the funnel, and the remainder of the twister sucked into his back.

He moved between us, his gray, shiny form glinting in the artificial light. "Thank you for saving me."

"How badly are you hurt?" I asked.

"I will be fine as soon as we get to our new home."

"He's lying." Ruby appeared beside him. "His wounds are extensive. We have a yellow with us who has the capacity to heal, but she says any change in pressure could reopen his wounds."

David glanced at me. "I can't guarantee pressure levels. We're going into space, and Mars is not Earth." His hands moved away from the controls. "We are almost at the Abyssal Plain. If you want, I can drop you off here with Silver's people."

"No," Silver said. "I will take the risk. Bring us to our new home."

"Are you sure?" Ruby asked.

Their hands touched, molding together.

"To live a lifetime with you, I would chance anything."

They molded together in a hug and slowly sank to the floor and disappeared.

Wow. That was romantic—in a cheesy romance novel kind of a way. Not that anyone would want to read a book about a couple of oversized jellyfish.

David motioned to the window. "We just breached the Abyssal Plain."

The searchlights shone up and over the edge as David leveled off the ship and steered us across the ocean floor. Sand puffed up around us, like a desert beneath the sea.

He tapped a few points on the wall beside him that looked no different than the rest of the ship.

"What are you doing?"

"Just making sure everything is okay. We're going to ascend slowly, just like we did on the way down."

So that was it. We were safe. At least for now. As we left the deeper part of the sea where Ruby and Silver's people lived, we now only had to worry about the aliens again, and picking up Dad and whoever else I could get to my house in time.

David's gaze stared through the window with an intensity I'd rarely seen from him. I wondered how mad he was going to be after he thinks he dropped me off on that island, and I pop out of a closet and surprise him when we're halfway to Mars. He seriously can't think I'll let him go alone.

"We're not going to be able to drop everyone off on that island," David said, not taking his gaze from the screen. "That would mean flying across your continent to the eastern shore, grabbing your father, and crossing the country again to get there. There isn't enough time." A map of the eastern coast of the USA came up on the screen. "I was thinking of dropping you off on this island here." He pointed at a large, narrow island off the coast of Florida.

"Cuba? I don't think so." I pointed a little further south. "How about here. Jamaica. Happy, smiling people and resorts and all. A much better choice."

He nodded. "That's fine. But you are staying there with your father. Even if Edgar and I have to tie you up."

Pfft. You could try.

He raised an eyebrow.

We definitely needed to work on this "not reading Jess's private thoughts" thing.

Something swam past the window, reflecting the searchlights back in our faces before flittering away.

"What was that?"

"My guess would be a large fish." His cocky grin slid away. "Make that a *very* large fish."

Whitish-gray, squirming flesh crept down the window from above. Long, suction-cupped-covered arms filled the screen. The tiny circles probed the glass like little mouths asking for a meal. The animal arched, and a pointed beak in the center of his eight star-shaped legs chirped twice before the giant octopus skidded away.

I furrowed my brow. "Was that the same octopus-thing we ran into on the way down?"

"It has the same mass, but I don't think there is any way of knowing for sure."

The giant creature sped away, banked, and spun back toward us. I cringed as a bright pinprick followed in the distance, quickly gaining on the octopus.

David turned the ship.

"Where are you going?"

"I recognize that light. It's attached to a giant mouth, remember? I'm getting out of its way!"

Still yards away, the behemoth snapped, seizing one of the octopus's legs. The animal reeled back, struggling as the huge-jawed beast thrashed, shaking the helpless cephalopod.

David pointed our ship toward the surface and accelerated.

I gripped the back of his chair. "We can't just leave him there to die."

"Yes we can. He just bought us some time."

"With his life? I don't think so. We need to do something."

He ignored me. But I never took kindly to being ignored.

I focused my thoughts. *Turn around. Turn around. Turn around.* "Stop it."

"Not until you do it." *Turn around. Turn around. Turn around.*

A growl gurgled from his throat and I felt his resolve bend and flutter through our bond. "I know I'm going to regret this."

The ship banked right, flipped, and aimed right at the fighting animals. David punched his fist into the fuchsia corner of the console. The ship trembled as a clear whoosh jettisoned from below us, but with a lot less "whoosh" than we'd seen in the depths. We slowed to a stop.

"What happened?"

"I don't know." He looked up. "Edgar?"

The lights flashed around us. David groaned.

"What is it?"

"Edgar said the weapon was made to work in below-rift pressure. It didn't take in enough water to make a difference."

The streaming bubbles spiraled forward and hit the behemoth with barely a nudge, but it was enough to startle it. Sliding backward, it released the octopus.

Our eight-legged friend scampered into the darkness, leaving the swimming mouth of gleaming teeth panting and pointed straight at us.

"Time to go," David said.

"I'm not arguing with that."

David trailed his arms over the controls, but I was still staring down the throat of something big and ugly.

"Umm, we're not moving."

He glared at me before turning to the ceiling. It was probably good that I couldn't read his mind all the time.

"Edgar," he said. "What happened?"

The walls flashed.

"Great. Just great." They flashed again. "How was I supposed to know using the weapon in less pressure would drain the energy cells? It's not like you left directions."

"We're out of power?"

The swimming mouth charged, opening wide. Bubbles drifted from its teeth and disappeared into the dark. The creature's jaws surrounded us. We shook as the behemoth chewed and chomped until we were staring into its gullet.

"Okay, this is sooo not good!"

"Edgar, a little help, please!"

My chair warped to life, immobilizing me as the giant fish thrashed, shaking us in the water like an animal killing its prey. My sight blurred. My ears rang.

The creature tossed us up before clamping down again.

"David?" I whispered.

I wanted to turn, to see the perfect, composed lines of his face. I wanted to believe everything would be okay, even if I knew it wasn't. But I couldn't move. I closed my eyes rather than stare at the ridged lines on the top of the monster's pallet.

David's hand covered mine. *I'm going to figure this out.*

Part of me expected him to say that. But I knew, even without searching our tether, that he was just as helpless as I was.

The screen before us flashed pink and orange.

"You have to be kidding me," David whispered.

His chair relaxed and he leaned forward, reaching into the console.

"What now?"

"Something is heading directly at us at high speed, from above. It isn't organic."

"What is it?"

"From size and velocity, my guess would be a missile."

"You're freaking kidding me, right?"

A square appeared inside the glass window, showing what I supposed was the rear view from our ship. A shiny dot appeared in the distance and then moved closer. Great. Just great.

Weren't things bad enough? I fought against the metal that had solidified around every crevice of my body. Okay, I got safety and all, but this was a little ridiculous.

"Get this Goddamn thing off me!"

"Did you hear the part about the missile?"

"David!"

The silver cylinder blasted toward us, a stream of bubbles in its wake.

Sweet Lord. No. Please.

My chair released. I jumped into David's arms and squeezed him as his seat surrounded both of us. His warmth injected into me. Tears flooded my lashes as I forced every possible thing I ever wanted to say to him into a flood of emotionally charged hysterical thoughts.

"I'm here," he whispered, tightening his grip as the missile hissed toward us.

25

The explosion roared through the ship, rattling my world into a cloudy oblivion. A shrill buzz sliced through my ears—a hiss combined with a ring that drowned out all other sound.

I held my breath as a deep numbness set in. Was I dead?

A heated grip worked its way up my arm, clutching and prodding as if making sure I was in one piece. I lifted myself to find the horror of night blanketing us. Darkness and the incessant, screaming buzz pressed me further into a void of chaos.

I wiggled my fingers into David's grip, pawing for the heat. My heart leapt when his hand gripped my own.

"David?"

My voice bounced between my ears, booming, taunting, and mocking with each merciless pound. I wasn't sure if I'd said his name, or only thought it, but terror riddled me when I considered trying either again.

The sense of David entered me. The comfort, the rightness. David was there, inside me, but quiet. Disconnected. He flattened my hand and drew a circle on my palm with his finger, followed by the shape of a K.

O-K.

"Yes, I'm okay." *I'm better than okay. I'm alive. We're both alive!*

I wanted to cuddle into his chest and take a moment to revel in the joy of simply existing, but a frightened shimmer rattled our bond. I'd said the words, but David hadn't heard me. Maybe he couldn't hear my thoughts either.

Grabbing his hand, I drew an O and a K on his palm. His arms surrounded me, and the fear slithering across our bond faded to joy.

I reveled in the warmth of his relief for a single heartbeat. We were all right, and the ship seemed to be in one piece. But how?

Two short flashes singed my retinas. Maybe I'd imagined it, but David's muscles tensed beneath my hand. Lights near the floor shone from an infinitesimal glimmer to a dull glow. David's form shifted beside me, not more than an outline, before the illumination increased.

I blinked away the spots dancing in my sight as the light from our ship brightened the sea outside our window. Half of the monster's massive rear fin and a hunk of bloody, scaled hide floated past the glass. Lines of drifting gore trailed behind the body's shredded edges.

David gaped before his gaze trailed to me. He laughed and pulled me into another embrace.

"We ... it," David's voice seemed to come from a distance.

I held my hand to my ear. "I can't hear."

"Can ... anything?"

"I can hear, like, every other word." But I could hear my own voice now, come to think of it.

He turned to the console, and his lips moved, but all I heard was the word "have."

He swirled his arms, and the ship moved away from the ghastly remains of the giant mouth-fish.

I jumped up from my seat. "Hey, we're moving! We have power!"

David smiled at me. *Oh.* He'd probably already told me that.

The wall flashed. My little *grassen* must have been hard at work.

Can you hear anything at all? David's voice hugged me from within.

"Yeah, I can hear you inside my head, now. I guess the buzz is getting less."

I had a ringing, too. It's almost gone.

He startled and looked to the screen, his lips forming a straight line just before a jolt of anxiety skidded across the top of our bond.

We'd just survived a freaking missile. Now, what?

"A communication is coming through." His voice seemed distant below the ringing, but it was getting clearer.

Erescopian symbols scrolled across the screen.

"What does it say?" I plopped back into my chair.

"It's being translated." A smile crossed his lips. "They are asking if we're okay. It's the submarine from yesterday." We rose further, toward the silver vessel. "They saw us get caught, but they couldn't dive this deep to help us, so they fired the missile, instead."

They'd fired at the mouth-fish, not us. They were the coolest submarine guys on the planet! But had they just been sitting there the whole time, waiting for us to come back?

No. Someone sent them.

I glanced up, as if I could see past the ceiling, through the ocean, and beyond. A warmth coated me. Someone up there was looking out for us.

Dad. It had to be.

I waved as we passed the submarine. Like they could see me, but I didn't care. "Tell them thanks!"

"Already done." He faced me. "Ready to get out of this ocean?"

"You bet that tight little alien butt of yours I am." I gripped my chair, ready for our ascent, before remembering our passengers. "How is everyone downstairs?"

David peered into the swirling liquid inside the console. "They seem fine. They probably don't even know anything happened."

Lucky them.

The dark sea outside the glass brightened to a dull gray before fading into a semblance of blue. Lines of sunlight cascaded through the water, celebrating our return to the real world. Our ship breached the surface and soared into the bright, blue sky. I inhaled, as if breathing for the first time in ages. Air and sky hugged the ship as the sea sprawled out below us, shimmering in the late afternoon sun.

We'd made it.

We'd actually made it!

David tapped the panel above. "The pressure is holding for our guests. We're good, at least for now."

"So now we get my dad."

"Yes. As soon as we … " He leaned over the panel and squinted. "What is that?"

I turned to him. "That's not even funny. We're out of the freaking ocean. What could possibly be wrong?" I ducked as a familiar rectangular shadow passed over us, not unlike the ones who flew past our house on McGuire Air Force Base. Another aircraft followed, nearly clipping our roof. "Did they just dive-bomb us?"

"No. I think they were heading for that." He pointed out the window, where the two jets rained ammunition onto a gray liquescent pearl the size of an apartment complex hovering over white capped waves.

Holy crap! We'd come out of the sea and flown right into an aerial battle!

Thomp.

I covered my ears and closed my eyes. That sound remained etched into my memory—the discharge of alien weapons that had taken out the small airport that David and I had run to the first summer we'd met. The ground had cracked beneath my feet. Balls of fire flew through the night sky, catching the trees alight. And the soldiers … so many dead.

We'd gone through too much to let this happen again.

I opened my eyes in time to see the plane on the left hit the waves. The one on the right burst into flames.

No! The pilots!

The flames from the second aircraft extinguished in a puff of smoke as the craft splashed into the sea.

"Tell them to stop!" I shouted. "Tell them they don't need Earth. We can make it rain!"

Erescopian letters scrawled across the screen. David settled over the console, the intensity returning to his gaze.

Thomp. David held on as our ship rumbled.

The liquescent opal pulsed as it rose and angled in our direction. "Are they shooting at *us* now?"

"Apparently."

"Why? Aren't those your people?"

"Yes, but it looks like they're still a little angry about me stealing their experimental hot-rod as you called it." He tapped the panel at his side. "We are still faster than anything they have. We can outrun them."

The pearly orb disappeared from view, and land appeared over the horizon.

"Is that home?"

David shook his head. "That's the west coast of your continent. We'll be over the east coast in a few minutes. If you are going to make phone calls, do it now."

Sweat drenched my brow. I leapt toward the yellow panel in the wall and shoved my hand inside. I gripped *Old Reliable's* familiar surface and shoved him back into my backpack at the base of the wall. Fumbling inside the wall again, I found the warm, square case and plucked my phone out.

Please, Lord, let this work.

I hit the power button and the little apple lit up the screen. Score!

The icon continued to flash.

Dad—he never answered the phone at work. Especially during an emergency. What if he didn't answer now? What if he couldn't get somewhere where David and I could pick him up? What if he wouldn't agree to come? I had precious seconds to convince him, and that stinking apple was still blinking!

Maggie. Matt. What if they were still in New York? No. Not possible. Matt would have driven Maggs home. Right? They'd both be in New Jersey. They had to be. With their families. Bags packed. Ready to go in case Jess shows up to save their lives. *Yeah. Right.*

Why wasn't that freaking phone booting up?

My home screen appeared and I tapped to my favorites and chose Dad. The ring hummed against my ear, the tone vibrating forever. *Come on, Dad.*

A roar punctured the ship as something huge flew over us.

I dropped the phone, slamming my hands over my ears. The ship rattled, shaking my mobile across the floor as David sunk his arms deeper into the controls. His face contorted to a grimace before the rattling ceased.

"What was that?" I asked.

"I have no idea, but it almost hit us and the temperature readings are off the charts. I've never seen anything give off that much heat." He stretched toward the back of the control panel. "Whatever it is, it slowed down and it's hovering about twelve miles to the east of here."

"Should we be worried?"

He huffed. "I already have too much to worry about."

The small blip on the screen flashed twice. If it was hovering, it had to be a ship. My gut twisted and an odd sense of foreboding coated me, like a warning from deep within. Like me, screaming at the top of my lungs that I needed to do something.

I did need to do something. Save my father. Save the world. Nothing new. Just another day with David. But something about that ship haunted me, like my tether had been cut in two: one strand tugging me toward David, and the other drawing me toward that ship. I rubbed my eyes. Dammit, if I didn't get some sleep I was going to lose my mind.

We continued our ascent and I shook my head to clear the echoes of the other ship. Breathing deeply, I snatched my phone from the floor. My call had ended, so I redialed Dad. Two rings and that familiar, barely noticeable click sound before the call connected, telling me the army would be listening in on the call. Didn't matter, as long as I got through to my father.

"Jess, thank God. Where are you?"

The sound of his voice warmed me like a hug. "Dad, I need you to listen to me."

"No time. Where are you?"

Desert sand whisked past at indiscernible speeds. "I'm not sure. Nevada. Maybe Utah, but we're coming to get you. I need you to … "

"No, you're not."

"Yes, I am. Dad, you … "

"Two Marines just got shot down over the Western Pacific. Please tell me you two weren't involved."

"No, of course not! There was another Erescopian ship there. It's like everyone is using us for target practice."

"Did David find what he needs to stop the attack?"

I paused. "How did you know about that?"

Grumbles reverberated in the background. "Answer the question."

I wondered if I should tell him it was more of a *them* rather than an *it*. Probably not. "Yeah, we got it. We're going to take it to Mars as soon as we get you safe."

"There is nowhere safe anymore. Put David on the line."

I gritted my teeth, hit speaker, and set the phone just beside the glowing console.

Why couldn't Dad just listen to me? All he had to do was come with us. Was that too much to ask? I slipped my hand around David's biceps and rested my head on his shoulder. If anything happened to my father …

"David?" Dad's voice boomed.

"Yes, sir."

"There's only one thing in this world that I care about, and I bet she's leaning against your shoulder right now."

I stepped back, releasing David. Was I that predicable?

"That little girl means everything to me."

David smiled at me. "I'm aware of that, sir."

A pause hung on the line. The desert below faded into green plains.

"I suppose you are also aware that there is a spaceship the size of China hovering about two thousand miles above Canada."

David closed his eyes. "You need to keep away from that ship."

"We've already engaged."

"No! You can't." He slammed his fist on the console, shaking the phone. "It's a trap. Your defenses will be slaughtered."

"You've been around humanity enough to know we won't go down without a fight. That thing isn't getting any nearer to Earth."

"That's not its purpose. It's there to draw you out. You don't understand."

"Your cargo is all I'm worried about. Jess, and whatever else you're carrying. McGuire is a military target. I don't want my daughter anywhere near here."

"But, Dad—"

"Enough. David, you need to get to Mars. Now."

Like hell. I leaned toward the phone. "We're coming to get you. End of discussion."

"You're wasting time. I'm not leaving. I'm needed here. David, she's going to hate you for it, but I need you to have the strength do the right thing."

The muscles in David's neck tensed. He pressed his lips together.

"No." Tears pooled in my lashes. "Don't you dare," I whispered. "Don't you dare."

David gulped and moved his gaze back to the console.

It was selfish of me to be so worried about my father, but fine, call me selfish. He was all I had left. I needed my father. I wasn't ready to be alone.

I could imagine Dad pacing on the other side of the phone, rubbing his hand across his tightly cropped hair. Did he know what he was doing to me? Probably. But Dad only focused on the big picture. Nothing more. Soldiers sacrificed. That was just the way it was. For once in his life couldn't he just say to hell with doing the right thing?

"Our entire race is counting on you, David," Dad continued, "and I have to say that I've never met anyone with such integrity—to have the *cajones* to go against your entire race and do what's right—twice—that takes a special sort of a man."

David's lips tightened. His hands twitched.

"I know we got off to a rough start. God knows I never wanted you anywhere near my daughter, but you've proven yourself, and you *continue* to prove yourself."

David stood a little straighter, taking a deep breath.

Dad continued, "No matter what happens today, I want you to know that I would be proud to call you my son."

David coughed and covered his mouth with his hand as tears streamed down his cheeks. The flood of joy and dismay shattered across our tether, nearly knocking the wind out of me. David had crash-landed on Earth a little over two years ago in a botched attempt to get into his father's good graces. By the time he'd left Earth, it seemed everything was fine between him and his dad. Then only three months later he'd saved Mars from a conspiracy to kill the planet. David was a hero, yet the essence of failure slithered across our bond, as if all his successes never happened.

His own father hated him. I could feel it. To hear such praise from my father, a human, a man he should consider his enemy, gashed a cavern through his psyche. David had been broken before, but this—this was the worst I'd ever seen.

The energy flowing between us subsided as David straightened. His features hardened. The emotions changed to a cacophony of warm feelings. Security. Admiration. Love?

His gaze centered on the phone.

My father. He was focusing his thoughts on my father, not his own. Had David finally given up on the man up there in space that he'd never be able to please?

David glanced at me, and the pleasant emotions faded. A deep burning wiped away the joy skidding across our bond.

Regret. Deep, undeniable regret.

A ball formed in my throat as the ship slowed. "No!" I pushed him. "Don't you stop this ship. Don't you do it! We need to save my father!"

"*Pequeña.*" The sweet, gentle sound of my father's voice bit into me. No longer the soldier, just my dad. "There are a few things I need to tell you."

I shook my head. "Don't you dare. Don't you dare." I wiped my eyes. "We're coming to get you."

The ship started to ascend.

"What are you doing? We need to get my dad!" I punched David's shoulder. He didn't budge an inch. "Fly back down. We need to go get him."

"*Pequeña,* stop."

I slipped into my chair, holding my temples.

"You are so much like your mother—the eternal rebel pitted against my dutiful soldier. She would have been incredibly proud of you, you know that?"

I rocked back and forth, pressing my temples. *A military target.* When those alien ships broke our atmosphere, they knew exactly what they had to destroy. Whose lives they had to erase.

"I may not always show it, but I am incredibly proud of you. And your photography is going to be the stuff of legends. I don't want you ever to give up your dreams."

His voice broke. I imagined tears in his eyes, but he'd wipe them away. A soldier was always composed. Confident. He'd want me to be more like him, but I wasn't. I wouldn't ever be.

Static hissed across the phone connection. "I love you, *Pequeña*. I always will." The hole in my heart cut deeper. "This isn't goodbye. One thing I've learned from you is this: anything is possible. Absolutely anything."

A bank of clouds shrouded the window, darkening the tiles on the floor. A crackle sizzled from my phone.

I jerked up. "Daddy?" The phone clicked twice. "Dad!"

Tears drizzled down my cheeks. I jumped to my feet and snatched the phone, tapping every icon on the screen.

"We're out of range." David grasped my shoulders, settling me back in my seat.

"What do you mean we're out of range? We can't possibly be—"

He stepped aside, revealing a window filled with beautiful, twinkling stars.

I wiped my eyes. "You have to go back down. You have to!"

He sunk his hands into the console. "You know we don't have time for that."

Time. There was always supposed to be time. I was only twenty. My entire life was ahead of me—time to hang with my dad as an adult. As a friend.

The screen blanked out in my trembling hand. "But I didn't get to tell him I love him."

David turned from the panel; his lashes glistened with unshed tears. "Major Martinez is a smart man. He knows you love him."

I nodded, but I wasn't so sure. When was the last time I told him how important he was to me?

Tapping the photos icon, I clicked on my favorites and stared at the only picture in the folder. Mom and Dad's smiling faces pressed together on the screen, cardboard crowns rested on their heads. A ran my fingers over Mom's face, and then Dad's. Leaving the photo on the screen, I set the phone into my backpack and closed the zipper.

"I'll save him, Mom," I whispered. "I promise." The stars shifted to the right as we leveled off.

How could this be happening? We had the stinking source in our cargo hold. We had a dozen stinking sources. Why were we even worried about anything? That was all we needed. Just get these giant, smart, talking jellyfish to Mars and *boom!* Everything would be okay. Right?

Bright flashes blanked out the stars. A sprawling, black mass hung in space, dwarfing tiny flies that skidded across its surface.

"What is that?" I asked.

"The ship," David said. "The one I told your father not to engage."

26

A fiery cloud lifted off the exterior of the alien craft, but quickly fizzled to darkness.

"What was that?" I asked.

"An explosion. Apparently your people managed to get a missile through."

A smile crossed my face. *Way to go, guys.*

Another explosion rattled across the liquescent vessel, and another. Within seconds the entire hull blazed.

"Yes!" I shouted.

"Idiots. All of them," David whispered.

"Why, because your superior technology maybe isn't all that superior?" I pointed out the window. "It seems to me a little human ingenuity is giving them a run for their money."

David's irises darkened. "Look at them, Jess. Look with your eyes and not your heart."

The glass flickered, and the scene zoomed in. Five space shuttles flew alongside several square, silver boxes with windows, while a few dozen more asymmetrical crafts made of multi-colored metals hung well behind the others. Computer-generated red dots appeared on two of the crafts at the rear, and one of the space shuttles nearing the Erescopian behemoth.

"Those red markers show which of those ships are still armed."

Three. Only three.

But streams of gas trickled from the alien ship, and the human fleet still seemed intact, as if the Erescopians weren't even fighting back. Maybe the battle was already over. Maybe we'd already won.

"Typical primitive thinking," David said. "It will get them all dead."

He pointed our ship toward the moon. Out David's window, the space shuttle fired off two long, sleek cylinders. They flew silently through space, exploding on impact. Fire billowed out of the alien craft and winked out, but a section of the ship the size of Texas broke off and floated away.

"They're winning!"

"It's a diversion," David said as we crested over the moon. "Simple standard attack strategy. Intimidate your enemy, and let them expend their resources until their defenses are no longer a threat. This is what I tried to warn your father about."

"I don't understand. That ship is falling apart."

Deep hurt radiated within his sluggish carriage. "Never let your enemy know your true numbers."

We banked over the edge of the moon. Along the horizon, space seemed to hollow out—deep, dark voids overtook all, as if someone had stolen the stars.

A shiver ran through me. Not voids: ships. Black opal liquescent ships hiding behind the moon, out of line-of-sight, where our sensors couldn't detect them. So many they began to blur together. Hundreds. Thousands. A throng.

This was the real threat. This was the terror that was about to scourge the Earth.

Sweet Lord, please help us.

We dove directly into the middle of the mass of alien vessels.

"What are you doing?"

"Looking for my father's ship."

"Are you insane? Aren't they still ticked about you stealing the hot-rod?"

A square appeared in the bottom left quarter of David's window. A violescent face appeared. Deep, turquoise eyes blinked twice and darkened to the same shade as the dim, mottled spot on the corner of the alien's shoulder. The tense set of David's posture told me the man was Sabbotaruo—the commander of the Erescopian fleet, and David's father.

The edges of Sabbotaruo's bridgeless nose flared. Erescopian words echoed throughout the cabin, but I heard English in my mind. *"Surrender the ship, Tirran. Enter through our forty-fifth sector and wait to be boarded."*

"Father, listen to me." Again, the words David spoke were his own language, but somehow my brain translated. How was this even possible?

"I have no time for childish games. Comply. Immediately."

"I will not. I have found the secret to make it rain. I can bring life to Mars."

"So you have said before."

"But I can do it this time. You need to trust me. We need to remain allied with the humans. We'll need their help."

"We will not need their help if we have their planet."

"This isn't right. You have to stop this."

"The decision has been made. We must do what the Caretakers have deemed necessary to save our race."

"Why can't you trust me? I'm not an idiot!"

Sabbotaruo moved closer to the screen. *"You have been a continual cause for embarrassment. The Caretakers have been gracious enough to let me hold my title despite your recurrent ineptitude. They will not accept more failure. Land that pilfered ship. Now."*

"*I won't let the humans die. It's wrong. Coud never would have agreed.*"

I flinched. Coud was David's mother's name.

His father's irises swirled, the colors separating before coming together again. "*For the first time in my life, I am glad she is dead. It saves her the agony of knowing she wasted her youth raising the likes of you.*" A grimace skewed his thin lips. "*I renounce you of her name. And mine.*" He waved his hand beside his face, and the communication faded back to the stars.

A jolt of agony flooded through David. A pain so deep I nearly slipped from my chair.

Four orbs dropped around us. *Thomp. Thomp. Thomp. Thomp.* The sounds drowned into one, continuous throttle of excruciating drums riddling the sides of our ship.

The walls baulked. Jittered.

A stream of mottled feelings ricocheted back and forth between us, rattling our tether, strengthening the bond in one wave, weakening us in the next.

I reached over and grabbed David's wrist. "Don't let him get to you. You're strong. You've made the right choice. Don't let him beat you."

Strong. Strong. Strong. I didn't know if silently repeating the word would help, but Sabbotaruo's rebuttal had sliced though David. I needed to get through to him somehow.

David blinked, his eyes staring at nothing. Anger simmered deep in my chest. I glanced out the window at the largest ship shifting behind the others in the distance. Why'd his father have to be such a dick?

The walls flashed yellow. David didn't respond.

"Edgar," I cried to the ceiling. "David can't answer!"

Dammit, I hoped there wasn't something he needed David to do.

I stood and grabbed David's cheeks. "It doesn't matter. He can't take away your name. He can't take away who you are."

David shuddered. "Yes, he can."

"No. He can't. The only one who can take away who you are is you. You decide who you are. No one else."

His gaze finally met mine. "I have no name. You don't understand."

"Then take mine."

He blinked. "What?"

"My father said he'd be proud to call you his son. Hey, Martinez isn't all that bad a name."

He closed his eyes. His lips trembled. Unfortunately, the ship trembled more.

"It's a good name. A strong name," he said.

"You bet your ass it is. And Martinezes don't give up. Ever. So I need you to pull yourself together, soldier, and high tail it out of here before your good-for-nothing father blows us out of the stars."

His eyes popped open and focused on me. "You've been so mad, I wasn't sure about us anymore. You really want to give me your name?"

Dammit! This wasn't the time to have a heart to heart about our relationship. "Okay, I was mad. I'm not anymore. Everything is fine. You, me, the connection thing, it's all great."

His eyes quaked. "Taking your name, it's permanent. You understand that, right?"

A boom rattled through the floor. Was he even aware of the ships shooting at us?

"Yeah, fine. Good. We'll sign the freaking adoption papers tomorrow. Whatever. Let's just get the hell out of here!"

Another shot flared across our windows. David glanced at the glass, unaffected by the attacking orbs. "Edgar, I need about four minutes. Keep us moving."

The ship jerked left, then right. The orbs still managed to hit us. What was he doing?

"David, we really need to go."

The sense of loss scooted over our bond, a hole longing to be filled.

He reached for me. "I need you."

"I'm here. I told you, I'm not going anywhere."

"You're really sure?"

Three more ships throttled towards us. "Yes, dammit, come on!"

He grabbed both my hands and looked deep into my eyes. No, *through* my eyes. My psyche locked, toiled, fought, and then opened, bearing myself to him. Everything that I was splayed out before David in an onslaught of my most cherished memories and my most embarrassing secrets … everything, anything, and more. Until there was nothing but me, naked with tears running down my cheeks.

My energy seemed to drain out my toes. "Wh-what just … "

He kissed my forehead. "Shh. It's done," he whispered.

"Done?" What was done?

His gaze darted to the flashing walls. "I'm here, Edgar."

Edgar? Oh, yeah. Ship. War. End of the world.

I stumbled to my chair. The room rolled and warbled.

"You all right?" David asked.

Stars. Pretty.

"Jess?"

My sight cleared. I pointed at David's window and I screamed as a dark opal dive-bombed us.

"Got it." He sank his hands into the controls. The walls continued to flash as Edgar communicated via the lights. "You don't need me to tell you to reinforce the hull. Just do it!"

We whisked away from the attacking opals, but four more appeared in front of us. The area between our ships blurred as they discharged their weapons. David maneuvered us down, missing their fire.

My stomach churned. I ran my hands across my wrinkled tee-shirt and jeans. I wasn't naked. Maybe I never had been. But he'd seen much deeper into me than what my clothing hid.

"They're crowding us," David yelled to the walls. "They know they're no match for us if we get into the open."

Open. Exactly. I'd been opened. Cracked, split, and put on display. I should have been angry, but all I could feel was pleased. Whole, but then again, not so whole. Lost. Empty. The spinning orbs and the flashing weapons fire crept into the background. A dull, meaningless hum.

The air around me quivered, and the chair beneath me bubbled to life. I shrieked as it seized me, until the room cleared of the fuzzy haze, and the battle outside came to a crisp, clear focus.

A thousand of them. One of us. Not. Good.

27

We spiraled, cascading toward one of the liquescent opals. The ship backed off, only to be replaced by another. I blinked twice. How long had I been dazed, and what happened?

A flash of light skidded across our windows, just missing us. "Don't we have any weapons?"

"Of course we do. But I'm not shooting at my own people."

They sure didn't have a problem shooting at us.

A small space opened between two ships on my lower right.

"David!"

"I see it." He waved his hands, plowing straight past another orb that tried to block our escape.

Clear, bright stars opened up around us. David breathed a sigh of relief and a smile burst across his lips. My restraints loosened.

"Don't you think they'll follow?"

He shook his head. "My father may be many things, but he's not a fool. They can't catch this ship in the open, and I'm not his priority. Earth is."

Okay, well, that didn't make me feel better. "Shouldn't we go back and distract them some more, then?"

"We rattled them pretty bad. We gained Earth a few hours."

A few hours? That wasn't much. "How long will it take to get to Mars?"

He frowned. "Almost a day."

A small white square formed on the screen. The box expanded, showing a small red and blue marble in the distance.

My stomach sank. "And how long does it take to scourge a planet?"

His lips formed a straight line as he stared into the console.

"David?"

He turned to the wall beside him and tapped the small shining panel. "I need to check on our guests."

I spun to the window, painfully aware that he hadn't answered me.

Our guests ... a bunch of pilgrims on a big, shiny liquidic Mayflower. But their new world may come in the wake of the Earth's destruction. What if all this was for nothing?

"Don't think that," David said. "This will work. It has to work."

Clear droplets gathered in the air between us, flinging from unknown places in the ship and gathering into a solid tube that shimmered and pinched until Maggie's perky curls and brilliant smile beamed back at me.

"It has become easier to breathe," Ruby said through Maggie's lips.

David plopped back into his chair. "I regulated the pressure. I'll be able to keep a better eye on you now that no one is trying to kill us."

"We sensed a great deal of fear. We were concerned."

"We're fine for now. The next stop is a clean, clear, beautiful blue ocean."

Ruby smiled. "That sounds wonderful."

A frothy spiral appeared beside Ruby, forming shiny gray arms that elevated of their own accord before Silver materialized behind them. "Is it truthful to tell our friends there is nothing to fear?"

Other than traveling to a planet where they might not be able to survive in a stolen ship where a bunch of aliens will probably try to blow us up? Nope, nothing to worry about. Nothing at all.

David smirked at me before returning his gaze to our passengers. "There is always the concern about the new environment, but I'm going to slowly change the chemical make-up of the seawater in your alcove to match the oceans on Mars. It should help to relieve some of the shock."

They nodded, and Silver splashed to the floor. The dampness dissipated and disappeared.

"How's he doing?" I asked Ruby.

"He's healing quickly. He still has some pain, but his wounds have closed over."

I shifted my weight. "I'm happy for you." And I was. It was very romantic, running away together to another planet. What a sacrifice.

She smiled at me and then David. "I hope I can be as happy for the two of you one day."

Her image split into thousands of sparking droplets that hovered for a split second, catching bright prismatic light, before falling to the floor and seeping through the tiles. The girl certainly knew how to make an exit.

David tapped on the panel beside the console. Erescopian symbols streamed across the screen.

"What's that?" I asked.

"I'm contacting Nematali Carash on Mars."

I smiled. Nematali had stood beside David two years ago as he begged the Caretakers to spare Earth, and fought at our sides when one of those Caretakers almost broke the treaty. Out of all of David's people, I trusted her the most. After David, of course.

"We're going to need ionic particle stabilization in the Martian ocean. That will help create the pressure we'll need to keep our friends alive until they sink into the correct depth." David rubbed the back of his neck as the characters continued to flow across the screen. "I've devised a way to start the chain reaction using the secondary propulsion engines on our ship."

"Perfect!"

"Almost. Stabilization will take time. Time we don't have." He tapped the screen. "There are three of these ships in existence. If Nematali can get to one of the other two prototypes, she can use my directions to start the reaction before we get there." He turned toward me. "We also need a food source for these creatures or they're going to starve on Mars. Falen Nematali studies the biology of alien species. I'm hoping he can help come up with something."

I shivered, remembering Nematali's mate and the examination from hell. 'Scientific curiosity,' he'd said, pocketing a stolen tissue sample. My pelvis still stung when I thought about it.

David glanced at me and then back to the console. "Sorry that happened. I can't condone his methods, but he's one of our best." He tapped a blinking light. "I'm sending them the data. We're going to need all the help we get."

I nodded. Even if Falen was an ass, it would be nice to get some help for a change, rather than dodging people trying to kill us all the time.

The characters faded from the screen as David stood. "There's not much more we can do until we enter Mars's atmosphere. We should probably get some rest."

The floor behind us rose into a coffin-like rectangle. The creamy liquescence swirled and kneaded like waves lapping a beach, before solidifying into a deep, gray recliner-like chair.

I raised an eyebrow. "You couldn't splurge on a couch?" I reached for his hand. "I'll rest if you do. Sit with me."

He smiled, a slight blue tinge touching his cheek. "I need to tell Edgar we're going to relax a little."

The chair widened as I approached, then deepened long enough to lie on. I sat on the edge, but the cushion barely budged. Extra firm for my first nap in space.

David slid beside me and propped himself up on an elbow.

I laid back slowly. It had all the comfort of cuddling up on a hardwood floor. "Is there any way to make it softer?"

The cushion shifted beneath me and I sank nearly a foot deep into the fluff. Piles of soft squish covered me nearly to my nose.

"Too soft! Too soft!"

I clambered back up beside him, the fibers below solidifying into a much more manageable, cushiony softness.

David hadn't moved a muscle. He barely fought his chuckle.

"You did that on purpose."

"Maybe."

I brushed my cheek against his. The quick intake of air that skidded through his lips sent a shiver across my skin. I'd forgotten how stimulating that simple gesture could be.

Still trembling, I leaned away. "Before, when you kissed my forehead, you said *it was done*. What did you mean by that?"

He smiled and traced his thumb across my bottom lip. "My bond to you is now the strongest tie possible between two people."

But when he had looked into my eyes, through my eyes ... "You know everything about me now, don't you?"

David nodded. "And you're even more perfect than I thought."

My cheeks heated. "Perfect? You're just saying that."

"I'm not." He cupped my cheek. "All those dark places, all of your hurt—everything in your life has made you who you are. What I saw was incredible. You are so much more than you know."

I slid my palm across his cheek. "So are you."

"I wasn't, but I am now—now that I can draw on your strength." He glanced to the side before his gaze skated back to me. "We could finish it now, if you want, so you can draw on my strength."

"Don't I already? I mean, sometimes I can feel you."

He nodded. "That's a result of our initial connection, but it can be more like … " He stared at the couch. "I can't find a human word. Sharing, I suppose is the closest concept. Deep, perpetual sharing."

"And you did that by looking inside me?"

"That's the beginning. Sharing is a commitment to the other. You should always know what you're getting into before cementing a bond." He twiddled his fingers. "I can guide you, if you'd like to see inside me, first."

All I ever wanted was to know what was going on in that head of his. Could I really see everything, like he'd done to me? I shuddered. Did I really want to know that much about a person—no secrets at all?

His brow lifted, his gaze wide and expectant. His bottom lip twitched. What he'd just asked me was something huge. Huger than huge, to him at least. As scared as I might be, how could I ever say no when he wanted to share something so deeply intimate?

I nodded. "Show me. I want to see everything."

Smiling hesitantly, he slid his hands into mine and eased us both to our knees. The flutter of his lashes relayed a fear deeper than I could understand—at least until he let me in.

"Don't be afraid," I whispered.

His hands trembled in mine. "If you don't like what you see, you can always stop. Just let go of my hands."

I closed my eyes as a tingle skittered through my palms, seeping into me and grabbing on before drawing back and whisking me along with it. I plunged into a river of cascading colors. Each swirling slash of pigment encircled me, welcomed me, cherished, and exploded in pure, expectant joy. The different hues melted together, spun, and flashed into a bolt of blinding yellow. I spiraled into the soft glow and landed on my knees in the center of a dull, gray room.

A boy knelt beside me, violescent except for a few faint bluish spots. My breath hitched. He was Erescopian.

A woman's voice filled the room. "Eyes down, Tirran."

Tirran … David's real name.

My stomach balled. The boy beside me was David. I reached for him, but my hand went right through his lavender arm. He didn't react.

Was this a memory?

The boy trembled and inched to his left, away from a hulking figure kneeling beside him. My gaze traveled over the man's thick, violet biceps, and a deep blue blotch across his broad shoulders. His gaze flittered toward David, his lips twisted in disgust. I quaked, pushing down my innate response to run and hide. *This isn't real. He can't hurt you.*

David slunk lower, cowering as if he expected the older man to strike. An odd sensation skidded through our bond, a swirling combination of fear, need, and admiration.

The older alien was Sabbotaruo, David's father.

Slender, violet legs stepped out of the shadows. David wiped his palms on his bare thighs as a female Erescopian moved before them.

"You may go," she said.

Sabbotaruo stood slowly, keeping his head down. The female stroked her cheek against his before the huge male backed away with his chin to his chest.

Deep adoration stirred my soul. A small part of me wanted to jump into her arms and never let go. Somehow, I sensed that she would always protect me.

I shook the fog shadowing my mind away. It wasn't me she'd protect, but the small boy she held her hand out to. This had to be Coud, David's mother.

Sabbotaruo continued to back away, face down. This huge Erescopian dwarfed everyone in the room—an undeniable military leader, but so acquiescent before his mate. Nematali had mentioned they were a matriarchal culture. I hadn't really digested what that meant until now. Coud dominated in the home. There was no question in that.

The wall shimmered and swallowed Sabbotaruo.

David exhaled, slouching. "I will never be able to make him happy."

Coud folded her arms. "The only one you need to make happy is yourself."

I tipped back and fell once more. A rainbow blanketed me, wrapping me in its brilliance before dropping me to the floor. I choked on a deep pain cutting through my chest. Tears streamed down my cheeks as my heart twisted, beating erratically.

The younger version of David crouched beside me, hugging his chest, and sobbing. His father yanked him to his feet and held his head, forcing him to watch as an elongated bundle of black rags burst into flames behind a window. David tugged away, screaming and splaying his hands across the glass, pounding and repeating an Erescopian word I couldn't make out.

I shivered.

Coud's funeral. I hadn't realized how young David had been when she died. A ball twisted in my stomach and forced itself up, choking me. Who would hug him when he cried; pick him up when he fell? Who would he run to when he was scared?

The sob I'd been holding burst free. My life ripped out from under me when my mom died. I missed her so much. How was I supposed to live without her? Losing a mother. It wasn't fair.

Sabbotaruo pulled David from the glass and shook him, forcing the child's jaw closed to stop his wailing. He held his son steady, forcing him to watch as the flames devoured the last remains of David's lifeline to love and happiness.

I hugged myself, stifling my own deep, unhealed wounds. My father wasn't the best, but at least he'd tried. David had been left with nothing but a domineering, harsh, uncaring parent. I wanted to reach for him, console him, and tell him that everything would be all right. But even if I could, that would be a lie. His mother was gone. Nothing would be okay again. Ever.

Colors exploded in another blinding array. I jolted to a stop, hidden in a dark corner. David cowered at my feet, hugging his knees. I trembled and tried to calm the overbearing fear strangling our tether.

Sabbotaruo was coming. I could sense it. But what could this child have done to warrant such terror? David glanced toward a heap of opened metallic silver bags piled in the corner.

The food. He'd eaten all of the family's rations. His father would come home to nothing. Again.

The walls shimmered. Sabbotaruo's footsteps tapped across the floor. David scurried deeper into the corner. My heart throttled, wishing the partitions could swallow and hide both of us, forever.

Flash. I flinched as a violet fist lodged into the wall beside our head. David turned away, shaking as his father growled in his face.

"*It's not my fault,*" David whispered in Erescopian.

"*Not your fault?*" His warm breath puffed across our face. "*She's dead because of you.*"

David fell to the floor as the next punch grazed his jaw. He took the pain, absorbed it. He deserved every ounce of punishment his father administered. He was nothing. Sabbotaruo was right, it would have been better if David had died in his mother's place.

A wave of deep, cutting despair rolled over me. I hugged my own shoulders, hoping David could feel me, absorb some of my strength. How could a father do that to his son?

A flash of yellow burst through the room. Over and over, I was forced to relive one painful memory after another. Each time David reached for his father, the Erescopian commander turned away. Somewhere deep within I sensed a seed of affection, but Sabbotaruo never showed weakness, always castigating David's failures and questioning his son's successes. A child needs to be nurtured, loved. Not pounded and screamed into submission. Not hated. Not blamed for an accident out of anyone's control!

Flash. I walked beside David, now slightly taller than me. A man. He beamed, holding his head high as he made his way toward a small, black liquescent ship. Sabbotaruo stood beside a row of hip-high black wire fences along the wall to our left.

Pride drifted across our link. How long had he craved his father's approval? But it had been simple. As soon as David had given up his childish love of the sciences and joined the military, his father's attitude began to change. For the first time in his life, he'd earned Sabbotaruo's respect. If he'd only known sooner…

My hands fisted. "No!" I tried to grab David, to stop him, but my arms sank right through him as if I were a ghost. Science was his life. He was brilliant, one of his people's greatest minds. He shouldn't waste himself. Not as a pilot.

As a pilot. I froze, turning back to Sabbotaruo. My breath hitched. This was David's first mission. The one he didn't return from.

The rainbow flashed twice before melting into hissing flames and deafening explosions. I ran beside David, barely escaping the searchlights hunting us from above. I dropped beside him as the last of the whooshing helicopters faded from our hearing.

"We're safe here," I said, but he didn't answer.

Alone now, I wanted to hold him, comfort him from Earth's decreasing temperatures. But all I could do was watch him shiver. Leaves shifted overhead, and David huddled into a ball. The movement of the trees, the noises of the woods … sounds so familiar to me, but terrifying to a person who'd barely set foot on a planet before. A resounding dread crept into my stomach, but it wasn't my own. I grit my teeth, realizing he was more afraid of his father's wrath than of being captured.

A blinding light surrounded us as time shifted again. David pushed up against a log, holding his shoulder. He'd been hurt in the crash. I'd almost forgotten. A new terror spliced through our connection as leaves crunched within the trees. My heart pounded in tandem with David's.

Lost, hurt, and alone, how could I help him if I was just a mirage?

I ducked behind a branch as a girl with long, dark hair ran through the neighboring trees and stopped only feet from us. I relaxed and laughed as I stared at my teenage self, leaning on my knees after chasing a stupid deer into the woods.

I breathed a sigh of relief. *It's only me. He's going to be fine.*

But fear still seized David. He gripped the log behind him and closed his eyes, fingering his jaw just below his camouflage implant. Triggering the change was a last resort. No pilot with an ounce of their senses intact would do so unless there was no other option.

The girl pulled back the branches. He inched lower behind the log as she threw dirt over the remains of the fire that had warmed him through the night. His last chance to remain hidden disappeared as she stood, and looked into the trees around them.

Calling on the countless training sessions no pilot ever dreamed they'd use, he reached into her thoughts and removed a vision of another native from her mind, a being who would comfort her.

There was no turning back now. No room for the terror rising in his gut. David took a deep breath, and bit down on the implant. The burst tingled in his jaw before exploding through his frame, driving searing pain through every cell of his body. I gasped as David's agony lanced through me. My teenage-self fell to her knees, screaming.

God, the pain, how had I endured it?

David curled into a ball, howling at my feet as a light bronze membrane crept over his beautiful violescent skin, and jet-black hair formed over his bare scalp.

"Are you okay?" the other Jess asked, peering over the log.

The rainbow swirled around me again, dropping me beside

David shivering on my living room couch, and the thermometer breaking. What an idiot I'd been. How could I not have known? Not that any normal person would have thought he was from another planet, but I should have questioned more. I should have …

I forced myself to stop second-guessing myself and warmed, watching David's expression soften as we spent more time together. His thoughts strayed less and less to the horror of facing Sabbotaruo after another failure.

Something about him changed. Strengthened.

This was when it happened—when David decided Earth was worth saving. He loved me, I realized, far earlier than I'd fallen head over heels for him.

All his past problems melted into a single sense of purpose: saving Earth. And he hadn't strayed from his new mission since.

How could he ever have thought himself weak? He'd saved me. He'd saved everyone.

Flash. The broken pavement crunched beneath our feet as we stepped into the blinding illumination of a liquescent spaceship.

David stiffened, searching through my mind and realizing I had no intention of facing the Caretakers with him to plead mercy for Earth.

"Don't do this," he said. "Come with me."

"No, David." Jess shook her head. "If I'm here, I know you'll work harder to keep me safe."

A deep pain riddled his chest. Didn't she understand? He couldn't focus if she was in danger. And if he failed, and she was still on Earth … No. That wasn't a scenario he could deal with. He couldn't face the possibility of losing someone he cared about. Not again.

"You'll be safe with me on the ship." His vision clouded as he faced the inevitable. He wouldn't be able to save her. He wouldn't be able to save any of them. The meeting with the Caretakers was a formality, a sign of good grace. They'd already made their decision.

Humanity would be eradicated before their moon rose again.

He quivered as she took his face in her hands and kissed him. Her touch, so gentle, so caring. His entire life had revolved around what his superiors wanted, or what his father demanded. He did their bidding, but at a distance. This—this touching, this contact wasn't something he was willing to give up. But how could he save her when her world was about to end?

She deepened the kiss, and her soul opened to him, she lay bare, vulnerable. His shoulders tensed as he gripped her and eased into her mind. It would be so simple, too simple to take control, to make her board the ship.

She sighed within their kiss, relaxing even more into his embrace as her mind relinquished itself to him.

He lightened his grip. No. He couldn't take her like this. He wouldn't force her. Not in this, not in anything.

He tried to break the kiss, but she deepened it, drawing him in. He felt himself slip, his mind baring itself. Opening. Drawing itself to her.

No! He tried to back off, to control his mind's need to reach out, to hold, to become one with this overwhelming rush of security and devotion.

Something snapped, and David gasped within their kiss as everything that was Jess rushed over him in a flurry of calming bliss.

She released the kiss, and David stared into her eyes. He could still feel her. Sense her.

He shivered, but not from Earth's cool temperatures. It was an accident. He hadn't meant to connect them, but he was fairly certain that was what he'd done. But she was human. It shouldn't have been possible.

She relaxed into his embrace, and the shock of what he'd done washed away in her warm sigh. She'd be angry with him when she broke from this stupor, and she'd have every right to be. Connection was reserved for intended mates, a pre-engagement of minds before the irrevocable bond that tied female and male together until their death. Oh, yes, this headstrong human girl would be angry, but he'd deal with that later. Now, he needed her on his ship. Safe. And maybe, just maybe, he could save her, and her people.

"Come with me," he whispered.

A flood of joy swirled through him as they slowly backed toward the ship. She didn't fight. She wanted to come. She wanted him.

He'd forgotten what it felt like to have someone care, to feel the strength of another through a simple emotional bond. How had he lived without that for so long?

She ran her fingers through the amber glow of the ship's entry portal. The lighting sparkled through her hair as the long, dark strands shifted in the breeze. He'd never tire of watching that.

"Are you ready?" David asked.

She responded with another kiss. He soaked her in, reveling in the intensity of their already growing bond. Until she tensed within his arms.

Tears streamed from her eyes as she pushed him away. "Save my planet, David. Keep me safe."

"Jess, no." But she backed away and stumbled into the arms of her father.

Every cell in his body called to her, tugging, pulling her back with all the strength of the newly established link between them, but she wasn't Erescopian, and maybe couldn't even be connected.

He shuddered. She might not be susceptible to connection, but he was. And he had no way to undo what he'd done.

I reached my hand to my mouth as I watched my younger self back away. The look on my face should have told him that the connection between us had taken hold.

No wonder I'd felt like my entire body had imploded as I left him. No wonder I couldn't stop thinking about him, even years later.

Somewhere deep within I wanted to be angry, but I couldn't. Our connection hadn't been intentional, but it was inevitable.

I'd opened to him. I'd let him in. I had complete trust in David, more so than anyone else in my life.

My lips parted, drinking in that thought. Maybe we were connected in a normal, human way, even before this night.

A deep dread filled me, a wave of disappointment and rejection like no other. I blinked, my eyes watering as Dad drew the other Jess further from the ship.

David reached out his hand, then lowered it, fighting the raging pull driving him toward her. He took a step, but stopped himself. She'd made her choice. This wasn't her fault. It was his. He'd lost her, like everything else in his life he'd ever cared about.

"No!" I screamed.

I ran to him, trying to stop him from getting on the ship, but again my arms melted right through him.

Why didn't he understand? I loved him more than anything, but I couldn't leave Earth. I couldn't take the risk. Couldn't he see that?

Flash. Teams of scientists flocked to David's side. Mars. They would build a new home for his people. Younger Erescopians stared wide-eyed, listening and tapping on computer pads as David spoke to the group.

I smiled. This was where he belonged. This was his element. He had so much to give. Why didn't he see that?

Flash. We stood in a dark room, but I could see almost as well as if it were daytime.

Teenage Jess spun, holding her arms out as if searching the dark. "David?"

"Shhh." He gently caressed her shoulders and ran his violescent hands down the arms of her shirt. She gasped.

David winced, releasing her. "Did I hurt you?"

"No."

She's lying. My touch burned her, probably worse than the icy sting of her fingers on me. Nematali Carash was right. Even if our people would allow it, we could never be together. We are too different.

"That's not true!" I screamed, but neither of them could hear me. This was the day I met him on his ship, the day when I'd made a horrible mistake.

The other me turned and grabbed his wrist.

"I don't want to hurt you." He pretended to tug away, not really wanting to rescind the touch.

"You're not hurting me." Jess pulled him closer and ran her hands down his chest. David trembled. Her touch, so cold, but he drank in every painful second, not wanting it to end.

He took her hand and brushed their cheeks together, releasing the joy that swelled within him upon seeing her again—seeing *me* again.

So, he hadn't made it up, he really did miss me. I gulped down a sob as their lips met. An embarrassing little whimper escaped the younger me. She nearly collapsed in his arms, and had to hold myself steady as a rolling need swelled up over David and tore through our bond, making me back up a step.

The longing, the desire, the need to give himself over completely, the yearning to be part of someone who loved him without judgement or prejudice ... the swelling hunger pressed and congealed, filling us with pride, assurance, devotion. David reeled in his feelings, fearful he might burst and ...

Jess ran her fingers up his neck and gasped, backing away when she found his scalp bare. The onslaught of emotions slapped out of him as if stripped from my flesh with a whip.

"David, I'm sorry."

Everything that was good slid away, forcing him back into the corner like a small child, waiting to be beaten by an angry parent. *She's not sorry. She doesn't want me. She probably never did.*

"Wait!" My own voice rattled though the dark room. I knew

I'd hurt David that day, but I had no idea how much. He'd dealt with so much pain from his father, no wonder he'd reacted like that when he'd thought I only cared about his looks.

Flash.

David was human now, at least on the outside. He sat on the metal table in the same room where he'd initiated the change into human form for the second time in his life. He held his gut, gasping for air.

Nematali sneered, bearing down on him. "*I told you seeing her again was a mistake. You need to find a way to sever this connection before it is too late. Both your lives depend on it.*" She spoke in Erescopian, but I understood every word.

David looked up, still holding his stomach. "*I need her.*"

Nematali's eyes narrowed. "*She is human. It can never be.*"

Flash.

David's grip tightened around Jess as we stood at the entrance to the ship that would take him to Mars, probably for good this time. His deep need to save my people smothered the searing desire to not let go, to lose himself in this now familiar luxury of touch.

His fingers ran aside her temple. "You will be on my mind every moment."

Jess smirked. "Well you better think of some of the brilliant scientist stuff now and again, too, or people are gonna be pretty peeved."

David flinched. I hadn't noticed at the time. Always ready with the smart comeback, I probably ruined a special goodbye for him. What an ass I was.

Nematali's nose flared before she looked away. I'd had no idea that she'd told David to keep away from me. No wonder she'd looked so ticked.

David straightened when his eyes fell on her icy gaze. He cleared his throat, kissed my temple, and walked away.

I'd been hurt by that almost-a-kiss. But David's mind screamed, demanded his return with every step he took. He'd wanted to hold me, kiss me, take his time. But she'd ruined that, forcing him to keep his distance.

I'm sorry, he whispered within his mind. *This isn't how I wanted to say goodbye.*

We tumbled through a kaleidoscope, and landed in another classroom. Dozens of young Erescopian faces looked up at him. The scene hadn't changed much since our last visit, but the glow in David's eyes had dulled. His musculature had thinned. His posture slackened. Mars's survival hinged on his every decision. The weight and responsibility aged him to the core. One wrong calculation …

Flash.

David punched a wall. "*The theories are sound. I need more time*," he shouted in Erescopian.

Sabbotaruo scowled, leaning close. "*You've had more than enough time. The Mars project is terminated. You will redirect your efforts on warming Earth after the removal of the humans.*"

Trembling slightly, David straightened himself. "*I won't do it.*"

The larger man hissed, charging at his son. A huge hand constricted around David's neck, throwing David against a wall and holding him there, feet dangling.

"Let go!" I tried to punch the larger alien, but my hand went right through him. David's eyes bulged. "Dammit, David, fight him!" But how could he? His father dwarfed both of us.

A growl erupted from Sabbotaruo's throat. "*I have had enough of you and your empty promises. If you were not my son, I would have jettisoned you with the trash years ago.*"

David struggled as the huge man lifted him higher.

"*Make no mistake, boy. If you do not hand me Earth, I will personally hold you down while the Caretakers gut you alive. Is that understood?*"

David nodded, gasping in his father's grip.

Sabbotaruo snorted before releasing him. "*Know that my*

promises are not empty. No amount of begging or screaming will award you with a quick death if you fail again." Backing away with a final disdainful twist in his lip, Sabbotaruo disappeared into a wall.

Sobbing, David slid to the ground.

"*I did everything right,*" he whispered. "*Why didn't it rain?*"

Swirls of dark foreboding pressed in on all sides. David rocked on the floor, holding his head.

"Hold on!" I knelt beside him. "You can do this. You can still save Earth."

"No," he whispered to the floor. "I'm not good enough. I never have been." He raised his gaze, but he seemed to look right through me. "Jess is probably better off without me. Maybe they all are."

I tried to punch him. "We're not better off without you. We're not!"

"I can't do it. I can't save my people and her, too." He pressed his temples, tears streaming from his eyes. "No matter what I do one of us ends up extinct."

"You figured it out! We're going to make it rain. Don't give up. You can't!"

He lifted his head. "Jess?"

Holy crap! I moved beside him. "Yes, I'm here."

He seemed to scan the room, before his gaze centered on me. The pain, the agony, the deep sense of loss radiating through that gaze—

Part of me chipped away and died, floated off into the far reaches of space. I shuddered, fighting the desire to look away.

But I couldn't.

I wouldn't.

David needed me, maybe now more than ever.

"It doesn't matter," he said. "Nothing about me matters." He closed his eyes.

"That's not true." I grabbed for his hands and pretended to hold them even though we couldn't touch.

David shook his head. "A man is only the sum of his deeds, and I am the sum of nothing." He blinked and centered on me again. "I am nothing."

The rainbow exploded, assaulting and burning as the colors twisted around me. I screamed, covering my face.

"No. No. No. No. No!" I bellowed into the void.

The pain, the loss, the weight of two planets pressed me into the looming obscurity. I struggled to breath. The pressure. Too much.

I reached into the darkness, and gasped when a vision of my own face appeared.

My eyes popped open, stinging in the light of our liquescent ship. I struggled to inhale.

David knelt before me, just as I'd left him; arms extended and hands still clinging to mine. His head lolled between his shoulders as he quaked, sobbing.

I knew he'd had a difficult life. At least I thought I knew. What he'd been through—failure after failure, loss after loss. How could anyone have endured such suffering?

"That's it," he said. "That's everything there is to see."

David trembled, not just outwardly, but on the inside. His soul, still laid bare before me, pulsed, reaching for me. I thought of setting him free—of releasing his hands and just staying connected. No one needed to know anyone else this well. Complete openness, it was wrong, but also so incredibly right.

Everything that was me still radiated from within, but his energy coursed through and around me. Intermingling. His strength burned with a power, a will to survive, a need to succeed. We were so much more alike than I'd realized.

I drew a slow breath, calling on everything he'd shown me. My heart swelled. Small holes within me filled. Where I was weak, he was strong. Was that what he meant about drawing on each other's strength?

I vibrated, suddenly feeling more alive than I'd ever been. Yes,

David was broken, but maybe, deep down, we both were.

At that moment, I felt more complete than I ever had, but David's failures still consumed him. Why hadn't I healed him as he'd healed me? There must be more—something I missed.

I dove back inside him, searching for a speck of truth within the scrolling chaos of his thoughts. I found a spark and grabbed onto it. The tiny ember flickered, grew, and brightened in my grasp.

It warmed. He warmed, building off the strength I held inside.

David had a glow within him, one that had always been there. But no one had taken hold and guided him on how to keep it alight after his mother died.

Until now.

Until we found each other.

Without me, he wasn't whole. Together we succeeded, because I was a part of him. I was his missing link, his lucky charm, and the one person who believed in him no matter what.

Sometimes, all you need is someone to believe in you.

David's tear-soaked eyes rose to meet mine. He gulped. His gaze wavered over our hands. "You can let go if you want to. I would understand."

I tightened my grip on his fingers. "I'm never letting go. I want this. I want *you*."

He inhaled, and the tears that had pooled in his lashes trailed down his cheeks. "B-but you've seen me. You know, now—I have no value. I have no accomplishments to offer you."

I placed a gentle kiss on the back of each of his hands, keeping a death grip on our contact. "You saved my planet twice, and you're about to save it again. You risked your own life to save mine. You broke your people's trust and followed your heart. I don't care how your people rate accomplishment. You're everything to me."

Still shaking, he straightened. "S-so, y-you want to stay inside me?"

I shivered. As much as I wanted to say yes, the real answer was no. There was too much darkness. Unless …

Squinting, I shot myself back in. I barreled through David like a ball of white radiance, smashing away any dark, constricting shapes, driving them to the farthest recesses of his existence.

You don't need to dwell on the past. I'm here, now. We can face anything together, we've proven that. Cling to our new memories. Cling to me.

David's energy encompassed me, swirling in a wave of sleek, unadulterated violet joy. I cried out and felt my head loll as the purple hue brightened, joining with my glow until we faded into one.

A dark shape loomed just above our combined brilliance. I tightened my grip on David as the relentless sense of Sabbotaruo shrouded over us. I prepared to move my light between them, but David's glow brightened, beating the dread of his father back until the shape faded into a speck in the distance. A memory—an important one, but no longer the focus of his life.

I opened my eyes, and my gaze fell on sparkling, turquoise irises.

David's smile rivaled any star. "He's held me back for years. You gave me the strength to do that." He touched our foreheads together. "I can't believe you still wanted me after you saw so much darkness."

"No biggie. You just needed a little house cleaning."

David laughed—a bright, tinkling sound that raised goose bumps across my skin.

I'd experience his emotions on several occasions, but always skipping along the edge of our tether, never so full, crisp, and real. His joy seeped into me; opening places I thought had closed.

But I couldn't be closed again. At least not to him.

I shuddered, realizing the vulnerability and strength in that notion. This was as close as I'd ever been to another person. And there probably wasn't a human way to get any closer. Not that I wanted one. Nothing could compare to being inside someone. Nothing.

He eased his hands to my waist. A mischievous grin played on the edge of his lip. "In our culture, you are supposed to consult with your parents before sharing yourself. My father is going to be very angry."

The heat in his stare overcame me. He wasn't worried about his father. Not at all. His thoughts, his senses, his everything, centered on me. Nothing but me.

My hands itched, yearning to draw him closer. Instead, I leaned toward him, tasting the warmth radiating from his mouth. "I don't want to talk about your father anymore."

"Neither do I."

28

His palm slid up the back of my shirt. The heat of his touch tingled, forcing my back to arch as his lips covered mine. Sweet euphoria settled into every pore, opening me up to a dull ache that blotted out all reasoning but my need for more. I combed my fingers through his hair, guiding his kisses down my throat and holding him right over the quivering, needy place near my collarbone. A slight moan escaped my lips as the heat of his tongue played cruel games with my skin, taunting as his breath ignited my core.

I pulled my tee-shirt over my head and threw the rolled up ball of cotton to the floor.

David's gaze dropped right to my chest. He gaped. Hesitated.

No. No hesitation. Not after what we just shared. I reached for him, but he backed away.

He held up his hands. "I don't want to hurt you."

I reached for him again and ran my hands across his solid, rolling abs. "Just keep your shirt on and we'll be safe, right?"

He nodded, his gaze drifting back to my cleavage. "This might not be the best time to admit that I'm not exactly sure what to do.

I mean, I read a few things, but … "

I propped up onto my knees and inched closer. "What do you want to do?"

A sweet, reluctant grin crossed his face. "You know I like the kissing thing, and I'm getting fonder of the touching every day." He trailed his fingers up my side, resting his hand just below my shoulder.

He lingered, trembling, his gaze frozen on his hand. My sweet, shy little alien. I could sense his mind rolling as his knuckles brushed the satiny side of my bra. Should he, or shouldn't he?

Oh, he should. He definitely, definitely should.

I placed a kiss beside his ear. "If you know what you like, then go with it."

His mouth claimed mine. His tongue glided and burned while his hands traced, stroked, and caressed, learning every inch of me. David's touch was like fire, a needy, consuming creature delving into the depths of the unknown. Everything I ever wanted, needed, or longed for washed over me in a fluttering wave of unconscious, streaming warmth; sliding, molding, and becoming part of me.

I stretched back on the couch, coaxing him atop me. David's weight, his heat, ignited me all over again. His kisses trailed down my neck, down my chest, lingering for several seconds between the cups of my bra.

Twisting, I fumbled for the straps, but David had already moved south, placing gentle, precise kisses around my navel.

His spine twitched. A deep pressure sweltered over me, rocketing through my center until my body cried out, begging for it to stop, but not wanting it to end.

With a guttural growl, he pulled me into a sitting position. I reached for another kiss, and he nipped my lips and tasted my tongue, drawing me deeper into him.

How had I lived without this for so many years: alone, lost, and devoid of the intensity of true, undeniable connection? This was breath, life, everything I needed to survive.

He lifted me with one hand, placing me on his lap without breaking the kiss. I straddled him, drawing our bodies closer, forcing two to become one. A slight whimper slipped from his lips as I smoothed my hands up his back, forcing our chests together as he ran his lips across my shoulder.

His hands glided up my sides, his fingers slipping beneath my bra. The heat of his hands ... so close.

Dammit, who needed a bra anyway?

I reached back to unhook the clasps and opened my eyes, ready to drink him in; but a grimace twisted David's face, draining the heat from my skin. A haunting ache coated my soul as he tried to cover the expression with a false smile.

"What's wrong?"

His gaze darted to his stomach, where twin ridges along either side of his abdomen strained his tight cotton tee-shirt.

He winced. "I'm sorry. I-I'm sorry."

"Again?" I reached for his shirt, but he backed away. "Does it really hurt that bad?"

Wrapping his arms around his abdomen, he closed his eyes. "They're trying to break through the artificial skin. It stings."

"Why didn't you stop?"

David curled his shoulders. "You were enjoying it."

"Well, I wouldn't have been enjoying it if I knew I was hurting you."

He puffed out a half-hearted laugh. "I thought I could get through it." His face contorted worse than the first time. "Maybe this was a mistake. Maybe all of this was."

I grabbed his face, turning him toward me. "No. We're not a mistake. None of this is wrong. It can't be."

"But they were right. We can't ever be together the way you want."

"The way I want? What does that mean?"

"No more secrets, remember? You want ... this." Still clutching his stomach with one arm, he moved his free hand between the two of us. "A human relationship."

"No, I don't." ... despite the panting and moaning and all that other stuff, but I'd thought he was enjoying it, too!

"You crave human touch."

"We've been through this already. I crave *your* touch."

He turned away. "And that's why we can't be together." His fingers trailed across the alien ridges in his torso. "My touch can hurt you."

The demonic bumps mocked me, but I wasn't about to give in so easily. "This didn't happen back on the green planet. Did I do something different? Just let me know and I'll stop."

He shook his head. "It's not you. I told you, I'm getting older. My body wants to mate. It's instinct. I'm not sure I'll ever be able to control it."

I nestled his cheek to my shoulder. "We'll figure it out."

"How? We were born millions of miles away from each other for a reason. We were never meant to be together." He leaned back. "We shouldn't have done this. Nematali was right. This is a childish dream."

I kneaded my fingers through his hair and drew him back, pressing our foreheads together. "I don't want to hear about numbers, and I don't care about species. I know how I feel. This isn't a crush. It's real. We'll find a way. We have to find a way."

"It's too hard."

"Anything really worth living for is hard."

He took a stagnated breath. "If I ever hurt you ... "

"Then don't." I ran my fingers over the ridges. A few pricked my fingers. "I want to see."

David shook his head. "They scare you."

I gritted my teeth. That must have been something else he'd seen inside me. I didn't think I was going to like this no-secrets stuff. "Then let's call this me embracing my fears."

I lifted his shirt. The protrusions strained his human skin, showing signs of the violescence beneath. Tiny swirling needles poked out of several of the mounds, squirming and searching like the arms of a strange alien sea anemone. My heart pummeled. My muscles tensed.

He tugged his shirt down. "I don't think they'd get through the cotton. I would have stopped if they did."

I sat back. "So that's how you, umm, attach?"

He ran his fingers along my bare stomach. "Our females aren't soft like this. Their skin is thick, like a hide. This part of me is made to … Umm … "

"I think I get it." A thousand little needles ready to rip into my skin and hold on for dear life, like a leech biting down and …

David cringed.

Leech—very bad analogy, Jess. "I didn't mean that. I'm sorry."

"I know."

I pulled my top back on. "There you go. Double protection." Some couples used condoms, we'd use shirts. Problem solved. "But next time you tell me if it starts to hurt, okay? We can take a break."

Blue tainted his cheek.

"What's wrong?"

"You make me feel … "

"What?"

"I can't find a word in English."

"Closest thing?"

"Warm. Cared for."

All the things he didn't get from his good-for-nothing father. My dad was a pest sometimes, but at least he cared. I'd never take him for granted again.

If I had the chance.

I laid down and closed my eyes.

David eased next to me and snuggled me to his shoulder.

"We're going to save him," David whispered.

"I know."

29

The sound of David's shallow, rhythmic breathing cradled me on the edge of sleep. Someday I'd wake like this on a Saturday morning with no worries whatsoever—some day when the world didn't need saving.

A shriek jolted me awake, followed by a weight thomping on my chest. Three blurry black eyes loomed above me.

"Edgar?"

Another warbling trill filled the room as his mandibles gnashed a few inches from my face. David sat up beside me.

"What's wrong with him?" I asked.

"How would I know?"

Yawning, David stumbled to the control panel. Edgar jumped off me and bounded past him, sinking his front two legs into the giant vat of gelatin. The walls burst into flashing, quaking light.

David nodded. "I see it."

"You see what?"

"Our passengers are in trouble."

He moved to the back of the room and tapped on the wall. The couch dissolved into the floor as I stood. Edgar scurried across the tiles and poked his leg into the swirling surface beside David. The walls flashed again.

"Give me a second," David said. "I'm trying to figure it out."

I moved to the back of the room and stood beside them.

Edgar chortled, his back legs tapping against my side of the console. The walls continued to flash.

"I know." David sat back in his chair. "I just can't get to them."

"What's wrong?" I asked.

"The pressure is destabilizing. The rear enzyme inhibitors have backed into the reflux system."

I chewed on that for a second. "And I take it that's bad."

He nodded. "Lack of pressure to them is the inverse of too much pressure on us. We would get crushed, but they can't hold together ... just like when Ruby was helpless on the rocks."

"Not good. Are they okay?"

"Right now they're all unconscious." His gaze perused the wall. "There is a juncture in the reflux system that acts like a valve. It needs to open and close every few seconds to keep the pressure stable in the tanks holding our friends." He rubbed his face. "The enzymes have clogged the valve."

"Can we unclog it?"

"Normally, yes, it's no problem. All it would take is going down there and turning a knob, but I reinforced the hull all around those tanks so the liquescent fortifications wouldn't burst under the strain of all that water." He pursed his lips. "The walls can't be liquefied, and neither can the maintenance tubes. I can't make them big enough so I can get down there."

Edgar reared up on his hind legs.

"Can Edgar fit?"

"Yes. There's only one problem."

Edgar raised his front four legs, waving his pointy feet.

"No opposable thumbs."

I flopped into my chair. "Why would they design part of the ship that a *grassen* can't manipulate?"

David smiled. "Simple. Enzymes are organic and good eating. It would be like waving those potato chip things in your face and telling you that you couldn't open the bag."

Potato chips. He had to remind me that the last thing I had to eat was seaweed.

David's eyes narrowed. He plucked a silvery package out of a wall beside him and threw it to me. I popped it open and leaves fell out. Figures. I guess a hamburger was too much to ask for.

The walls flashed five times before Edgar jumped up on my back and pawed at my shoulders, cooing at David.

"I'm not sending her down there." David turned and tapped on the console.

Edgar growled; his eyes set on me.

"Wait. Would I fit?"

"Probably. But you don't know how to navigate a liquescent environment."

"I thought it was a tube."

"It is, but you have to get through several liquescent walls first, and remember, the only place with air breathable is this chamber."

I set the leaves on the console. "Can I wear a mask?"

The muscles in his neck flinched. "You don't even know what you're looking for."

"Edgar can show me. All you need are my thumbs, right?" I wiggled my fingers. "Well, I have two. Let me help."

Edgar jumped beside David. The walls shimmered in a new set of colors.

David ran his fingers through his hair as his gaze bore through Edgar. "You don't understand. If anything happens, I won't be able to get to you."

The walls flashed yellow and a hint of green.

David slammed his fist on the edge of the panel in the wall.

"What do you mean *what could happen*? It's me and Jess. Something *always* happens!"

I turned from him. "Come on, Edgar."

"Where do you think you are going?"

My hands shot to my hips. "To save our friends."

David closed his eyes, shaking his head. "I knew you were going to say that."

"Then help me with that mask and let's get going."

***

I breathed deeply through my nose as the mask formed around my face. How insane was it that I was starting to get used to all this crazy science fiction stuff?

"Just please, stay with Edgar. Don't fall through any walls."

"I won't." Of course, I didn't think I'd fall through a wall two years ago on the Ambassador's ship, and that certainly led to no good.

David half-smiled and brushed his thumb against my cheek. "I just want you safe."

"I want me safe, too." I flashed an *I'll be fine* grin and followed my little arachnid buddy into the wall.

The chill of the liquescent metal hit my cheeks. I'd always wondered how David could stand the cold inside these partitions. He acted like he couldn't even feel it. So much about his people was still a mystery. One I'd like to unravel if he'd stick around long enough—and if my planet was still in one piece when we got back.

I shivered. Thoughts like that certainly weren't helping.

Blind in the murky dark, Edgar tapped my ankles, guiding me through the void of frigid nothing.

I oozed out of the goo into a plain, gray space not much bigger than my closet. Edgar chittered beside a hole in the wall about two feet in diameter. My stomach plunged into my socks.

I had to go *in there?*

You can do this, I told myself. *Ruby and Silver need you.*

Edgar disappeared into the shadowy orifice as I got to my hands and knees and slithered inside. The *grassen's* glowing eyes lit up the passageway, shadowing his rear and his spindly legs. Four years ago the sight of a giant spider's rear-end in the dark would have horrified me. Now I found his spindly legs and hairy, segmented shape oddly comforting—like crawling into a pit with my best friend.

My hair skidded along the top of the tube, and if I shifted more than an inch or so to either side, my shoulders bumped the rounded walls. I tried not to think of the little creepy crawly things that might be hiding in there with me. Didn't David say once that *grassen* ate rodents? Were these tunnels where alien rats hung out?

Definitely time for a new train of thought, Jess.

Dragging along with my elbows and shimmying my hips, I followed Edgar further inside. I took a deep breath and let it out slowly, ducking as the tunnel seemed to dip and tighten around me. My heart began to pound within my ears. The tunnel shrank, pressing closer.

Oh God. I was going to get stuck. What was I thinking?

Holding my breath, I inched further and closed my eyes. Trickles of strength seeped into me. David?

Yes, it was definitely David. I drew in a deep breath, let it out slowly, and opened my eyes. The walls weren't closing in. It was my imagination. Was this what he meant by drawing on each other's strength?

I looked down the tunnel, this time with no fear. Edgar spun and chirped at me before continuing on his way. We were going to make it, but it occurred to me that unless this tunnel opened up some, I'd have to reverse-shimmy to get out. That didn't sound like fun. But I could do it. Piece of cake.

Edgar stopped, clicked his mandibles, and shone his laser vision on a slick protrusion in the wall.

"Is that the knob?"

He bobbed his head up and down in an adorable replica of how he'd probably seen David and I respond to each other.

Okay. This was what the primate was here for. "Let's do this."

I reached over with my left hand and gripped the knob. The handle shifted, sinking into the wall with my fingers still attached.

"Was that supposed to happen?"

Edgar raised two upturned feet. That must have been the *grassen* version of *I don't know*.

Great. Just great.

Completely off balance, and unable to find any leverage, I worked my fingers around the knob.

"Why did it sink? I thought this part of the ship wasn't liquescent anymore?"

A click reverberated in the walls.

"Jess, get out of there." David's voice boomed through the tube.

"What? Why?"

"Something's wrong. The walls are softening."

"So what?"

"There's an artificial ocean a foot to your left. If that wall gives, you'll be flooded."

And these breathing masks don't work if they get wet. Why couldn't anything ever be easy?

"Can I still turn the knob? Will it still help?"

"I don't know. We're looking at complete systems failure. It's the water. Without the extra pressure holding that room together, the weight per square inch ratio is too much for the liquescence. We're losing molecular stability in that section."

"Is that like losing cohesion?"

"If you are right there when it happens, it will be pretty close. Come back now. We'll find another way."

And in the meantime, Ruby and Silver, Earth's only chance of survival, were suffocating on the other side of that wall.

No. I couldn't let them down.

I shoved my arm deeper into the wall and found the slick knob again. It was more like the rounded end of a cylinder than a doorknob like I'd expected. My fingers slid across the surface, doing a whole lot of nothing.

"Jess, why aren't you moving?"

"We can still do this. Give me a chance."

"You're out of time. Get out. Edgar, get her out of there!"

My little buddy tapped his one silver leg beside me, but didn't move.

"Thanks for backing me up," I whispered.

I withdrew my hand, wiped the goop on the bottom of the tunnel, and shoved my fingers back inside. This time I met a little friction and the cylinder turned a fraction of an inch.

The wall to my left creaked and moaned. That couldn't be good.

My hand slipped, but I tightened my grip, grunting as I turned.

"Come on, you stupid piece of crap. Turn, dammit!"

The cylinder gave, spinning until my knuckles hit a hard barrier, scrapping my skin. Oww.

David's voice clicked back on. "You guys, you did it! The pressure is stabilizing."

The creak to my left increased.

"Is that what I'm hearing?"

"What do you mean?"

"There's some kind of creaking noise."

Edgar started trilling like a grasshopper on steroids. He ran at me, climbing on my hair.

"Ouch! What are you doing?"

David's voice seeped through the walls. "What's going on?"

"Edgar's gone all crazy!"

I flattened myself down and let him crawl over me. WTF?

A thump echoed through the tube, and a fizzy splash hit my hand.

Water?

Water!

"David! The wall cracked. Water is coming in!"

"Get out! The whole thing is going to cave in!"

The salty draught splashed into my face. I tried to shimmy backward as the sounds of a manic jabbering *grassen* fought against the roaring waves. Weren't things bad enough?

My mask stuck to my face.

Oh, no. If it gets wet …

I sucked in the deepest breath of my life and held it just before the water surged over my head.

I pushed backward, trying to use buoyancy to my advantage. It didn't help much.

How far had we crawled? Would I be able to find my way out on my own?

The sensations of prickly hairs itched against my ankles. What was Edgar doing?

Something hard grazed my skin before a searing pain blasted through my ankle. I screamed, releasing some air. I smashed my hand to my mouth when I'd realized what I'd done. I started moving backward at turbo speed. I closed my eyes as I rolled over four times. How long could I hold on with no oxygen in my lungs? The dizziness gave me my answer. I had to inhale. I had to open my mouth.

Vise grips clamped around both my ankles, wrenching me back even faster. Rescued from the tube, I free floated in the dark until humanoid hands grasped my shoulders. David?

He ripped the mask from my face and brought his lips to mine, puffing air into my lungs. My body relished in the gift as he grabbed my wrist and propelled off the bottom and into the spongy cold of the wall. The liquid metal pressed down on us a hundred times harder than before, terrifyingly reminiscent of the walls solidifying around us as the Ambassador's ship died two years ago.

But we weren't going to make it this time. We were out of luck.

Stop thinking that, David's voice boomed in my head.

Can't breathe.

Hold on!

David yanked my arm, and we broke through the partition. He splatted to the floor in front of me. I stumbled and fell beside him, gasping. My head started to clear as the oxygen soaked into my lungs.

We inched off the slick tiles as Edgar scampered out of the wall. A splash of water spilled out with him before the partition resealed. The little *grassen* backed himself into a corner and shook glistening droplets from his hairy midsection. I wrung out my hair and panted, hardly believing we'd all made it out.

The shimmering ivory partition solidified into a stiff, aluminum gray as David hopped to his feet and sprinted to the control panel. I willed myself to move, but all I could do was breathe.

Edgar flopped beside me, panting. His three long fangs slowly retracted into the roof of his mouth. I rolled up my soaking pant leg and perused the bleeding wounds on my ankle. He'd bit me and dragged me back through the tunnel. The little dude had saved my life.

David reclined in his seat, facing the ceiling and breathing heavily.

I crawled across the floor and into the chair beside him. "What happened back there?"

"The water. Too much weight. It was starting to give before you restored the pressure." His chest rose in a huff. "I had to solidify most of the ship to keep the rest contained. It's going to be like flying in the pre-molecular era."

"Ruby and Silver?"

"They're okay from what I can tell. They just have a lot less mobility in the main chamber. We need to get them out of there as soon as possible."

"Can we still make it to Mars?"

He waved over the console, and the dark film coating the windows disappeared, revealing a huge red and blue marble hanging in space, nearly filling the glass.

"We're here! We made it!"

David nodded. "There's only one problem. We can't land."

30

"What do you mean we can't land?"

David leaned on his knees and held the sides of his head. "These ships are made to flex when entering a planet's atmosphere. Without a liquescent hull, there's nothing to diffuse the friction on reentry."

News footage of flames lapping NASA landing pods flashed through my thoughts. "How bad will it be?"

"The liquescence is part of the environmental controls. Solid, like we are now, the temperature inside will double every second."

The red and blue planet spun gently below us, deceptively warm and inviting. "Can you make us liquescent, just until we break through?"

"Not if we want to hold on to all that water."

The memory of Ruby's boneless, squashed bulk on the dry rocks flashed through my mind. And with so many of them trapped in such a small space, they'd probably crush each other.

No. We couldn't risk it. We needed to keep the ship solid.

"Are you sure the temperatures will rise that fast? Can't you adjust the pitch or something?"

"You can't change physics. We either risk losing the water, or boiling them alive."

Not to mention cooking the crew within five seconds, if I'd calculated correctly. But the planet was right there. There had to be a way.

Three Erescopian ships moved into view, blocking the blue and red planet from our sight. The space between us blurred, and our ship rumbled.

"Are they shooting at us?"

David sunk his wrists into the console. "Of course they are. Why wouldn't they be?"

The sarcasm in his voice bit through the air. His eyes narrowed. Grim, but determined.

I turned back to the window just as white, sparkling streams drifted from below us, glinting in the light from our ship.

"What is that?" I asked.

Edgar jumped onto the console. Several more lines of shiny crystals floated past us. The walls began to flash.

"I see it." David turned to me. "They've punched a hole in our hull. It's the water. It freezes almost instantly in space."

"We're leaking?" Did Ruby and Silver know? Were they panicking?

A tint of blue shimmered beneath David's human skin. "We have no protection against their weapons in our solid state."

Another blast, and the ship jolted. I grabbed the console to keep my head from slamming into the dashboard. We obviously had more to worry about than just losing the water.

Alien symbols scrolled across the screen as we banked right, moving away from the planet.

I held the sides of my chair. "Where are we going?"

"Away from the guys who are shooting at us."

"Just tell them that we can make it rain!"

He tapped the controls. "I'm working on it."

We spiraled between two small, dark opals. My seat swelled around me a second before another jolt rattled the ship. A stream of bubbles fizzled out from beneath us, quickly dissipating into sparkling crystals. More water wasted in space. How much was down there?

The walls quaked again. More alien symbols crawled across the screen. Was that us pleading *"don't shoot,"* or them telling us to surrender? I supposed at this point, it really didn't matter.

Ruby sprang up between our chairs, smaller than before and slightly transparent. "The water is nearly gone. Some of us are getting crushed."

David faced her, the pain in his eyes ricocheted through our bond.

Failure. Death.

I guess we both knew the chances of this working were slim.

"We can't give up." I grimaced. *Even if we don't make it home.*

Ruby gaped as four ships barreled toward us, artillery blazing. She shimmered before her form faded to a puff of gas.

The lights dimmed when the armaments hit us. I held on as we spun to the right. Why did they keep firing? We were on the same side!

When the light returned, we arched to the left, almost clipping two of the advancing opals before Mars came back into view. More liquescent vessels came from our sides as we rocketed toward the planet. My God, how many ships were they going to send after us?

Edgar shrieked as a dark opal cut in front of our bow, blocking our path. David didn't slow. I screamed, bracing myself as the shimmering black surface filled our windows.

An instant before we collided, the attacking ship pinched, flattened, and seemed to melt across our windows as if covering us like a blanket. A whooshing sound coasted over our hull before the blanket retracted and the ship rolled right over our heads.

I released my breath and wheezed in the next. David gaped.

"We're still here." I reached over and touched his shoulder. "Let's do this."

The planet filled our windows.

David tensed under my grip. "You do realize I have no idea what we're going to do once we get into the atmosphere."

"There's no water in our hold anyway, right?"

He looked at me.

"Then let the ship flex. Our passengers already can't move. What have we got to lose?"

"They have some liquid. They can still breathe."

"Like you said: they won't be able to breathe if they're boiling." I held my breath as the ship took another hit. "If we flex, the water will leak, but the temperature won't rise. They will be no worse off than they are now." And maybe, just maybe, we could all get out of this alive.

A warbling, elongated opal shot into our flight path.

David banked left. "How are we supposed to get them into the ocean while I'm dodging all these idiots?"

The glowing munitions shot past us, lighting up my window. "Did you tell them what we're trying to do?"

"I don't think they're listening."

"Then shoot back!"

"I told you, I won't hurt my own people."

Too bad all Erescopians didn't have his moral code.

I closed my eyes as more weapons fire pummeled our hull. Those ships were going to follow us into the atmosphere, and they weren't damaged. How do we save a hull full of aquatic beings when we might not even be able to save ourselves?

The walls flashed.

"The water is gone," David said. "All of it." A shiver started at his temple and ran through his entire body. He turned to me. "They're dying."

A span of red land crept into view, standing out against the deep blue Martian sea. Beautiful, just as David had described. Maybe we did have a chance. But only one. We might be able to save the passengers—if we sacrificed the crew.

A vision of my father laughing filled my mind.

Maggie hanging upside down from the top of her swing set when we were ten.

Matt smiling at me from the next desk my first day back at school.

Mrs. Baker holding a cake loaded with birthday candles.

Even Bobby, with that crooked smile that'd nearly won my heart.

They were counting on me. Them and tons like them. People I didn't even know. Billions. And they all deserved the chance to live. A chance that only David and I could give them.

I held back a sob and faced David. "Crash the ship."

He gaped, turning to avoid another attacking orb. "What?"

"Crash into the ocean."

"We're in bad enough shape as it is. That would be just as bad as hitting a landmass. We'll come apart. Every square inch of this ship will lose cohesion at the same moment."

I gulped. "That will free Ruby and the others into the sea."

It worked for Captain Kirk. There had to be some kind of science behind those movies, right? Our passengers would drop into the ocean, and they'd release the kinetic energy. It would rain, and they'd call off the attack on Earth.

I slid my hand down David's arm, over his wrist, and grabbed his hand. I wished I wasn't shaking, because I really wanted to give him strength, but I needed all of my fortitude to keep myself from falling apart.

David's grip on me tightened. "If we lose cohesion just as we hit the water ... "

We'd fall from the ship, and hit the ocean at about a million miles an hour. It would probably be over in less than a second. At least it wouldn't hurt, but we'd be dead, and the rift dwellers would be dead. Everything we'd gone through would be for nothing.

Edgar jumped up on the console. He raked one of his legs over his face, exposing his center fang.

His center fang. Two years ago he'd saved David's life by biting him, injecting a venom that put David in a coma, and then coating him in a cocoon. Within the safety of that natural escape pod, David had survived a crash landing that had obliterated his ship. Could Edgar do the same for both of us now?

"No," David whispered.

I blinked, not even startled that he'd read my mind. "Why not?"

"Because when we hit the ocean, I need to be here to incite a compression field."

I raised my brow in the best *huh?* I could muster.

"I need to simulate the pressure of Earth's ocean until Ruby and the others sink deep enough that the environment will suit them." He sank his arms into the controls. We veered up and over an attacking ship. "The field will only last a few minutes. I'll have to trigger it just before we crash. There won't be enough time for Edgar to … "

Do his thing.

I got it. We were skunked.

My brain fogged. David continued to maneuver the controls and dodge ships as his thoughts sifted through mine. In a brief flash of his will, I suddenly understood pressurized moleculization. I knew how to create the field that would save the lives of the beings we'd transported from Earth.

He glanced at me. *Just in case.*

And then I understood why I wasn't already in one of Edgar's cocoons. David needed a backup. If something happened to him, I'd be the one to press the button before we crashed.

I closed my eyes. Why did it have to be this way? Why did it have to be so hard? I didn't want to die. There was so much I had to do still.

Hike through the Grand Canyon.

Race kayaks with Dad on the Delaware River.

Dammit, I never got one of my pictures on the cover of National Geographic!

A sob burst from my lips. My tears ran into my mouth, but I didn't wipe them away. Their salty tang covered my tongue. Bitter, but right. This was the way it had to be.

I opened my eyes and watched the planet come closer. Would anyone even know what happened? Would anyone know what we'd done?

Wiping away my tears, David's deep blue irises came into focus. Not the odd, human blue I'd become used to in the past few days, but the deep, true turquoise of the boy I'd met in the woods.

"Is this what you want?" he asked.

I nodded. "It's the only way it can be."

He ran his hand down the side of my cheek. Gentle, despite the rattling of the ship around us. I'd never tire of the warmth radiating from his skin.

His gaze centered on mine. I tensed, expecting a momentary invasion of my mind; for him to slip inside me for one last intimate breach of my very existence. But he simply lingered, staring, as if committing my face to memory.

"What?"

His face hardened before turning back to the window. "Let's do this."

31

I felt the smirk coat my face hearing my little catch phrase. Too bad I didn't have time to tease him about it.

A huge, translucent ship materialized, filling our windows in an instant. I pushed back, screaming in my chair as two blasts shot from their bow. The swirling, clear energy skimmed the top of our ship before the craft throttled past us.

"They missed," I said. "Holy Toledo that was lucky!"

David looked to the panel above him. "More like they were aiming at the guys chasing us." He smiled. A warm tingle of familiarity scurried across our bond. "Nematali Carash is on that ship."

Blondie! Yes!

"She bought us just enough time." David sunk his arms deep into the panel "Here we go."

Edgar chittered, and the walls flashed.

"He says Nematali Carash is holding them back."

I tightened my grip on my armrests. "Maybe we don't need to crash. Can she help us?"

David clutched the sides of the panel. "The rift dwellers' life signs are faint. There's no time." He leaned toward the console and frowned. "And she's outnumbered."

We hurled toward the deep blue ocean. Turquoise, like David's eyes. The cloudless sky glistened in a mauve shimmer. Pinkish-orange, not blue. The color etched a sharp contrast against the approaching sea and the ruddy land in the distance.

I wished I could take a picture. But I'd never have a chance to show it to anyone. No one would know how beautiful David's world had become. I closed my lashes, ashamed of the stupid thoughts going through my mind. I should be thinking of Dad, back on Earth, counting on me to make everything right.

More than anything, I wanted to make him proud. But even if this worked, would it be enough? Would the Caretakers call off the attack, or was Earth already gone?

I shivered. *No.* I needed to believe. I needed to know in my heart that this was worth it.

We leveled off slightly. I sensed David judging the distance before he released the pressure bubble.

"This is it," David said. "Three, two, one."

He smashed his fist into the panel. A wave of clear brilliance wafted up and over the ship as the last few feet of sky between us and the Martian sea disappeared.

32

David grabbed my hand and tugged me onto his lap. I wrapped around him as the chair came to life, bubbling up and congealing around us.

We hit the ocean like a roaring train. The impact blasted us with a numbing crescendo that sliced into my skin. David's grip on me tightened as we rolled over, slamming and banging again and again. I screamed into my clenched teeth as a tearing explosion rumbled around me, followed by a whoosh that ended in utter silence.

A dull ache started in my scalp and crept over my entire being. David's grip relaxed. I released a breath, and struggled for the next.

My ears popped. I recoiled in the deep, fading gray around me. A television buzz screamed like Godzilla stuck inside my head. I tried to gasp, but there was no air to take in. David flinched, his heartbeat drumming against my hand.

Holy crap. We were alive.

David! I winced, unable to distinguish my own inner voice above the monster wailing in my skull.

David woke, flailing and pawing at the cushioned membrane around us.

I fought the ringing in my ears, concentrating my thoughts. *I think we're sinking.*

He grasped my hand. *Do not let go of me. Take a deep breath.*

Deep breath? Deep breath of what? There was no air!

A ripping sound broke past Godzilla, throwing the screaming monster out of my mind. We slipped out of the remains of David's chair into water that burned like a hot tub cranked to the boil setting. I scrunched my eyes shut and kicked toward what my instincts told me was up.

David floundered.

Keep kicking your feet. Not that kicking my own feet was helping much.

The sea drove the searing heat against me. My brain pounded as if my skull was too snug a fit. Why was the ocean so hot?

I broke through the surface. My mouth opened to worship the air, and was rewarded by a dry, tangy heat. My throat constricted.

David's hands slipped against my cheeks. "Take shallow breaths. Let your lungs get used to the heat."

The heat? Was there even any oxygen?

"Not as much as on Earth. This atmosphere is synthetic. We don't have any photosynthesis yet. But your respiratory system should adjust." He slipped under the waves, and popped back up, choking.

"Are you okay?"

He grimaced. "Like I said, I've never had the need to learn to swim."

Blue sea rolled in soft waves, kissing the pink horizon. I would have been a lot more comfortable treading beside a weak swimmer if I were able to see land. Or if there was some debris to cling to. "How can there be nothing left of the ship? Even when the Titanic went down there were doors and stuff to float on."

"As usual, I have no idea what you're talking about."

I tried to gulp away the dread building at the base of my throat. "It's just another movie." I shuddered, remembering what happened to Jack on that ill-fated night.

David slipped beneath the swells again. I caught him and held his head above the water. Unlike Rose in that movie, I *would not* let go.

A forced smile covered David's face. "You can't keep doing this."

"No? Watch me."

His gaze scanned the steam drifting up from the sea. "So, you watch a lot of these movies, huh?"

I laughed. "Yeah, I guess I do."

He spluttered as froth splashed into his face. "Tell you what. When we get back to Earth, I'd like to see one. Can we do that?"

"Absolutely. Totally." I drew him closer. My tears trailed cool lines down my cheeks.

David's legs weren't kicking as hard as they first were. His exhaustion crept along our bond, poking at my fortitude. If I had to tread for both of us, how long would I last?

No. No. No. No. No. Bad thoughts. Definitely needed new ones.

What could we talk about? The weather? Why not? After all, it was the reason we were here. "How will we know if Ruby, Silver, and all survived?"

"I don't know. It's not like they can swim up here and tell us they're okay."

Well that was a very short, uninspiring conversation.

The sky darkened, as if the mood wasn't somber enough.

"I'm sorry it turned out this way," David said.

Was he serious? "You mean you're sorry we didn't get torn to pieces on reentry? Gee, yeah, I sure am ticked off about that, too."

"I'm not sure drowning will be much better."

A lump formed in the sea between us. Water sheened down a two-foot, hairy back before three black eyes rose above the ocean.

"Edgar!" I tried to hug him, nearly dunking both of us.

He wiggled away from me, raising one of his legs. A thick leather band twisted around his leg.

"My backpack? Seriously?" I clutched the heavy burden, a bag filled with worthless equipment. But my little dude had saved it for me. As much as I wanted to let it sink down to the ocean floor, I couldn't. I slipped it over my shoulders.

Edgar cooed and flipped out of the sea, spread his legs, and landed atop the rolling waves. His legs held him above the ocean like a giant water bug.

I gaped. David's mirrored expression told me he didn't know Edgar could do that, either.

Could it be that simple? Could we cling to Edgar like a life raft?

David reached out and gripped the *grassen's* leg, but Edgar instantly sank with the additional weight. So much for a simple solution.

The last bit of hope drained from David's eyes. But there had to be a chance. There had to be some way to work through this.

His gaze drifted to me. The fear and sadness faded into a peaceful serenity. Acceptance.

He looked up toward Edgar. "Ruby, Silver, did they make it?"

Edgar warbled, tilting toward us as his legs tapped the crests of the waves.

"I have no idea if that's good or bad." Water splashed in David's mouth as he spoke. He spit and coughed.

"He seems happy, doesn't he?" I asked.

Something cold tapped on my hair. I submersed myself to scare it off. Who knew what it might be on an alien planet?

I popped back up. "Is there anything flying around me?" I asked.

"Nothing," David said, sputtering. His face barely held above the surface.

I swam to him. "Lean on me."

"No."

Stinking, stupid, stubborn alien! "Lean on me, dammit!"

"You're a strong swimmer. You might be able to make it to land."

I slipped my arm under his shoulders, dragging him in a random direction. "Then we'll both make it to land."

He pushed me away. "You won't make it carrying me, Jess."

His words cut through me like a jagged edged sword. "Yes, we will."

Something splashed beside him, but his intensity centered on me. I tensed, barely able to keep myself afloat. Something changed in his eyes—a certainty of conviction that I'd never seen before.

"You're mine," he whispered. "My responsibility. There's one last thing I need to give you."

He grasped my face, stared into my eyes, and kissed me. A stream of energy surged between us, sizzling across my nerves and shooting through my veins; entering, strengthening, and worshiping every hidden part of my body until cascading back in a rolling ball that exploded in my chest.

Something slapped against my head again, but I couldn't care. Whatever he was doing, it didn't have the warm, sensual effect his touch usually did. This was wrong. Very wrong. But I couldn't stop. I tried to let him go, but my hands clenched, pulling him closer.

I screamed inside our kiss. His grip only strengthened.

My mind swirled, blocking my protests. I drank him in, devoured him. The energy coursed through me, sickening me and strengthening me at the same time. The power swelled, intoxicating, brilliant, but I had to get rid of it. I had to stop myself from drinking in more.

The energy, this strength inside me—it wasn't mine. Deep dread built in my stomach as the tingle shimmied in and strengthened me in ways I'd never dreamed or even wanted.

I was vaguely aware of small splashes around us. I denied my longing to draw more of this unending strength I'd tapped in to. I concentrated on separating every speck of energy that wasn't mine, and rolled it into a ball. I imagined the glowing mass in my hands, and I flung it back to David, but he fought me, and as usual, his mental strength backed me down.

Beaten, I relaxed and let the sweet decadence of the energy sweep over me. Delicious and wonderful in its wrong-ness. I felt dirty. Sleazy. Disgusting.

He'd given more than he should. He'd given all he had left. One final gift—a gift I never wanted.

Tears streamed down my cheeks as David broke the kiss.

"You can't die," I told him. "I won't let you." I struggled to keep us afloat, clutching him to me. "Come on, swim! You can do this!"

Edgar chittered beside us, somersaulting over and over atop the sea. The sky had darkened to nearly purple. Little circles appeared in the water on either side of David's face. He stared, agape, before his gaze slowly lifted to the sky. Clear droplets splashed across the rolling sea.

The sky boomed, and I gasped as an abrupt deluge rushed from above. The roar of the sudden storm drummed along the surface of the ocean, echoing off the sea like a thundering train.

"It's raining!" David pulled me into a hug. "It's really raining!"

"You did it!" I wrapped my arms around him, blinking away the deluge. *You did it*, I repeated, injecting the thought with all my strength and love into his mind.

He smiled. "It worked. It actually worked."

The rain hammered the sea, raising a wake in its ferocity.

Maybe a little too ferocious. The slaps on my head seemed to get larger by the minute, thumping against my skull like being whacked with a pencil. "Why is it coming down so hard?"

David moved his hands frantically to keep from sinking. "The rift dwellers must all be directly below us. The energy is centralized in a single location and the atmosphere doesn't know what to do about it! We need to … " He slipped under.

I dove, grabbing him, shoving him up. Clear dribbles trailed along his cheeks as he broke into the air, leaving a bluish tinge to his skin. His irises darkened to nearly black.

"Something's wrong with your eyes."

"No, it's normal." He ran his hand along my cheek. "The strength I had left, I gave to you."

Oh, God—that weird, horrible energy thing he hid in the kiss! "Take it back." I pressed my lips to his, forcing my psyche to return what wasn't mine. "Come on, take it back!"

He held me away. "I can't."

Those eyes: so dark, so vacant. I brushed my forehead against his. "There has to be a way. You can't just give up. You made it rain. It's working." The storm's droplets trailed between us, fostering our separation.

"That doesn't change that you are a better swimmer than me. You're working too hard to keep me afloat, and you're getting tired."

"Screw tired. Don't do this to me!"

He kissed my cheek, the corner of my lips. "Tell your father thank you for believing in me."

My throat constricted. The pain building, burning. "Tell him yourself. Tell him yourself, dammit!"

"Goodbye, Jess."

He pushed away and sank beneath the waves. The sea swallowed him, as if he'd never been there.

33

That scene from the movie *Titanic* bashed into my mind like a sledgehammer—Rose, stranded out in the middle of the ocean, clinging to Jack's frozen corpse. Tears streamed from her lashes. *"I won't let go, Jack. I won't let go."* And then she did. She freaking let go! She let the guy she loved sink into oblivion.

A heated splash jolted me back to reality. Three black eyes glared at me as Edgar hissed in my face. My gaze drew back to where David had been.

Holy shit. I let go.

"Screw this."

I dove beneath the swells. The storm above darkened the sea so that I couldn't see more than a few feet in any direction. I let him go. He was gone, and it was my fault!

Three white beams shot past me, illuminating the depths. Edgar's spindle-like legs twirled like propellers at his sides. I swam back up, took a breath, and dove back down, following the illumination from the *grassen's* eyes. *Come on, Edgar. Find him, buddy!*

The weight of the ocean pressed in on me. Either Nematali had succeeded in the ionic particle stabilization, or we were still inside the ship's pressurized moleculization funnel. I tried to dive again, but the artificial mass that kept the water more dense for the rift dwellers strangled me below five feet. Shit!

My lungs ached from the pressure, forcing me back to the surface. But I couldn't stay up here. How many times had David saved me when I told him to leave me behind? I couldn't let him go. I wouldn't.

I took in a deep breath, then another and dove, kicking my feet and tensing my chest muscles against the ocean's weight. I used the weight of my backpack to speed my descent.

In the depths below, the dark sea shimmered yellow, blue, and green as the rift dwellers spiraled together, causing the storm above. I pumped my arms twice and angled toward their glow.

Maybe they could help?

Three more beats. My head pounded. My ears ached. *David! Where are you. Please!*

A red glow blasted from the depths, heading straight for me like a missile. Ruby?

Three white beams of light from Edgar's eyes joined the vivid crimson, speeding the rift dweller's ascent.

Their glow blinded me for a moment before they rose, dragging a precious burden between them.

David! Thank God!

I fumbled until a large, unilluminated round mass pushed David into my arms. Silver twitched as I took David's weight from him.

Pressing my lips together, I fought back a sob. *Thank you. Thank you so much.*

The glow around Ruby brightened. *No. Thank you, land dweller.* A red tendril slid across my cheek. *Now go. We both have promises to keep.*

Yes, we did, and I fully intended to keep mine.

Ruby wrapped herself around Silver, and they sank toward the others.

Feeling dizzy, I accepted Edgar's help and kicked toward the sky. I gasped as I reached the surface, puffing as I held David's face out of the sea. Every molecule inside me screamed as the clear water trailed the edges of his pale, lifeless face.

I had to save him. I *would* save him, but how was I supposed to do CPR in the ocean? How could I give him back the strength he forced me to take from him?

Edgar spun up out of the ocean and hovered before landing on David's back and plunging us both under. I spluttered, kicking furiously to bring David back up. Edgar pummeled him again, and David coughed.

Yes! I gripped David's shoulders and shook him. "David!"

He opened his eyes, but I almost wished he hadn't. Lifeless demon orbs stared back at me. Completely black with no irises.

"Just let me go," he whispered.

"I think we've had this discussion before. Nothing's changed. We're in this together no matter what."

A wind kicked up, and the rain stopped. We both looked up to the dark clouds. The rain continued to thrash the sea, but the deluge no longer ravaged us.

I clung to David and searched the clouds. *What now?*

The sky shimmered; liquefied as if someone held a giant piece of plastic wrap in the air and let the wind wave the clear sheet in the breeze. A full radiant rainbow arced over our heads, holding back the storm like a massive, glistening umbrella.

The figure rounded and took shape. I gulped as another liquidic ship, like the one we'd just crashed, materialized above.

Checkmate.

There wasn't a darn thing I could do other than pump my legs to keep David above the water. I'd never felt so helpless.

Game over. I surrender. I'm done.

The ship swiveled and flexed, reflecting sparkling prisms across its liquescent hull. The cylindrical elevator in the base of the ship began to form, and a wave of relief settled over me. We still might not make it through the day, but at least we wouldn't drown.

The access tube hung just over the ocean and a yellow line formed down its center as the entryway opened. The blinding interior light stung my eyes as a sleek violescent alien crouched toward us.

"Give me your hand," a woman's voice said in familiar, perfect English.

I swam David toward the craft.

He grabbed her hand. "How did you find us?"

The alien smiled. "I just needed to follow the rain."

She hoisted David into the cylinder and turned to me. "Come, little one."

Little one?

"Nematali?" My brain couldn't compute her alien form, instead remembering the long blond curls of the human disguise I knew so well.

I snickered at the irony. With all she'd done for us, she was beginning to make a habit out of saving our hides.

I grasped her palm. Startled by the heat of her touch, I fell back into the water, submerged, and popped back out. It had been so long, I'd forgotten how hot their skin was when they weren't wearing a human coating.

She placed her hand out again. "We have no time."

No time. Got it. No problem—just hold on to the hundred-and-twenty-degree alien and try not to lose any skin. I inhaled and shoved my hand toward her. She hauled me up as easily as plucking a doll out of a bathtub.

Panting, I dropped to the floor beside David. Edgar scurried past me and jumped into a wall. Where did the little guy get all that energy?

I leaned up and gasped as my hand sunk into the floor by about a quarter of an inch. The chill of the liquescent metal stole the burn from my palm before my hand rose back to the surface.

Nematali tapped a panel on the wall. "That should have repaired any damage to your skin."

I flexed my fingers as the redness smoothed away. "Yeah. Thanks." I slid closer to David and brushed the dripping hair from his forehead.

Our tether twisted.

My mind drifted to my mother's funeral—me kneeling beside the casket, sobbing. Dad staring straight ahead, his expression stark and emotionless.

I couldn't lose someone I loved again. I wasn't strong enough.

The floor rumbled as the elevator tube retracted into the ship. We stilled, and the walls sunk, leaving us in a chamber slightly larger than the entrance to the craft David had arrived in. The surrounding partitions glistened like melted vanilla bean ice cream.

"What's wrong with him?" Nematali knelt beside us.

He's dying! What do you think? I choked back a sob. "His eyes," was all I could muster.

She tilted his face up. David's lashes opened, but the ghostly smoked-glass orbs still held his beautiful eyes hostage. He didn't move. He didn't blink. There was no sense he was still with us. "Did he say anything to you?"

"Yeah, he said the strength he had, he gave to me or something like that."

"Idiot," she whispered.

"It's like he just gave up."

"He didn't give up. He gave the right to survive to you. A ridiculous tradition among our people that has left many families fatherless."

"I don't understand."

"You need to force the energy back into him."

"I already tried that. It didn't work."

"You must try again."

I flinched as her searing hands gripped mine.

She placed my fingers on his temples. "Search for the strength inside you that is not your own, and gather the tendrils together."

I closed my eyes and looked inside myself. But how could I separate energy?

I cleared my thoughts. *David. Come to me.*

The brighter, hotter energy swept to a focused point and swirled. A deep seeded love reverberated around the flexing light, effusing sacrifice and adoration. For a moment, I was hesitant to give it up.

Nematali's fingers wove through the back of my hair. Her hand heated, tingled, and the sense of her alien conscious seeped into me.

My will shrieked at her invasion. I drew on the billowing mass of perfection I'd gathered, and used David's strength to drive her out. My body baulked.

"I'm only helping," she said. "Let me in."

But her very essence inside me seemed wrong: an unwelcome intruder, the third wheel where there was only room for two. David's energy swelled, ready to toss her out.

But was that what David needed, or what he wanted? Had he readied his energy for such an attack, making sure I wouldn't be able to return his gift?

Nematali had never given us a reason to not trust her. And now I needed that trust more than ever. I inhaled and relaxed, opening myself up to her harsh, prickly soul. She swept in like a B52 bomber, smashing into David's energy, struggling, brawling, and finally wrestling him into a tight, shimmering ball. The foreign luminescence exploded, tearing through and out of me, leaving a gaping hole in its wake. I fell to the tiled floor, gasping.

I trembled, soaking in the sense of being alone again. Had I thrown too much of David out? Did I break our bond?

My stomach quivered before a luxurious calm enveloped me. A sweet, perfect sense of … *David!* The connection between us reformed. Thicker. Stronger.

Beside me, David took two deep breaths. His eyes fluttered open and a warm smile crossed his face.

Nematali stood. "This is not the Breaking of Time. That type of chivalry is outdated by two thousand years."

David coughed. "I guess I'm old-fashioned."

She grabbed him by the collar and dragged him across the room.

"*You completed the bond,*" she said in Erescopian. The *sense* of the words, rather than the actual words skidded through our link. "*Are you out of your mind? I warned you.*"

"*I love her,*" David whispered.

"*We are not susceptible to human emotions.*"

"*Guess what,*" he laughed. "*They were wrong.*"

She released him, shoving him against the wall. "*You will not be laughing when your father finds out.*"

He pushed from the swirling partition before stumbling back and bracing himself against it. "*He renounced me of my name. Now I hold hers.*" He pointed at me.

Nematali sneered in my direction. She probably had no idea I could understand them.

She stepped closer to him. "*That will not stop him from hunting her down and killing her out of spite. Your father has no love of the humans.*"

David raised his eyes. "*He'd have to get through me first. I'm not a child anymore.*"

"*Neither are you a warrior, Tirran Coud.*"

"*Tirran Jessica Martinez,*" He corrected.

My heart twisted, but not in a good way. That almost sounded like we were…

"*Do not use a human-bonded name in front of any of our people. If you have to hold it, keep it to yourself.*" She slammed him against the wall again, sneered, and walked to the front of the ship.

Hol-ee-shit.

David released a breath and slumped to the floor. His exhaustion skidded through our bond, but we could share strength now. He needed me. I crawled to his side and dragged him into my arms.

Screw Nematali and all the rest of them. I never expected anyone to understand. What had happened between us transcended race. It transcended everything, but what David had done in the ocean—some kind of alien *harakiri*. Not cool. So not cool.

"We're a team now, you and me. Whatever we get into, we get out of together. Period. Don't you ever do that to me again."

He gave a half-hearted laugh. "I can't guarantee that."

Stubborn son of a ... I amassed all my anger, wrestled it into a ball, and shoved it through our bond.

He jerked back, eyes wide.

Had I hurt him?

I redirected my energy, feeding off the agony of almost losing him. *Never again. You're part of me, now. I'm not letting you go. Ever.* I calmed, and allowed the sensation to ease through our link.

Our bond trembled. David's eyes quaked. His emotions swirled: stronger, but still unsure. A dim light flickered at the edge of his soul, mingling with the fear of letting me down ... of letting everyone down.

No. Not again. Not ever. It wasn't just him or me anymore. We were one.

You made it rain. You did it! You've become more important than you realize. To me, and to the world—to both our worlds.

My father had told me once that confidence wasn't inherent. It was taught. Self-assurance was one thing I'd never lacked. It got me into trouble sometimes. Mom always said I had confidence to spare, and I couldn't think of a better person to share it with. Every lesson I'd learned, every battle I'd won, every loss I'd endured, everything that made me the sometimes arrogant, sure person I'd become rose to the surface of my mind. I packaged each experience up and shoved them through our bond.

David inhaled as if taking his first breath, then steadied himself. "W-what was that?"

"I just gave you something I have plenty of. My mom used to call it good old fashioned *chutzpah*."

He stared at his hands, flexing his fingers as if seeing them for the first time. His eyes brightened back to a crisp, bright turquoise.

Damn. I looked pretty good on him.

I hopped up and pulled David to his feet. "Enough slacking, soldier. We still have a planet to save."

34

Clouds gave way to space and sparkling stars as David and I helped each other to the front of the ship.

Nematali directed David to the control chair and helped him sit. "Are you well enough to pilot?"

"I think so."

"Excellent." She stepped back, not even looking at me. "I have sent an emergency transmission on all frequencies informing the Caretakers of your progress. They have confirmed the precipitation is genuine, and naturally occurring."

A smile burst across David's face. His eyes glossed with tears.

Finally, after all this time, the recognition he deserved. My heart swelled for him.

I fell into the co-pilot's chair. A whoosh of adrenaline wafted from my frame. It was over. Earth was safe. We'd saved the world. Again.

Hopefully it would stay saved a little while.

"But there is a problem." Nematali lowered her gaze. Her brow tightened. Her lips thinned.

"It's already started, hasn't it?" David asked.

A chill coated my veins. "What's already started?"

Nematali folded her arms. "The scourge was scheduled to begin approximately three hours ago."

What? I scrambled to my knees and leaned on the back of my chair. "But, they never attacked. They called it off in time, right?"

Nematali shifted her weight. "It takes approximately an hour for a transmission to reach Earth, and an hour back to confirm. As of yet, they have not confirmed."

Ice curdled my veins. I fisted the back of my chair.

"There is a great deal of intergalactic static between our worlds," she said.

David sighed. "From what? An ion storm?"

"Unknown. The nearest space anomaly on record is a nine-mile wide celestial projectile Earth's scholars refer to as Halley's Comet, but the static has made even an object of that size unreadable."

"Have they tried displacing the signal off the outer lying stars?" David rubbed his temples. "It's archaic, but at least they will know we're trying to get a message through."

She nodded. "All avenues have been explored."

"You've got to be kidding me." I pushed back from my chair. "There has to be a way to get through to them."

"Possibly," Nematali said.

*David turned to her. "*What are you t*hinking*?"

"Our people will continue transmitting the ceasefire, but in the meantime, this ship can travel between our worlds in one day. It is probable that you will reach Earth before any of our communications do."

David scratched the bridge of his nose. "They'll never believe us. The Caretakers will have to encode a message into our logs."

"Excellent thinking," she said. "I will stay behind, just to make sure the communication remains a priority."

I hugged myself. "So, we'll still be able to stop it, right?"

They both turned to face me.

They could have said anything. Mary had a little lamb, recited the A B C's. Something. Their blank stares tore through my soul.

Nematali turned away. "Go. Quickly. I will take an escape pod."

35

The ship jarred as Nematali's pod shot from our hull. David waved his palm over the console, and our view in the windows slipped to the left, past Mars. The liquescent black orbs that had attacked us on arrival spun, catching the light of the sun, looking more like small moons than warships protecting the planet.

"Ready?" David asked.

I nodded, and a small white square formed over a little blue dot in the distance.

Earth. It seemed so insignificant from here, but it was everything. My world. My home. It was hard to even imagine out there in the quiet of space that something horrible could be happening within our sight.

"Do you think the attack started already?" I asked.

"With communications down, there's no way of knowing."

"If it did start, how long would it take, to ... you know?"

"Scourge a planet?" He massaged the back of his neck. "Not long enough."

I spun back to my little blue marble. My hands clenched the

armrests. What would I do if we didn't get there in time?

No. We would get there in time. We had to.

David's chair turned toward mine. "They just uploaded the ceasefire protocols to our ship, and I've plotted a course. There isn't anything else we can do until we get there." He leaned his elbows on his knees. "Do you want to try to get some sleep?"

"I don't think I could." Earth. So beautiful, and so far away.

His hand slid beneath mine, prying my fingers from the supports. "I could help you rest, if you wanted me to."

"You mean doing your mental mojo thing? No thanks." It just didn't seem right, sleeping while ... I really didn't want to think about it. It was easier to shut it out and pretend none of this was happening.

Edgar popped out of one wall, scurried across the floor, and jumped into the opposite partition.

A smile spread across my lips. "He's a busy little bug, isn't he?"

"*Grassen* always seem to have something to do, but I think half of it is hoarding food."

I laughed, but cut myself off, ashamed for the outburst while my dad might be back home facing the fight of his life—the fight of everyone's lives.

I tightened my grip on David's hand. "Do you really think we can stop this?"

He shrugged. "I'd like to say the odds are in our favor, but they're not."

My stomach clenched. "Sometimes I just wish you'd lie to me."

He spun my chair toward him and grabbed my other hand. "One thing I'm sure of is that anything is possible when we're together. We have been through some insane stuff."

"Tell me about it." The stars twinkled outside the window. So serene. So beautiful. "Sometimes I wish I could just press a pause button and stop time, just to give us a few minutes where we didn't have to worry. You know what I mean?"

He nodded, tightening his grip on my fingers.

My chair jolted.

"What was that?"

"I'm not sure." David waved his hands over the controls. "It felt like something hit us."

"Please tell me someone just chucked an empty can out their spaceship window or something."

He raised an eyebrow.

"What? Aliens don't litter?"

We jolted again.

"Okay, that was sooo not funny. Are you messing with me?"

"I wish I was."

The walls flashed yellow twice.

"Is that Edgar? What did he say?"

David turned to the window.

My chair came to life, towing me back and tightening. "What's going on?"

David settled into his own seat as his gaze remained fixed on the controls. "Meteor shower."

Meteor shower? Yeah, cause that was probably the only thing that *hadn't* happened to us yet.

A roar echoed through the ship and a white fog filled the window screens. We shook like maracas before the fog dissipated and the roar faded to nothing.

"That was a little too close," David said.

"Can't we fly around them?"

"Too many, and the field is too wide. We either keep going through, or we add an extra week to the trip."

That's a week we didn't have. "Didn't you know this was here? Don't you alien guys keep maps of things like this?"

"Yes, if I was an astrological alien guy, but I'm not. Eco-biologist alien guys don't pay attention to things like meteor showers." He wiped his face with his palms. "Besides, I'm not a complete idiot. I did check the maps and this wasn't here."

"I never said you were an idiot." I tensed as a white, fluffy, smoking bowling ball soared past the window. "I'm sorry. I'm just scared, and I want to go home."

He flashed me a half-hearted grin and returned his attention to the screen. "We'll get there. I promise."

I let his words soak in, trying to find comfort in them.

We're coming, Dad. We're coming.

Thunk. Something crashed against the window and skidded over the top of the ship.

"This thing is ultra-smash proof, right?"

"To an extent."

A bright puff appeared in the distance, getting bigger by the second.

"Do I even want to know what that is?"

"Probably not." He tapped the edge of the panel to his left. "You know, stuff like this didn't happen to me before I met you."

"Are you saying I'm bad luck?"

"No, I'm saying you make life more interesting. Much, much, much more interesting."

The blurry dot cleared, looking like a miniature sun.

"So what is that?"

"A spherical meteor, class seven."

"Does that mean it's really big?"

"We've recorded larger, but this one still outweighs us by about four hundred tons." We jolted to the left. "I'm trying to get around it, but there are too many smaller ones to dodge." David tapped the panel. "Edgar, what kind of weapons is this ship armed with?"

The walls flashed.

"I guess that will have to do." He stared into the screen. "You might want to hold on."

Yeah, like I had a choice.

The restraints on my chair tightened as the windows filled

with brilliant white. A glowing silver star throttled from below us, rocketing toward the miniature sun bearing down on our little ship.

I held my breath as the star's tail sparked to nothing, while the sun grew.

The flash seared my eyes and I gasped. The comet detonated like the Death Star exploding, minus the theatrical flames.

"Yes!" I screamed.

David's chair released and he leaned toward the console. "This is not good."

"Aw, come on. You blew it up!"

"Yes. But now one big hurling object is a few thousand high-speed explosion-launched objects."

Of course it is, because it's us. Captain Kirk never had these kinds of problems! Kirk got scenarios where everything was always over neat and tidy at the end of every show. But Jess? Noooo, Jess got a thousand projectile objects hurling at her at high speeds!

David flopped back into his seat. The ship rattled. A searing noise sounded overhead, and something the size of a cantaloupe cut through the roof and landed between us. The sizzling noise echoed through the chamber. We weren't dead, so the liquidic hull must have instantly closed over.

"Edgar," David shouted, "we need some help up here!"

The lights flashed and the sizzling stopped. We jolted, jerked, and shimmied. A blast hit the windows and sparks blanketed the glass.

Space became dark again—silent, except for the stars twinkling in the distance and a bright white pebble beside my beautiful blue golf ball.

"We're through." David stood and sunk his hands into the control panel, sighing. "We're okay. We lost some air when a few smaller meteors sliced through our hull, but we're fine."

My chair released and I threw my arms around him. His embrace made me feel safer than any demonic chair could. "Please tell me there are no more meteor showers."

A laugh barely escaped his lips. He rubbed his puffy eyes. "No more meteors."

"You look exhausted."

"Of course I do, I've been hanging out with *you*."

I smiled and returned my attention to Earth. "How long until we get home?"

"About fifteen hours."

My little marble twinkled in the distance. A sense of serenity coated me, knowing I'd be back with Dad soon. "Maybe it *would* be a good idea to get some sleep, then."

Edgar popped out of the floor and jumped onto the control panel. The illumination dimmed. He must have been listening in on us, the little stinker.

The long, deep couch oozed up out of the floor.

David steered me to the cushions. "Edgar can wake us if he needs anything."

He laid on his back, and I cuddled up to his shoulder. The tension drained from his face, replaced by something deeper. His gaze centered on the roof of the ship as his lips tensed just on the edge of a grimace.

I drew a line down the edge of his chin. "Please don't say there's something you're not telling me."

He took in a deep breath. "No. You know everything I do, but that isn't much. I hate not knowing what we're flying into."

His gaze remained fixed on the ceiling. A profound dread trickled along our tether, but quickly abated. I cringed. What was he hiding?

Swirls of tingling emotions passed between us. I reached deeper. The dread I had felt hid below veiled fears of his father's continual rejection, and the occupation of Earth. There was something worse, something he wanted hidden from me.

I imagined my hands sifting through layers of his thoughts.

I rammed aside his terror of confronting his father, and sieved through his uncertainty about saving Earth. The shroud within him parted, leaving behind a dull, lifeless ball.

"Don't," David whispered.

"I want to see. No secrets anymore, right?"

He shuddered as the chilly ball of sadness rose above the clutter of other concerns and floated free. The sphere signified something more important than anything else—something he tried to hide, but could never escape from. I imagined my fingers easing along our bond, stroking and relaxing every fiber of his body as he'd done to me so many times before.

He opened up, the ball shattered, and the sense of my own conscience swept through our bond.

It was me.

His deepest, most secret concern was *me*.

He'd always wanted me safe—that worry always churned across the surface of the others. This was something more.

I tensed as the sense of duty injected itself—the need to do the right thing—to sacrifice.

An image of me, shrouded in green and sleeping, penciled through our intermingled psyche. Inside the vision, he dragged his fingers though my hair. A deep desire to hold, keep, and conceal consumed everything. Warmth seeped into me, a deep sense of comfort.

We were in the alcove on the green planet. Alone, with no way to get home. He was happy. Was it possible that maybe I was happy there, too?

Duty drilled its way through, a bar of incessant brown nagging at the comforting green, pummeling until the tranquility faded away.

I gasped. David had been happy on the green planet. His only concern was me. There was no responsibility, no one to answer to. But we'd escaped, and threw ourselves back into what David feared the most—a life of seemingly unending obligations.

We hadn't escaped from the green planet, we'd allowed ourselves to be caught again. Caught by reality.

I stiffened. I'd been angry because David left me for so long. He'd always known he would have to leave, but he hadn't realized until he returned how upset I'd be.

The brown bar looming in David's mind flexed and jabbed within him. Now he was more afraid, because he was planning on leaving again.

Duty.

He was more like my father than I wanted to admit.

I leaned on David's chest. "You know, you don't have to go right home when all this is over. You can stay with me a little bit."

Or maybe a lot of bit. I smiled, circling a pattern on his chest with my fingers. I could make tacos again. We could watch that movie he wanted to see. Be a normal couple for a few days.

For once I wanted to spend some time with David that didn't involve us running for our lives or racing against the clock for some reason. Was that too much to ask?

David closed his eyes and huffed a deep breath that lifted me up on his chest. "That would be nice," he said, but the undertone in his inflection said "fat chance of that ever happening."

"Why couldn't you stay?"

"I have to finish what I started. I need to give my people a world they can live on."

"But it's already raining."

"But they need trees to make air. They need animals to fertilize the trees. There's still so much to be done."

"Can't someone else do some of that?"

"I killed all the people who could do all that, remember?"

I trembled. We hadn't known each other when the accident happened. David had made a critical error, and it claimed the lives of most of their terrestrial scientists. "But aren't you training people?"

"Of course, but a few years is hardly enough time to learn a career's worth of knowledge. They need me."

A cool shiver ran across my skin. "Will you ever be done?"

"No, but in a few years everything will be running well enough that I can take prolonged sabbaticals."

I perked up. "Like how long?"

"A few months at first, and then longer."

"So you'll come back to Earth?"

"I'll need a place to stay. Is your couch still free?"

I giggled into the soft folds of his shirt. "My couch is always free." I ran my index finger along the edge of his sleeve. "But by that time I hope you won't want to stay on the couch."

His grin melted me. "I don't think that would make your father all that happy."

"He loves you, but he *will* threaten your life. That's just his job."

David laughed—a deep belly chuckle that warmed me to my toes. "Humans are very odd."

"But that's why you love me."

"Among other reasons."

His lips covered mine. A nice, sweet, warm, very human kiss. No sparks. No alien fireworks.

He reclined on the soft cushioning. "I'm sorry. I'm really tired."

I snuggled closer. "Me too."

36

David's voice itched through my dreams. "I don't know why. Keep trying."

I stretched out a yawn. David waved his hands over the console while Edgar scampered across the copilot's side of the dashboard. The walls flashed yellow and David nodded.

"Everything okay?" I asked.

David twitched as he turned toward me. "Umm, yeah. Sort of. The ship is fine, if that's what you mean."

I sat on the edge of the couch. "You guys look really busy."

David's gaze fell to the floor. "Jess—"

I eased off the bed. As I stood, a big, dark circle came into view. "Is that Earth?"

"Yes," David whispered.

"What's wrong? Why is it so dark?" I settled in the chair beside David.

"It's nighttime."

An unspoken "but" hung in the air. Apprehension chittered across our bond. Confusion. Dismay.

Something had confounded him, and he wanted to hide it. Whatever it was, he was trying desperately to keep what felt like terror from seeping through our bond. I gulped, pushing the overbearing emotion back. I needed to keep strong for him, if not for me.

I leaned forward and took in the mammoth orb, squinting at the bright yellow sphere just peeking around the edges of the planet's circular horizon. I could barely see the outline of Florida, as if the eastern shores of the United States had faded from an old black and white photograph. Yes, there was something very wrong. "Where are the cities?"

"The entire power grid must be down." He raised his gaze. Deep ridges formed in his forehead. He lost hold, and a flood of dread shrieked through our tether, smashing me back in my chair.

"No." Bile pooled in my throat. "We had to get here in time. We had to."

David stood. "I'm not sure what's going on. If the planet had been scourged deeply enough to cause the readings I'm seeing, the campaign would be over and Erescopian ships would be everywhere, but they're not. There isn't even any sign of encoded transmissions. I can't say what's going on until we get closer."

I nodded. "Okay, so then we go closer."

37

The sun peeked over the horizon, welcoming morning in a wave that swept over the Atlantic Ocean and kissed America's eastern shores. A few wisps of clouds greeted us as we dropped into the atmosphere.

Silent skies. Beautiful, but I tensed as the trepidation skidding across out bond deepened. I felt it too. For maybe the first time, ever, no one was chasing us. I never dreamed I'd be praying for another ship to pop up out of nowhere are start shooting. Anything normal would be welcome right now.

"There's a huge wind shear heading our way."

"What does that mean?"

"Nothing. And everything. It's an odd wind, like thousands of ships moving at high speed and messing with the atmospheric conditions."

I leaned closer to the windshield. "I don't see anything." Not like I'd be able to see wind, but— "Why would so many ships be moving, and who's ships?"

David opened his lips to answer, staring at something on the screen I couldn't see. He closed his lips. A helpless consternation hung in the air, pulling at me, searching for answers where their might not be any.

"Nothing seems right," he finally said. "The planet looks fine."

I straightened. "Well, that's good. Maybe it was just a blackout."

He waved his hands over the console. "I'm going to fly up the coast from that peninsula."

We flew down toward Florida. In this ship, it would be less than a minute before we made it to New Jersey. *We're almost there, Dad. Hold on.*

David shrieked and grabbed his head.

"What's wrong?"

"Something, *someone* is in my brain. Manipulating." He screamed and doubled over.

Someone was inside him?

I remembered the day we met, the intense pain when he'd taken my language and stole the vision of the actor Jared Linden to create his human appearance. It no longer hurt when we shared thoughts, so this couldn't be something I had done by accident. But if not me, who?

I reached for him, but sat back as a wave of well-being coated me. Joy slid through our link, while David screamed on the floor beside me, not sounding joyful at all.

My eyes fogged, and the Florida coast deepened from a rich green to a smoky, dull gray.

David blinked, taking deep, labored breaths.

"Are you okay?"

He rolled his shoulders. "Maybe I came in at too steep an angle?" He stared into the console before his gaze slowly scanned to the window. "Oh, no."

The ground below us folded up in cracks and pitches of grass and dirt. We slowed.

"What did this, a tornado?"

David's mouth remained open as he turned to me.

"The scourge? The scourge did this?"

I scanned the area below. Flattened. The only sign of humanity lay in a door sticking up out of the ground, and a car bumper hanging out of the limbs of a partially uprooted tree. "Where are we?"

"From the latest internet records of your planet, it appears this used to be Charleston, South Carolina."

"But there had to be hundreds of thousands of people here. Where are they?"

David grimaced. "Hopefully your United Nations evacuated in time."

Everyone, in only a few days? A deep pain formed in my chest as David elevated the ship a few hundred feet. We followed a desolate highway up the coast. There should have been hotels, resorts, houses.

This was a dream. It had to be. Maybe I was still asleep, and we weren't even near Earth yet.

A skyscraper peeked out over the trees on the horizon.

I nearly jumped out of my seat. "There. That city is fine."

David nodded. "Raleigh, North Carolina."

As we neared the structure, a fog of dust puffed up from the streets below. A rumble echoed through the glass, and I screamed as a million tons of steel folded into the smoke. The cloud billowed up like an atomic bomb, leaving nothing behind.

"There had to be people in there," I said. "Maybe we can help them?"

"There's no one, Jess. I'm not getting a human life reading for miles."

"But that doesn't make sense. There has to be hundreds of thousands of people."

"It looks like it's over, Jess. There's no one. Anywhere."

"What do you mean no one anywhere? How far can you see?"

"The sensors are reporting back on the entire planet. Human population: approximately one million, scattered mostly on the outer lying islands that haven't been scourged. The main continents … "

"That has to be wrong. How many people does it show in the United States?"

He closed his eyes and took a deep breath. "Three thousand six hundred and forty-seven in a little over two thousand clusters."

Three thousand left out of three-hundred million. Scattered. Alone. A numbness settled over me.

It wasn't possible. It just … wasn't. "How could we be too late?"

"Your continent was one of a handful considered a threat. They would have been targeted first. After the main strikes, they'd go back to eradicate any survivors."

Eradicate?

His silent apology niggled across our bond.

No. This wasn't happening. "What about my dad? How many people are left in New Jersey?"

David grimaced. "None. That was a military target. They wiped the entire area clean."

I sat back in my chair. A pressure built in my head as if someone crushed my skull within a vise. My ears pounded.

I swallowed down the need to burst out crying. Everyone couldn't be dead. We weren't gone that long.

No. It had to be a mistake. I needed to keep cool. I needed to think. "Is the scourge still going on anywhere else? Isn't there anyone we can save?"

David concentrated on digital Erescopian symbols scrolling over the desolation of the planet below. "Houston, Belfast, Stockholm, Dallas, Vancouver, Amman, Madrid, Cape Town, Philadelphia, Glasgow, Knoxville, Sacramento—all gone and everything in between them."

"What about Australia?"

He turned away. "That was the first location marked for

settlement. It would have been leveled by now."

I let my face fall in my hands. It just wasn't possible that three hundred million people died in a day. We did everything we were supposed to do. We found the rift dwellers. We got Ruby and the others to Mars. We made it rain. It just wasn't fair. "There has to be someone we can save."

"It doesn't make sense. Where are all our ships?" He tapped his fingers over the console. "There's no Erescopians, and barely any humans. There's no one—wait."

I lifted my head. "Did you find someone?

"A ship, hanging back about half a mile from us. I thought it was a distortion before, but it's following us."

"Maybe they know what happened?"

He dipped his pointer finger into the console. "They're not answering our transmissions."

I straightened. "Should we send them the ceasefire?"

David glanced at me. I knew it was too late to help most of the planet, but what about the people on the islands?

He waved over the control panel. "I'm enhancing the scanners." The lights flashed. "Yeah, Edgar, I'm not too comfortable with this, either."

"Why?"

"They're just hanging there, watching." Several Erescopian letters scanned across the screen. "And somehow they are reflecting our image back to us. It must be some new type of camouflage." David sat back. "Wait. According to the readings, it's another fluidic prototype."

"What does that mean?"

"There are only three of these ships in existence. I stole one and crashed it on Mars. We're sitting in the second one."

"So, if that's number three, what does that mean?"

"They are an exact match for our speed and weapons. That means no more tactical advantage."

And they were probably highly trained at how to shoot their target out of the sky.

He glared at me, lips pursed.

"Sorry, stray thought."

"It's all right. It's the truth." He tapped the panel above him. "Keep scanning, Edgar. We're heading north." He turned to me. "Let's see if we can find your dad."

The walls flashed yellow, then red.

David checked the console. "I see them." He waved his hands over the controls. "The other ship is advancing. Fast."

The clouds in the windows whisked into a blur. I leaned forward, but my chair grabbed me from behind, forcing me back and immobilizing me.

Thomp.

The sound echoed through my soul, streaming up memories of the alien weapons that tore apart the surface of the planet the first night the Erescopians landed. That was two years ago. We were supposed to be at peace. Friends. How could all of this have happened?

We rumbled, banking to the left. "Edgar, did they just miss us?" David narrowed his eyes. "Either we are finally getting lucky, or whoever is driving that thing is a worse pilot than I am."

Thomp.

We jolted.

"That time they didn't miss, but I think it was only a warning."

"Why are they shooting at us?"

"I don't know. They're not talking."

The smoking landscape sank beneath my sight. I held on as we blasted straight into the sky.

"Are we going back into space?"

"Haven't really figured that out yet."

Edgar scurried out of the floor and jumped onto the panel.

Thomp. A flash of orange grazed the top of our hull.

Edgar chattered and clicked.

"Yeah, I know. That's not good."

"Why? What?"

"That was a short-range scourge weapon. Whoever's in there obviously wants us dead. Thank goodness they're a lousy shot."

But who hated us that much? One of the Caretakers? But they already had what they wanted. Humanity was all but wiped out. What could destroying us possibly—

Thomp.

We jolted forward. Edgar slammed against the thin bar between the two windows and fell back onto the panel.

Thomp.

Our ship jarred to the side. Edgar's limp form slid to the floor.

This was insanity. We'd been through so much. There had to be a way out of this!

The ship shuddered, and our ascent slowed. My body rose from the chair, weightless, before my restraints tightened. I gulped down bile as the pull of gravity drew us down.

David released his restraints and sunk his arms up to his shoulders into the console. "We lost propulsion. Hold on!"

The ship rolled over. Now facing down, we raced toward the tops of the clouds. An orange glow encircled the room.

"What are you doing?"

"Using the last of our power to set off our scourge weapon."

"Why?"

"Because I don't want to die. They're right behind us."

Whomp.

The vibration of our own defenses riddled through me. Was this it? Had it all come down to a game of cat and mouse with weapons designed to destroy civilizations?

Thomp.

And they fired back. Was it because I was on board? Were they here to obliterate the survivors? Did they need to get rid of me to make sure humanity was completely wiped out?

Whomp.

I gritted my teeth, holding on.

David jumped back to his seat. He reached out, his right hand grasping mine. "That's all I can do. We're about to blast them with everything we have."

"Can we get back control of the ship?"

His silence gave me my answer.

Our hull hummed, then flexed. A deep *whomp* echoed through the chamber, the sound instantly overcome by a louder *thomp.*

David's eyes widened. *They fired, too!*

A scream tore through the ship, followed by a rocketing explosion. Heat and flames blanketed the windows. We tumbled and jarred in a mad frenzy. Holding on for my life, I closed my eyes and whispered a prayer. Tears welled in my lashes. It couldn't end this way. It just couldn't.

I held my breath, willing the ship to stay together a few more seconds. Would I burn alive, or fall to my death? Would it hurt? Would Mom be waiting for me? Dad?

David's grip on me tightened, and I returned the pressure. Somehow, I always imagined us having a happy ending. I mean, why not? Books ended that way. Two teens up against impossible odds, always somehow or other making it through to save the day. Why couldn't I have that? Was the fairytale too much to ask for?

The shaking stopped, but the flames continued to flap across the windows as if the glass were on fire. We spiraled out of the clouds, plummeting toward the sea and coastline below.

We didn't explode!

Holy crap, it must have been the other ship! The other ship exploded, not us!

My chair rattled, constricting until I could barely breathe.

"David!"

His grip on me tightened more. "We're still falling. There's no power."

Flames continued to lick the outside of the window as we twirled toward the ocean below. The detonation of the other ship hadn't saved us. It only gained us a few extra moments. I suppose it was something. A few more seconds to remember life, love, and home.

I'm here. David's voice soothed me, taking some of the fright.

I'm scared.

I know.

For some reason admitting I was scared freed me. It was probably better this way, dying quick rather than sifting through the ruins with the survivors. There was no one left for me on Earth, anyway. Dad, Mom, Maggie, Matt … all gone.

Even my passion: photography. Gone.

After all, I couldn't be much of a photographer when there was no one left to look at my pictures. David was probably all I had left to live for. At least he was here to share my last moments.

The whoosh of David's soul coated me, sheltered me from my fears. *I'm here.* And there was no one I wanted with me more.

Tears streamed from my cheeks as the crests of the waves came into view. I'd spent so much time at the beach back home, staring at the ocean. Maybe this was fitting.

At least I'd die on Earth.

38

The ship quaked and moaned like a tortured, dying animal.

"*Orieb casala thorent, est!*" David screamed, releasing my hand.

My mind translated it to something akin to *holy effing crap*. Not that it mattered. I wished I would have had a chance to really learn his language. Not that *that* mattered either, a few seconds before I died.

David sprang from his seat, clearly oblivious to the planet we were about to smack into.

"What are you doing?"

He sank his wrists into the panel. "The power is trying to come on."

"Seriously?"

The lights flickered. David bent his knees as if bracing for impact. He grunted and growled at the stress. The gentle ripples of the ocean waves traveled along their path, unworried about the spaceship that was about to plow into them. I closed my eyes.

"Grrrrr-ahhhh!" David screamed.

My eyes bolted open as we banked up just inches from the water. We flew back up into a crystal-blue sky kissed with beautiful billowing clouds.

We weren't dead.

Holy shit. We weren't dead!

We leveled off and hovered. My seat released and I jumped into David's arms.

My tears stained his shirt while his soaked my shoulder.

"I don't believe it. I don't believe it. I don't believe it."

David's heartbeat pummeled my chest. His deep breaths echoed through my ears. "I'm not sure I do, either. It's like the ship choked, passed out, and woke up groggy. I've never heard of anything like it before."

"Stupid experimental technology."

Edgar rolled over and shook. He lifted his one gray leg and itched the bald spot behind his center eye before tilting his head as if questioning us.

David smiled. "I think that experimental technology just saved our lives."

"What about the other ship?"

He waved his hand over the panel. "It's gone. I only hit them once. That detonation must have been their primary core exploding."

"Lucky shot, huh?"

He nodded. "Yeah. I guess so." He continued to fiddle with the panel. "Wait a minute. Something is strange."

"What?" I settled into my chair.

"The readings. There has to be a mistake." He turned to me. "The population numbers. They're higher."

"Well, that's good, right?"

"Yeah, but it makes no sense. Right below us in the area designated *New England*, it's showing about seven hundred thousand people."

A smile burst across my face. "What about the rest of the country?"

"There only seems to be people on the east coast. And the numbers are small. The rest of the country is nearly wiped out. Just small concentrated pockets of life."

I nodded. "That's okay. That's some people. That's more than extinction, right?"

His eyes narrowed. "Yes, but it's very strange. I've never known the instruments to be that wrong."

We flew toward Earth. The green struck me first. Trees, everywhere. Sand and brush dotted the shoreline.

"There's no sign of the scourge. Maybe they got the ceasefire before they hit this area?"

He squinted at the panel. "There are no large buildings, no sign of technology. It has to be scourged."

"Are there any signs of the Erescopians?"

He leaned closer to the panel. "None. Let's land and see if we can find out what's going on."

We moved over the trees, jostling the leaves until we settled beneath the branches. Edgar wrapped around my ankle as the shimmering elevator whisked us to the surface.

I stepped away from the ship into a small clearing beside our landing site. A gentle, crisp breeze caressed my cheeks. The air smelled fresh and new after being on a ship for so long.

Edgar scampered beside the nearly invisible edge of the ship. The base of the craft mirrored the trees above, and the liquescent hull angled around the trunks as if it had oozed itself between them. If I didn't know what I was looking for, I'd have no idea there was a spaceship there.

A bird flittered in the trees behind me, chirping to a friend on another branch. A squirrel scampered down a trunk and disappeared under the brush. He stuck his head out and eyed me warily before scooting back into hiding. It all seemed so—normal.

Crazy, how half the country had been blown away, but life went on here like nothing happened.

I walked back toward the ship. David tapped on some sort of hand-held computer. "Do you know where we are?"

"Somewhere just outside a place called Danvers, Massachusetts.

There is a high concentration of survivors just north of here. They should be able to tell us what's going on."

I walked backward a few steps, taking in our landing site. The trees and vines wove around the liquescent hull as if they'd overgrown the alien technology for years, leaving our vessel completely invisible inside the edge of the forest. "Is there a reason you hid the ship? I'm afraid we won't be able to find it when we get back."

David peeked over his shoulder. "To be honest, I'm a little unnerved by all of this. There's no sign of my people anywhere. I figure it's probably not the best idea to scream *here's the alien* until we know whether or not I'll be shot on sight."

"Good point."

I watched my step as we walked the dirt path, wishing I hadn't lost my Nikes at the bottom of Mariana's Trench. My bare feet kicked up the dust in a cloud that stole away on the breeze. David walked over the rough terrain like nothing. He probably couldn't feel anything through that fake human skin of his. I tried not to limp as another rock stabbed at my heel. Martinez feet were definitely not made for barefoot hiking.

David raised his hand, stopping me. "What's that noise?"

A *clop clop clop clop* sound mixed with a squeak carried on the breeze. A horse whinnied.

Edgar scampered around my feet as we climbed to the top of a hill. I stopped short. Trees sprawled in every direction for miles, losing themselves within the horizon.

David held up his computer tablet and tapped on the screen. "This is definitely not scourged."

This forest—the woods going on for miles on end—was wrong. There should have been towns. Houses. Shopping malls.

Where was everybody?

David's eyes widened. "Jess, this atmosphere is showing only a point zero-two-six pollution quotient."

"What does that mean?"

"It's impossible. It's like a new planet, uncontaminated by modern technology."

The side of his computer opened up, and he scraped some dirt into a scoop that drew back into the unit. His lips formed a straight line.

"What?"

"This planet hasn't been scourged."

"What do you mean? Then where is everyone?"

He lowered the device. His gaze scanned the trees. "I don't think they've been born yet."

Icy fingers crawled down my spine. "I don't understand."

"This planet is younger than the one we left. This isn't your Earth, Jess. According to these readings, this is Earth's past. My people won't arrive for another three hundred years."

I stared at him, waiting for a punchline that didn't come. "Please tell me you're kidding."

He shrugged. "Is this one of those times that you want me to lie to you?"

"No. Yes. I don't know!" I dragged my fingers through my hair.

The clopping sound elevated, and a wooden, horse-drawn cart rolled along a dirt path between the trees below us, kicking up dust behind it like a fog.

My stomach flipped. It couldn't be. "Time travel isn't possible."

"I'm aware of that." His gaze fell back on his device. He tapped his fingers across the screen.

A sinking feeling crept through my center. I tucked my hair behind my ears and closed my eyes. The leaves blew in the wind, blocking out the faint sound of the cart. No car horns. No radios. No anything.

Shivering, I took in the sprawling forest, the clean scent of the air, the overwhelming sense of … nothing. Nothing but pure, undeveloped nature. My lower lip trembled, struggling against a sob.

"We're going to be fine," David said, still intent on the screen.

"According to these readings—"

I spun and grabbed the computer from his hands. I nearly threw it. "Will you get your head out of that thing for a minute?"

He gaped, staring at me.

"David, we're back in time. In the past!" I wasn't sure if I wanted to laugh, or cry. Slumping to the ground, I set the computer pad on the sandy gravel. I'd gone from everyone I knew being dead, to everyone I knew not being born yet. Somehow, I felt just as alone.

The horse whinnied in the distance as the breeze swept through my hair.

I straightened. Dad, Maggie, Matt: they weren't dead … *yet*.

And right now, the aliens might not even know about Earth.

"We can fix this," I said. "We can stop the apocalypse before it ever happens."

David gazed into the trees. "Theoretically, I suppose we could."

"Theoretically? Why couldn't we? All you need to do is bring us back before your people attack."

He nodded. "Theoretically."

I jumped to my feet. "Will you stop saying that! This will work. This has to work."

A trickle of fear crept across our bond, a deep, frightened certainty of—failure?

I took his hands in mine. "David we can do this. We can save everyone."

His gaze darted to the computer on the ground, and back to me. "I don't know how to get us home, Jess. I don't even know how we got here in the first place."

I let go of his hands and slumped back to the ground, covering my eyes. "How did I know you were going to say that?"

He settled beside me. "There is a bright side."

I laughed. "Oh please, let me have it."

David smiled. "We have about three hundred years to figure this out."

A NOTE FROM THE AUTHOR

Gah! Sorry about that ending. Please don't hate me!
[She runs and hides her head under a pillow]

If you'd like to be the first to hear about future books, follow this link for the latest news, cover reveals, and maybe even some bonus content. http://tinyurl.com/pwvs98h

And if you're in the mood, don't be a stranger. Drop me a line and let me know what you thought about *Embers in the Sea*. I'm on all sorts of social media. Pick your favorite mode of space travel at my website http://www.jennifereaton.com/

Waving madly from the pre-industrial age!

ACKNOWLEDGEMENTS

Writing *Embers in the Sea* was a huge challenge for me. Without a doubt, this was the hardest book in the series to write. I mean, Jess and David have already been chased through the woods, and then through a spaceship, and then through outer space. Where else was there to go? The ocean was the next great frontier, but this setting proved more difficult than anything I've written before.

I have to admit, the first several drafts were rough and ugly. Thanks so much for my team of beta readers J. Keller Ford and Kelly Said, who weren't afraid to tell me how much work was still ahead of me, and pointed out all those places where things would have been fine on land, but weren't really working underwater.

Thanks also to my Month9Books editors Cameron and Georgia, whose extensive comments and in-person meetings about the story brought things to light that I hadn't noticed. Thank you both for believing we could make *Embers* into something great.

There is a certain point in the editing process where I begin to question just about everything. I'm not writing for myself anymore, but for a sea of people who love my characters just as much as I do. Sharon, I have to say, handing over a pre-pubbed version of this book to a fan may have been the most stressful thing I've ever done. Thank you for re-infusing me with the electric charge of a fan felt "squee". I could feel your smile from thousands of miles away. Thank you for your suggestions, concerns, and for confirming that this roller coaster ride was ready for prime time. And, yeah, that ending … sorry. Hope you can repair whatever it was that you threw across the room.

In the crazy world of authorship, ya gotta have friends. This is a big old, heartfelt shout out to the Sisterhood of the Traveling Pens, who cheer me on when things are going great, and offer shoulders to cry on when things are hard. You certainly had to listen to a lot of my bellyaching over this book. You guys are worth your weight in gold. Nope, you are! Go hop on a scale and check! (Okay, okay, you can skip the scale part if you want.)

As always, I have to thank my family who are so supportive of my writing. Thanks to my husband for never even blinking when I have a deadline. You are what keeps our house running. Without you, none of us would eat. Thanks for all you do.

Also a special nod to my oldest son, who peeks into my office every night to make sure I've gotten enough pages done, and also reminds me that I need to sleep. Love you, buddy!

To my two younger dudes: your hugs and smiles are worth the world. Sometimes they are all that keeps me going on a rough night.

And to the fans: you have no idea how much joy it gives me to see you guys online talking about my books. I appreciate it like you wouldn't believe. Thank you for all the support. You guys make it all worthwhile.

Alien Kisses!

—Jennifer

JENNIFER M. EATON

Jennifer M. Eaton hails from the eastern shore of the North American Continent on planet Earth. Yes, regrettably, she is human, but please don't hold that against her. While not traipsing through the galaxy looking for specimens for her space moth collection, she lives with her wonderfully supportive husband and three energetic offspring. (And a poodle who runs the spaceport when she's not around.)

During infrequent excursions to her home planet of Earth, Jennifer enjoys long hikes in the woods, bicycling, swimming, snorkeling, and snuggling up by the fire with a great book; but great adventures are always a short shuttle ride away.

Who knows where we'll end up next?

OTHER MONTH9BOOKS TITLES YOU MIGHT LIKE

FIRE IN THE WOODS
ASHES IN THE SKY
PROJECT EMERGENCE
STATION FOSAAN
GENESIS GIRL
DAMAGED GOODS

Find more books like this at http://www.Month9Books.com

Connect with Month9Books online:
Facebook: www.Facebook.com/Month9Books
Twitter: https://twitter.com/Month9Books
You Tube: www.youtube.com/user/Month9Books
Tumblr: http://month9books.tumblr.com/
Instagram: https://instagram.com/month9books

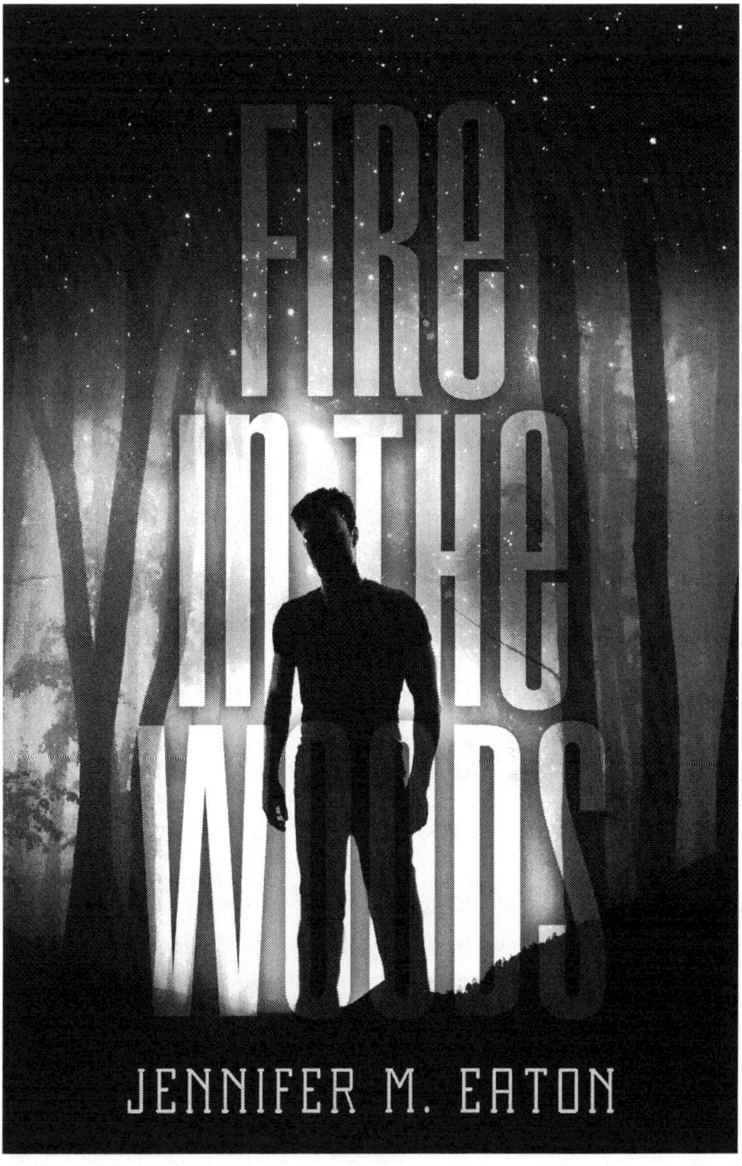
FIRE IN THE WOODS
JENNIFER M. EATON

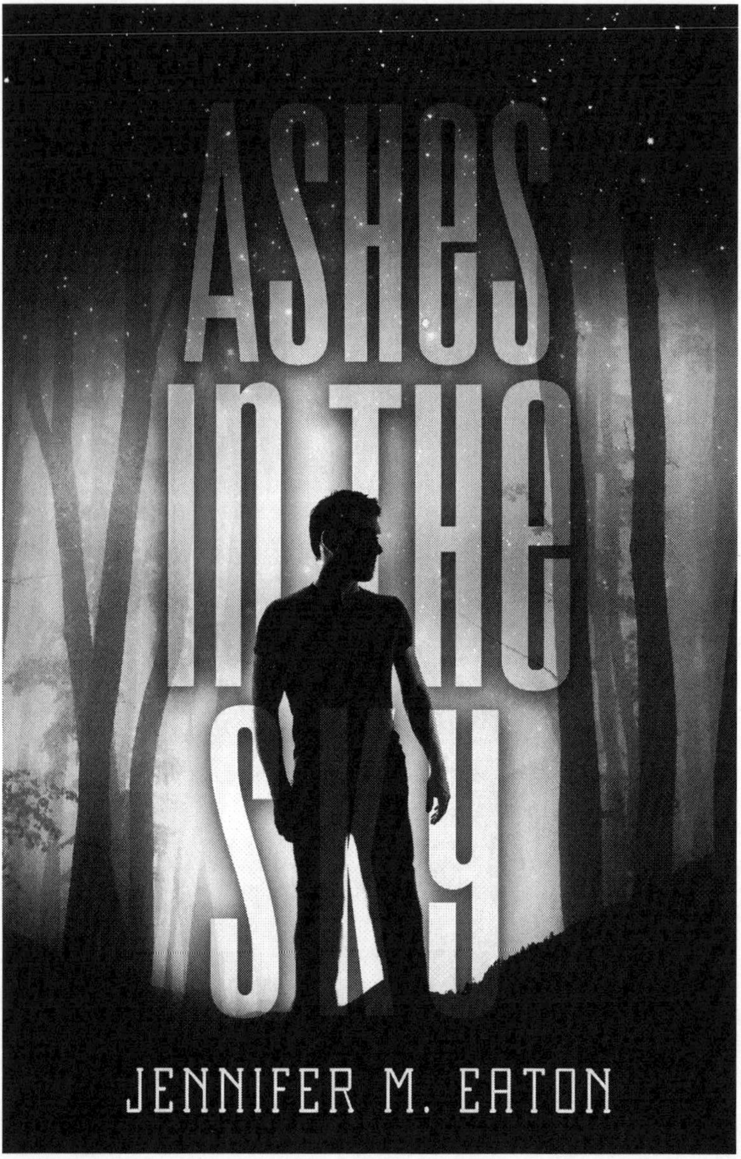
ASHES
IN THE
SKY
JENNIFER M. EATON

A Promised Future. A Traitor on Board.
The Fight of Their Lives.

PROJECT
EMERGENCE

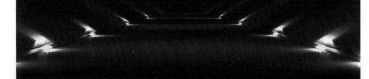

EMERGENCE

JAMIE ZAKIAN

DEE GARRETSON
SIXTEEN-YEAR-OLD QUINN WAS GIVEN THREE RULES TO FOLLOW, AND HE'S ABOUT TO BREAK EVERY LAST ONE OF THEM.
STATION FOSAAN

Their new beginning
may be her end.

BLANK SLATE: BOOK 1

GENESIS
GIRL

JENNIFER BARDSLEY

BLANK SLATE: BOOK 2

DAMAGED GOODS

JENNIFER BARDSLEY